I0527785

Wings on Mountain Breezes

by

Dr. Sue Clifton
&
Kelley Reinemann-Banks

Daughters of Parrish Oaks, Book 5

This is a work of fiction. Names, characters, places, and incidents are either the product of the author's imagination or are used fictitiously, and any resemblance to actual persons living or dead, business establishments, events, or locales, is entirely coincidental.

Wings on Mountain Breezes

COPYRIGHT © 2017 by Mantia Sue Clifton

All rights reserved. No part of this book may be used or reproduced in any manner whatsoever without written permission of the author or The Wild Rose Press, Inc. except in the case of brief quotations embodied in critical articles or reviews.
Contact Information: info@thewildrosepress.com

Cover Art by *Kim Mendoza*

The Wild Rose Press, Inc.
PO Box 708
Adams Basin, NY 14410-0708
Visit us at www.thewildrosepress.com

Publishing History
First Mainstream Women's Fiction Rose Edition, 2017
Print ISBN 978-1-5092-1194-4
Digital ISBN 978-1-5092-1195-1

Daughters of Parrish Oaks, Book 5
Published in the United States of America

"Take off your pack," he ordered, and Sue Ann did not hesitate. It was far too heavy for where she was having to go.

"Go through it and be quick about it, and take out at least half of what's in there. Leave the water bottles here except for two. Water is the heaviest thing you're carrying. I have a pump and filter and can fill from the streams. Socks should stay, along with your bedroll. Everything else can go. Keep the backpacker food. It doesn't weigh much."

When she finished, she left everything in plain view but figured he would make her hide it so anyone tracking could not find their trail.

"Where are you taking me?" she asked again as she fastened the straps on her much lighter pack.

"I told you, not for you to know. Get your pack on and move. I want to be there before dark. If you break a leg in the dark, I'll bind you and leave you for the bears."

"Pleasant thought!" Sue Ann mumbled as she slung the pack over her shoulders and tightened the chest and shoulder straps. She picked up the items left out of her pack and wadded them into a ball, prepared to stuff them in the crevice.

"Leave them out. In fact, spread them around so they are in clear view. The sooner he catches up, the better."

"He who? Who are you trying to trap using me as bait?" Sue Ann put her hands on her hips and stared at the man.

The man chuckled deep in his throat. "Wouldn't you like to know? But you wouldn't believe me if I told you. We'll just let it be a surprise."

Praise for Dr. Sue Clifton

THE GULLY PATH, Dr. Sue's first novel, won four first-place awards at the Arkansas Writers' Conference a few years back. Since then, that first novel has grown into a series of five books:

~~

THE GULLY PATH
UNDER NORTHERN LIGHTS
HEART OF THE BEARTOOTHS
MOUNTAIN MISTS
WINGS ON MOUNTAIN BREEZES

~~

All are available from The Wild Rose Press, Inc.
www.thewildrosepress.com

Dedication

by Kelley Reinemann-Banks:

I dedicate this book to my mom, Teresa Reinemann. Without her immeasurable patience, unconditional love, and never-ceasing prayers, I would not be who I am, nor would I be capable of contributing to a project such as this book.

Thank you for the late-night study sessions; for helping me to grow outside of my comfort zone; for always encouraging me to do my best and accepting the outcome; for believing in me when I didn't necessarily believe in myself; for building my courage to try new things and to look for the good in people despite opinions given by others; for guiding me in my attention to detail and judgment of character. And, last but not least, thank you for leading by example in the ways of Christ. I can only hope and pray to be half the mom you were to Nikki and me. I love you.

~*~

by Dr. Sue Clifton:

The final book in this series is dedicated to Hilda Broome and Gayle Beard, two special friends who not only follow me as readers but who stayed with me in my place in the Beartooth Mountains of Montana, critiquing sections of novels as they were written and offering ideas and suggestions to enrich and add believability to Sue Ann and Betsy's stories. But most of all, thank you, Gayle and Hilda, for also sharing my love of Mississippi, Montana, and Alaska. May we never forget Madame Aurora's sign of approval (upon the release of *Under Northern Lights, Book 2*) when she wrote "S" (*for Sue*) above our heads.

Acknowledgements

A special thank you goes to Northern Cheyenne tribal historian Linwood Tallbull. Linwood is an honored elder in his tribe and teaches ethno-botany, the study of plants and how they were used by the Plains Indians. Thank you, Linwood, for taking the time to explain the Sacred Places of your people and the similarities to your neighbors the Crow. I used your entire explanation of the Little People at the Medicine Wheel, and I always carry fruit for the Little People when I visit, as did my characters. Wings on Mountain Breezes is made extra special and more spiritual and realistic because of your contribution.

Another thank you goes to my friend Gayle Beard, a former educator at Northern Cheyenne Tribal School and a writer contributor to this, the final book. Gayle, your depiction of Custer's wild horse vision at the Medicine Wheel will put readers, as it did me, in the midst of this magical tableau. Your vivid description took me back to times I too stood "on the precipice of the ten-thousand-foot cliff overlooking the vast western plains," and "praised the turquoise and vermillion sky" while feeling uplifted, a feeling possible only in a truly sacred place.

My final acknowledgement goes to Ronald Glenmore Seminole, Cheyenne culture and language teacher at Northern Cheyenne Tribal School. Ron, a poet and honored elder of the Northern Cheyenne people, gifted me his poem "Beware of the Winds" to use in Wings on Mountain Breezes, a great honor to share with my readers. Ron left this earth on January 6, 2017, before the book was released, but his poetry will live on for his family and those of us who call him "friend." My promise holds, Ron. I will see that your wonderful poems are published for your children, grandchildren, and your beloved Cheyenne people to enjoy for generations to come. "Listen to elders in dreams when they whisper" you wrote in your poem. We wait...we listen...for your whispers, "White Antelope", Vo'kaa'e Ohvomaestse, "Two Man."

Part I

Eagle Wings

Oh, Great Spirit whose voice I hear in the winds,
and whose breath gives life to all the world,
Hear me, I am small and weak,
I need your strength and wisdom.
Let me walk in beauty and make my eyes ever behold
the red and purple sunset.
Make my hands respect the things you have made
and my ears sharp to hear your voice.
Make me wise so that I may understand the things
you have taught my people.
Let me learn the lessons you have hidden in every leaf
and rock.

~

I seek strength, not to be greater than my brother,
but to fight my greatest enemy—myself.
Make me always ready to come to you
with clean hands and straight eyes
So when life fades, as the fading sunset,
my Spirit may come to you without shame.

~Native American Prayer, translated by
Lakota Sioux Chief Yellow Lark in 1887

Chapter One

Montana, Autumn

Custer sat on the porch of his cabin in the aspen grove and leaned back, his straight chair angled precariously against the log wall hewn by the pioneer who had built it in the late 1800s. Custer loved the old cabin, especially the front room, original to its pioneer history. He himself had hewn the logs by hand for the small addition on the back, to make it blend with the old part so it looked as if it also had been there for over a hundred years. The cabin was symbolic of his life; the original part represented the old ways, his Crow heritage that had saved him from his young adult period, the bad days that still haunted him. The addition represented rebirth, erasing the bad and providing a life that was good, filled with rightful living and happiness with his only love and now wife, Sue Ann.

His eyes stared, entranced, as if seeing his Beartooth Mountains for the first time as he had the day he bought the land and cabin forty years ago, when the old pioneer's descendants had no interest in its history or its demand for living simply, detached from society.

Putting his hand to his heart, his fingers kept time to the irregular beat growing fainter with each passing day like a Crow drum made from hide not properly tanned. A good drum was necessary for the steady beat

1

of traditional songs and chants of his people, the Apsáalooké, meaning long-beaked bird.

His cardiologist had told him he needed a heart transplant, but Custer had told him this was not an option he would choose. "My body will leave this world as it entered—with the same heart, weaker yet full of contentment and gratitude to Creator of All Things for allowing me to live as I have with my last years being my most fulfilled. I have no regrets; my life and my heart will end when it is my time—no sooner, no later." After explaining his position, Custer asked the doctor not to inform Sue Ann of his need for a transplant, not wanting to worry her unnecessarily.

But one person did need to know of the likelihood of his departure from this world. Custer stepped into the front room and pulled the cell phone from its hiding place under the primitive table. He had never tossed the phone away as directed by Raven three years ago. Flipping it open with his thumb as he returned to the porch, Custer pressed the keys connecting him to the lone number it held. Custer's heart tried to beat stronger as he listened to the incessant ringing with no answering on the other end. A click sounded, and the ringing stopped. Either an answering machine had picked up the call or Raven stood staring at the phone but saying nothing. Custer figured Raven would not answer and closed his eyes, wondering at the conflicting emotions he felt when he did not hear Raven's voice; happiness, desperation, and solace all fought for dominance.

Without knowing if anyone was on the other end to hear him, Custer spoke.

"It is time to join my ancestors, Raven. Sue Ann

will need you when I'm gone. She is often weak from her battle with cancer. Think wisely and follow your heart." He flipped the phone shut, walked slowly back into the cabin, and placed it in the hidden compartment under his table in the makeshift charger. The table was pushed close to the wall, so the phone stayed attached to the generator by a hidden wire. Custer ran the generator each time he visited the cabin. For Sue Ann's sake, it was imperative he stay connected to Raven, but soon he would be too weak to make the trek to the aspen grove. He knew he would have to trust someone with the information about Raven. He had always assumed it would be Hawk he would tell, but now he thought Tobi should be the one to make the decision. Regardless, Sue Ann would have to be told about this terrible secret her husband had carried to the afterlife. He only hoped she would not hate him for it.

After walking back out to the porch, he leaned against the post and gazed again at the frosted mountains, the snow growing deeper as each night dropped below freezing. Winter would soon be upon him, and he wondered if he would be here to enjoy the full season with its crisp purity. Then again, maybe even another spring was in his future, although he doubted it.

An eagle, his animal spirit, soared high above him, calling, beckoning him to listen to the whispers of the mountain breezes surrounding him, whispers that would either comfort him or prepare him for the inevitable.

Not yet, Eagle! Your final sun has not yet set. Be strong and enjoy the red-and-purple sunsets ahead, but use them wisely to prepare yourself and your loved ones for when your feather falls. Until then, seek the wisdom of the Sacred Hoop, and keep your ear to mountain breezes.

Chapter Two

Montana, Spring

Tobi left the Adirondack chair on the front porch of his small cabin and paced as he reread the letter from Star ending their relationship before it was even allowed to cool to red embers. Tobi crushed the letter in his hand and threw it across the porch. He stooped to pick it up a few minutes later, thinking he would burn it in the fireplace tonight when spring coolness demanded a little warmth after the sun went down.

As he moved to lean against the porch post and look to the mountains for consolation, his thoughts traveled back to another important letter that had changed his life, but he had no regrets about that one. His grandmother, or the woman he had thought was his grandmother, had died leaving him a letter explaining how she had stolen him from an unwed mother, Sue Ann Parish. His grandmother was working as a nurse in the hospital in Memphis, Tennessee, where Tobi was born. It was a "switched at birth" story and an act his grandmother never regretted. As a son, he had given her childless daughter so much happiness after miscarrying so many babies, but she and her husband had lost their lives in an automobile accident when Tobi was fourteen.

Tobi knew he could call his twin sister Betsy, and

she would be there in minutes ready to console him.

Hell, she's probably on her way now. Betsy always seems to know when I'm hurting, just as I can sense when something is bothering her.

Before he could stuff the heartbreak into his pocket, he heard the Jeep bumping its way up the path to his cabin.

Custer! How does he always know when I need to "spill my guts" as he says? I could never talk to Mom or Betsy. They would get too emotionally involved, knowing how I feel about Star. The one girl, the missing piece I thought could make my life complete here in the mountains, kills all my day and night dreams with a few strokes of her pen.

"Hey, Custer. Just the man I need to talk to. Come on up and sit with me." Tobi gestured to his stepfather and made his own way back to one of the chairs, a cabin-warming present from his mom and Custer three years before, when he'd moved here to be with the mother and twin sister he had just found.

"I need someone to talk to right now." Tobi looked down at the letter still crumpled in his hand.

"That doesn't sound good. Am I expected to provide profound words of wisdom when we have this talk?" Custer took a seat in the other chair but did not sit back, choosing to sit with his elbows propped on his knees, his hands clasped together. Following Tobi's lead, both men cast their eyes toward the mountain peaks. Silence followed as neither spoke—one choosing the words for his précis with the least negativity and emotion possible; the other allowing silence to guide him with advice, solace, or both, whichever was needed to help this stepson whose face was painted in emotional pain.

"Star is no longer part of my future." Tobi kept his eyes fixed on the mountain as he blurted out his news. Opening his hand, he straightened the crumpled one-page letter against his thigh before handing it to Custer.

Custer took his glasses from his pocket and read the brief passage. After putting his glasses back in his pocket, he handed the letter back to Tobi.

"I'm sorry, son. I know Star meant a lot to you."

"That's it? Surely you can give me something better than 'I'm sorry'!" Tobi stared at Custer, who leaned back in his chair. "Can you believe she said this?" Tobi cleared the emotion out of his throat before reading aloud. "'Being with you taught me what has been missing in my life. I have been alone too long, and I miss being loved. I have reconciled with Dylan, my ex-husband, and we have remarried.'" Tobi wadded the letter up and threw it over the log rail into the yard. "Damn! If I'm such a great teacher, why can't I help myself and pick the right somebody to fall in love with?"

Custer propped an elbow on the chair arm and rubbed his chin, putting himself into thinking mode. After a minute of gathering his words, he spoke in the melodic, Native monotone, his trademark delivery for life lessons. Every word unfolded syllable by syllable into meaningful Custer philosophy.

"Love is what every man seeks, Tobi. It feeds our manhood, makes us lift our shoulders with confidence, and gives us a reason to live. Right now, I know you feel empty, probably madder than hell. Your shoulders are slumped, your self-esteem crushed, your green eyes from your mother are full of sadness and betrayal. I lived with that same kind of pain for over twenty years when your mother kept leaving me and returning to Alaska. But I refused to give up, and she was worth the wait. I've never been happier, Tobi, than I am now, married to Sue Ann." Custer paused, giving his words time to sink in. "Some say a woman's highest calling is to lead a man to his soul, and I believe this is true. My soul is Sue Ann."

"But what if my soul was Star? She's married, Custer! What the hell do I do now?" Tobi took Custer's former position with elbows on knees but rubbing his hands through his blond, curly hair. "I feel like my soul just died and there is no afterlife."

Custer remained silent, thinking. He knew Tobi depended on him for answers, and he did not want to let him down.

"Perhaps Star was a good teacher for you, son. You, too, learned to love again after suffering through a nasty divorce. I do not think you are meant to be alone. You have a strong, innate sense of protection." Custer sensed his stepson was hanging on his every word. "A man's highest calling is the protection of a woman. Do not put barriers across the pathway to your heart opened by Star, Tobi, for that path leads to your soul." Custer again looked to the mountain peak.

"I wish I could believe you, but right now, I wish I were a drinking man." Tobi became quiet again, trying to let Custer's words sink in. "What makes you think there will be someone else for me, Custer?" Tobi stood, putting his hands in his pockets, leaning with his thigh against the porch rail.

Custer stood by him and put his hands on the rail. A breeze surrounded him and Tobi. "Whispers…the voices in the mountain breezes, son. They guide me, and they will guide you."

Chapter Three

Sue Ann smoothed the moisturizer over her face and down onto her neck but allowed her fingers to stop when she felt a small lump just below her jawbone. Gently, she worked her fingertips over the bump, willing it to go away.

It's just a swollen gland from the cold I just got over. Do not panic!

But Sue Ann's thoughts could not prevent her from remembering the awful chemo she had been through a few years earlier, as well as the double mastectomy to rid her body of the monster. Immediately, she moved her fingers to each armpit and held her breath, praying she would not find any swollen lymph nodes. Breathing a sign of relief, she dressed quickly and hastened down the stairs to the kitchen to make a fresh pot of coffee to go with the raspberry wholegrain muffins she had baked earlier. Custer should be returning soon from visiting Tobi and would dive into the muffins, wild raspberry being his favorite.

****

Sue Ann had eaten only half of her muffin, having lost her appetite after Custer told her about Tobi's pain at losing Star. When her children hurt, her own heart ached with them. She took her coffee and left the table where Custer sat and headed for the sofa facing the fireplace in the great room. The glow of the low fire did not give her the therapeutic warmth it usually did. Leaning back, her eyes traveled to the picture over the mantel. There she and Betsy stood in their green heavy Alaskan coats with white fur trim surrounding their faces so much alike. Surrounded by deep snow, the mother-daughter duo's emerald eyes played off the green curtains of Her Majesty Aurora as the Northern Lights swirled over and around them. But it was not the painting that caused her mind to wander. The master artist, Shade Dubois, reentered her mind as she was reminded of the severe pain of losing someone you love more than life itself. Even knowing her thoughts would crush Custer if he read her mind, she could not help but return to that world, hers and Shade's, as he held her in his arms in his easy chair in his private, magical world. Before them, the huge painting of the Aurora had danced across the wall, aided by strobe-type lights that gave the painting the illusion of the northern lights moving. The feeling of contentment and warmth emitted from him that night, after he had saved her from the terrible wreck in the high mountain pass in Alaska, was a feeling she could never forget even if she tried. Sue Ann crossed her arms, hugging herself, and closed her eyes as visions of sweeping greens and yellows with just a touch of red waltzed across her subconscious. She felt Shade pull her head to his chest as he caressed the top of her head with his chin. Only when he took her hand in his did she open her eyes.

Custer pulled her to him and held her hand, caressing the backs of her fingers with his thumb even though he knew her thoughts were not of him. Sue Ann loved him. He knew this, but it would never be with the depth she had loved Shade. Custer accepted this. All he wanted was Sue Ann beside him. But was it right for him to keep the secret he had held within for over twenty years? He knew it had to be this way, but not because of Sue Ann. He had promised Raven, and he had sworn an oath to the CIA.

Custer sometimes thought back to the day he had pulled a severely wounded Raven from the raging Tekooni River in Alaska. Would he have saved this man destined for death if he had known Sue Ann then? Custer knew the answer to this question was "yes" even though Sue Ann was his heart and soul, the essence of his existence. His greatest fear was her finding out Shade, whom he knew as Raven, was alive, but it was also something he wanted to happen once he himself was no longer alive, so Raven could protect her.

Custer's gaze rested on the painting of Sue Ann and Betsy. Part of him wanted to take it down and shred it with his hunting knife, but this was not his nature. Sue Ann and Betsy loved the painting, but it was a constant reminder of how much his wife was still attached to another man even though that man was a ghost to her. To Eagle, Raven was a spirit, yet he was very much alive and would never go away, even though he remained silent.

Custer's fingers grazed the ring finger of Sue Ann's right hand and hit the gold nugget ring Shade had given her. The huge blue diamond stared at him daily, reminding him of Shade's light blue eyes, unique eyes, an identifying feature that kept him in hiding from those who might harm his loved ones if they knew he was alive. Custer figured Shade moved around. When Custer had decided to leave Tiger's Eye, Shade had offered him access to his place in Costa Rica, where he guaranteed no one would ever find him. Perhaps Shade would see he had called and would call back, letting him know he was there in his jungle fortress. If Shade carried the phone with him, or had calls transferred to a new phone, he would get the call wherever he was.

Sue Ann lifted her head from her husband's chest and smiled at him. "Do you think he will be all right, Custer?"

"Who?" For a second, Custer was taken off guard. "Oh...Tobi."

"I don't want Tobi to ever leave here. To think I missed over thirty-five years of my son's life. Seeing him and Betsy together was the medicine I needed to finalize my recovery from breast cancer."

"I don't think Tobi would ever leave you and Betsy, or the mountains. Don't worry, Sue Ann. I just have a feeling someone, the right someone, is in his near future. And no, I did not see it in a vision. My heart tells me." Custer put his hand to his heart for emphasis and was brought back to the reality of the present as he felt the thud of a missed beat aided by strained pumping that caused his ears to become warm with anxiety.

****

Betsy pulled in at Tobi's and headed for the door. Tobi opened it before she had time to knock, and they fell into a twin hug.

"I am so sorry, Tobi. What can I do to make you feel better?"

"You just did, Sis." Tobi took Betsy's hand and led her into the cabin, where the smell of fresh coffee greeted his sister. Her brother had sensed she was on her way.

"Well, it didn't take long for you to hear, and I knew it wouldn't. I guess Mom called you after Custer broke the news to her."

"Yes, she did. If you trust Custer's words like Mom and I do, then you have nothing to worry about. Star's replacement is on standby." Betsy took a long sip of the coffee Tobi had placed in front of her, while keeping her eyes on her brother, now sitting across the table.

"Really? Well, I do believe in Custer's sixth sense, but I'm not going to jump into another romance. The last one punched the air out of me." Tobi drummed the table with his fingers.

Betsy put her coffee mug down, reached across the table, and placed her hand on her brother's. "With your good looks and charm, it will happen, Tobi Parish."

Chapter Four

Washington, D.C., Late Spring

Clickity!Clickity!
"NOOOOO!"

Angel's blood-curdling scream echoed, but not through the dimming branches of the twilight where the stranger dragged her small frame like the carcass of a wild animal. Only her consciousness witnessed her plea for help. The stranger, the kidnapper, gave a maniacal laugh, enjoying the terror in her eyes glaring at him through glistening tears that cascaded down her pixie face and spilled over the duct tape tightly sealing her lips. The last remaining light of day was falling, as was all hope of escape, leaving only fear and trepidation in its wake.

Her mind was running a mile a minute, her stream of consciousness littered with emotive thoughts. Torture? Death? Escape? Survival? Would this really be the end, or did a light of hope linger at the end of the proverbial dark tunnel?

Silence filled the gap, and Angel looked away from the monster, her gaze taking refuge in the forest surrounding her. With her life in peril, Angel could not believe she was even able to think of the old adage "if a tree falls in the woods, and no one is there to hear it..."

So cliché! How she hated clichés. *So hallucinatory!*

Darkness! Oh, how she hated the dark. Ever since she was a small child she'd had an overwhelming fear of the dark and what it contained. She could remember a woman; the smell of perspiration and earth; and men, lots of sweaty men, gasping, panting, all clamoring and hunched over a small woman, probably her birth mother, like a bunch of savages. She could smell the candle burning, the only dim light cast over the cot where the woman lay stretched out waiting for them to finish while her little girl—Tulen, she had called her— stared at them from her straw mat on the floor. The woman had retaken her from the orphanage, perhaps for one fleeting moment of desire to know the girl child she had borne and then abandoned to the Sisters four years earlier.

Her adoptive mother, Hattie, had never divulged what became of Angel's biological mother. In fact, she refused to speak of her. All Angel knew was that her birth mom was half Vietnamese and she, the daughter, was a product of a war-ridden mindset of "take or be taken."

Darkness vanished as light shone against Angel's closed eyelids, reminding her of the brilliant dancing fire of the Northern Lights. "The sky has so much beauty to offer, beauty almost as important as the Aurora Borealis," Raven, her father, had told Angel one night in his cabin as they lay on the floor and gazed upward through the open skylight at what was his greatest inspiration for painting.

But the light on her eyelids faded, and the dark tunnel returned, filled with the night terror of a lifetime ago. A massive bear pawed the air before ONE, as he called himself, shot the bear, allowing him to fall near a bound, gagged, and terror-filled Betsy, Angel's best friend. Then there was the sharp knife blade the miscreant used, teasing the two teenage girls and luring TWO, the name given to her father in the days when he worked for ONE, a time Raven had tried to forget but could not.

"You like my toy, Tulen? Or do you prefer to be called Angel? Angel—how appropriate! Exactly what you'll be in a few minutes if your daddy doesn't show himself." He crouched beside Angel, waving the knife before her face. She kept her eyes open, replacing fear with contempt, refusing to so much as blink.

"Maybe I'll take off one of your ears—just to show you how truly heartless I am."

Angel felt a trickle of warmth from where the blade nicked her ear. She heard the blood plop as it fell onto her jacket. Who knew blood could be so loud? Was she becoming delusional?

If a drop of blood falls in the forest, can it still be heard by the one being tortured?

But Angel's and Betsy's torture at the hands of ONE was nothing compared to their last moments as captives. This was the nightmare that would never leave her, recurring every time she thought she was ready to go on with her life without the father she had longed to be with forever.

ONE ordered Betsy and Angel up the hill to the bluff overlooking the Tekooni River, pricking their backs with the point of his knife every few feet if they balked or hesitated. ONE had finished TWO off for good this time by plunging his knife deep into him as they fought. And now it was time to further his hatred of this man—he would kill his precious Angel, and with her would go Betsy, the daughter of Raven's lover, Dr. Sue Ann Parish.

The girls hugged each other, each taking solace in the other's embrace, knowing they were about to die. But neither of them screamed or cried, and neither begged for her life as they heard the creaks and groans of the ice floes in the newly thawing river below.

"Any farewell speeches, girls?" ONE raised his rifle, but as he clicked the safety off, Raven reared to life again! Using his last ounce of adrenaline, he rushed the would-be killer, yelling, plunging the knife he had pulled from his own body into ONE's groin, twisting, holding to him like a mad dog as the two men catapulted off the cliff and into the raging river below.

"Dad!"

****

Clickity! Clickity!

Angela woke with a start and knew she had fretted in her sleep while aboard the Amtrak running from Philly to DC. It took a minute for her to renegotiate her surroundings. Perspiration stood in beads on her forehead, and she took a tissue from her pack and blotted her face. She could feel her seatmate staring at her.

"Are you okay?" he asked.

Angela nodded, giving a hint of a smile, as she reached for a bottled water in her backpack. The cool water trickled down her throat, refreshing and calming her. Again, she leaned her head against the seat and closed her eyes. The clicking of the train wheels against the rails soothed her, helping her to recover from the nightmare that had startled her awake.

For most of her adult life, Angela had experienced

that nightmare, even as a teenager safe in her grandparents' home in Philadelphia, where she had gone to live, with Sue Ann's blessing, after her father's death. His death had taken a profound toll on her psyche, as she was sure it had on Sue Ann and Betsy also. Although Angela, known then as Angel, hadn't known her dad for as long or as intimately as Sue Ann and Betsy had, her heart had been ripped from her chest after witnessing him plummet from the Alaskan river bluff to his death. However, if it had not been for his dying, she and Betsy would not have lived to see the light of another day. Nor would Angela have had this opportunity to go into DC on a temporary duty assignment, a TDY, for her job with the CIA.

Through the generosity of her grandparents, Angela had been granted the opportunity to pursue her higher education at any university her heart desired—Harvard, Yale, UCLA. However, Angela had her heart set on the University of Mississippi, Ole Miss—the Harvard of the South. Her grandparents had been against this decision. Why on earth would anyone want to attend a university so far away, one not nearly as prestigious as the Ivy League universities of the Northeast? Angela remembered the few times she had been allowed to visit Betsy at Parrish Oaks during the summer. Parrish Oaks was close to Oxford, Mississippi, home to Ole Miss. Angela longed for the warm summer days, the mild winters, and the hospitality of a world that embraced an era no longer in existence anywhere else in the U.S. Angela hoped to find refuge with people similar to those she had come to love in that time in Alaska just before her world fell apart and her safety and her future were in question.

After she convinced her grandparents Ole Miss would be the right place for her, Angela submitted an out-of-state application and was accepted. Her stellar grades, as well as her ethnic background, both detailed in her entrance essay, cinched her a place as an Ole Miss coed. Ole Miss was always looking for ways to improve its image after its tumultuous twentieth century, scarred by racial division and tension, and being Asian, Angela was given an edge as a minority applicant. This was okay with her, being on a mission of her own to improve both her image and her outlook on life. And eventually she would piece together more of her past, she was sure.

Angela was awake now, her mind racing with thoughts of the past, but she soon turned them to present day as the Amtrak approached Baltimore and turned south toward Washington. For ten years now, Angela had made the trip, mostly by train, to CIA headquarters. Ole Miss, followed by graduate school at Harvard, had prepared her well for her career with the CIA, but mostly it was her own convictions and values that made her successful. She had watched as other international studies students at Ole Miss practiced bigotry and self-righteousness, the very description of the people they swore to fight in their crusades against the conservative, agenda-driven "man" not only of the United States but of the world. These students had been so focused on the "bigger picture" they had forgotten how to be decent human beings. Angela prided herself on being a decent human being first and CIA second.

Angela had always known she wanted a government job. The benefits were great, and while the pay wasn't wonderful at entry level, particularly for those living in larger cities, the job security would grant her the time, access, and contacts that could lead her to more information about the stranger she so frequently dreamed about. After the death of ONE and her dad—Raven or Shade or TWO, whoever the hell he was—the hunger for discovering more about this man who had been her father consumed her.

She had lost touch with Betsy and Sue Ann following her graduation from Ole Miss, something she regretted. But the death of her dad was not something she could forget, even all these years later.

The train huffed to a halt at Union Station. Angela took in the smells and sounds of the place and the hustle and bustle of the crowds. Lunchtime was fast approaching, and the soul of the city manifested itself inside the station. Grateful she had time and didn't have to rush, Angela transferred from the Red Line to the Orange Line, securing a seat against a window on the new train, where the only time-passer would be to stare out at the landscapes going by too fast to really appreciate. The humming and screeching of the train pulling out of the station engulfed her, drowning out the conversation of other passengers within the car. As the next stop was announced, the darkness of the tunnels ahead consumed her view. Angela closed her eyes and swallowed. She was momentarily back in the woods, with the stranger's fetid breath against her face and the knife nipping her ear. The train emerged from the tunnel into the sunlight, releasing her from the disturbing memories. She welcomed the sun's embrace and refocused her mind on the task ahead and how she had gotten to this point.

Eager to join the CIA, Angela had buried herself in

her studies at the Farm. She hadn't expected the classes to be tedious and the instructors to treat the students as if they were in high school. Uniformity proved to be the way of life, and if anyone deviated from these expectations, the perpetrator was reprimanded on the spot.

"There's a reason we're the number one intelligence agency in the world." The disciplinarians used this line on a daily basis. Angela had made sure she was at least twenty minutes early to class each morning, even after late nights of studying. Determined to graduate as an intelligence analyst at the end of the fifteen-week hell, she refused to allow herself to slip into dangerous habits like some of her classmates, whom she considered to be underachievers. She wondered how they had ever been admitted to the program in the first place.

The next few weeks had brought relief as her classes focused on the core of intelligence analysis, and Angela caught on quickly. Not only had she excelled in her studies, but after only three years with the CIA she had earned the status "Best of the Best," an intelligence analyst in demand for cases of highest magnitude.

Unfortunately, the TDY didn't involve her much-sought-after expertise this time. Instead, Angela was participating in an inspection assignment for old evidence—one of the more mundane aspects of maintaining a managerial position in the agency. In this particular instance, Angela and her assigned team of inspectors were delegated to peruse seemingly ancient evidence and classified documents, many of which contained redacted information, to ensure they had met a certain threshold before being cleared for permanent destruction. The destruction allowed additional storage room for newer and more relevant case material. It was a dirty job, and someone detail-oriented had to do it. Angela's Type A personality could handle the challenge. Overall, the tasking proved to be quite monotonous and tedious, but one set of documents recently assigned to Angela's team hit too close to her own life, leaving her mind wandering and lingering in a past best forgotten. She felt vulnerable for the first time as an intelligence analyst, not a good position to be in with the CIA.

The first document, a cable from the Vietnam War, had been handed to her three weeks earlier and had been hard to wrap her professional mind around. The date and names had been redacted, with fictitious names written above the blackened lines signifying the person had been assigned to protective custody within the agency. The cable contained a set of instructions given to a hired assassin, or a group of special operatives of the soldier-of-fortune variety. Their mission was to take out a Vietcong leadership target hiding behind North Vietnamese enemy lines at the time.

She made her inspection determinations in the margin and moved on to the next document, an internal memorandum addressed to someone at the Defense Intelligence Agency, the DIA. The contents mentioned the unauthorized execution of a Vietcong source, a woman, by a member of a specialized taskforce referred to the DIA by the Agency. An incident had occurred between the Task Force Officer (TFO) and the source, based on the memo's context clues. The memo was also addressed to the CIA Director at the time, but the other names were blacked out. Just their affiliated agencies remained in type. The details piqued Angela's interest, being a Rambo fan, and she pictured Sylvester Stallone executing guerilla-style tactics with precision in the Vietnamese jungle. She smirked to herself, visualizing Stallone's muscles rippling under the sheen of his sweat. Realizing someone could be wondering why she was grinning, she cleared her thoughts, regained focus, and moved on.

She sifted through a few more documents and rested her eyes before coming to another cable involving the same Task Force Officer. This one broke her fully from her Stallone-induced trance. While the TFO's real name was redacted, with an alias written above it, his codename was still included in the meat of the document. TWO! What were the odds she would be reading documents revolving around the Vietnam War and an operative with the codename TWO? Fifty minutes crept by, and no other documents in her stack mentioned a TFO named TWO.

She needed a break and sat staring at the wall for a minute, allowing her eyes to refocus before turning back to her paper stack. She had to peruse the details of one last document before reconvening with the rest of her team. Halfway through, she stopped. Her mind was exhausted from trying to take in too many details at once. She needed to pace herself.

Angela moved her chair back to the main table, where the other members of her team also began looking up from their stacks. One of the other analysts, Robertson, began telling about a set of memorandums in his reviewed stack that sounded like something right out of a spy book. The details surrounded a former private security company's hired assassin who killed his boss's brother, turned state's evidence against the boss, became a savior to American prisoners of war, and subsequently went into hiding for many years before his former boss caught up with him. The hair on the back of Angela's neck bristled, but it was the next detail of an associated hostage situation that really caught her attention.

While her other teammates began writing their inspection findings and determinations, Angela took Robertson's stack of papers, under the guise of a secondary review. She shuffled through the intel until she came to a cable marked up in the margins by her team member, and she scanned the details as quickly as she could. Nothing! It wasn't the one she was after. Again, she shuffled papers and then flipped to a page with several markings in the margin.

"Ah, ha! VIETNAM...okay. MURDER...okay." Angela's gaze sped through the pages. "Alaska... Hostages... Two Teenage Girls... Tekooni River..." Her eyes could not keep up with her racing heart! At the bottom of the page, she noticed a handwritten note, initialed by someone she assumed was a supervisor at the time. The last report was written many years, possibly decades, earlier.

ONE confirmed dead. TWO pulled to safety by Special Operative, Code Name EAGLE. TWO disappeared from protective custody three months after his entry into the program. After action report needed.

The date was redacted, but Angela didn't need it for reference. She knew what she was reading. The capitalized numbers ONE and TWO indicated codenames, names she knew well. Angela stared at the paper in disbelief. Was her mind playing tricks on her? Could such a coincidence be possible? Closing her eyes, she was transported back to that night in the woods, the nightmare resurfacing in her conscious mind now that this case had been brought to her attention. She could feel the tree behind her and the stranger's breath on her neck. Was this the same TWO who had been coaxed out of hiding by using his daughter as bait? Was this—could this possibly be?

HE'S ALIVE!

****

Three weeks later, Angela prepared to leave her office at the CIA much later than she liked, considering this was DC, but the Postman, the name she gave the anonymous person who was feeding her information, had given directions to leave work at exactly 8:00 p.m. on this date, and she would receive more information. One package containing a classified document, one she should not have in her possession, had already been delivered to her condo in DC, using a delivery service. The condo was temporary housing she used only when needing to stay over because of work or recreation. The document delivered was part of the same classified information she had been working on in her job, the documents leading her to believe her father was alive. Even though she was an expert in research, part of the training with her job as an intelligence analyst, she had not been able to find the information she had been seeking for the last three weeks during her extended TDY, but she had to know more. Yet she had to be careful; she was teetering close to where she was not authorized for need-to-know. The first document was about her and gave her just enough information about her father and his years in Indochina to make her do some serious digging on her own, but it was to no avail. More information had been promised about her father, and her interest was piqued. Hurriedly, she grabbed her briefcase and headed to the entrance.

I hate leaving the office so late at night, but I have to know more. Whoever sent me the first document knew I would do whatever it takes to get more information.

As she headed for her car, her cell phone beeped, signaling a message. She stopped and read the screen, knowing the identity and phone number of the messenger would not be displayed. On the phone screen she read:

Document is in large envelope on floor under driver's seat of beige Ford parked beside your Mercedes in garage. Further information will be forthcoming. Tell no one or information flow will stop.

Angela hurried to her parking spot in the garage and was not surprised to find an older beige Ford parked beside her SUV. Quickly, she opened the driver's door, reached beneath the seat, and pulled out a thick manila envelope. After punching in the code to unlock her SUV, Angela threw her briefcase on the back seat, pulled another older briefcase from the floorboard in front of the passenger seat, and tucked the envelope inside, locking it.

As she drove to her condo in the city, she thought about the mystery surrounding the documents she was receiving. Who could be sending this information to her, and for what purpose? The message on her phone would not be traceable, not that she would be taking this information to anyone in the CIA, but someone inside had to be sending it, since the information was classified with the agency. She knew plenty of agents with the CIA but no one who fit the Postman's profile. Regardless, she would follow instructions in order to get more documents. This information was about her father and was for her eyes only.

Angela hadn't realized just how nervous she was until her phone rang, causing her to jump and swerve her SUV. But when she looked at her phone screen, a smile replaced any fear.

"Hi, handsome!" She glanced in the rearview mirror, more from habit than fear, although she did notice a vehicle behind her, something that might bear watching. She considered taking a surveillance detection route, just in case, but decided against it. She had had a long day. "I drove in to work today, so I'm staying at the condo. See you in an hour or so?" She glanced at the mirror again and noticed the car seemed to be staying the same distance from her, just far enough back, too far to ID.

"I wish, Angela, but I've been called out on a case. I leave on a flight at midnight." Randal paused, and she knew he must be checking his watch. "Damn, I hate to leave without seeing you, and you know how the CIA works. It could be a while before I get back to DC."

"Where are you now? If I hurry, I could meet you at the Marriott by the airport. You know, for a little meet-and-greet before we say our goodbyes." Angela smiled as her imagination took over.

"I'd like nothing better than making love to you, sweetheart, but there just is no time. I have to meet up with another agent for a debriefing before I board my plane. This is hurried but vital, or so I was told. I promise I'll call as soon as I can. Keep those thoughts until I get back."

"Call when you get a chance. I'll miss you." Angela hung up, but her mind was reeling with thoughts of the man now in her life.

Randal Davison is always good for a change of pace, and he can be exciting. Just the kind of recreation I need to keep me energetic.

She thought back over the years she had spent married to her job, and to her art when she had free time. She had almost relegated herself to being alone forever. There was to be no Mr. Right who could take her mind off her eternal loneliness. Then, out of nowhere, Randal Davison entered the picture, introduced to her by one of her old friends, her supervisor at the CIA, Herb Feller. Herb would be retiring soon, and Angela would miss him.

She looked around as she parked in the underground garage at her condo building, something she had trained herself to do. Living in DC, even just part time, could be dangerous. For some reason, she was more nervous than usual and could hardly wait to be safely inside her condo. She much preferred staying in her home in Philadelphia, the home left to her by her grandparents, but since receiving the first documents, she found she was seeking opportunities to stay in DC to work more and more…just in case she received a message from the Postman.

Seeing no one in the garage, she grabbed her briefcase from the backseat, left her car quickly, and headed for the elevator, clicking the lock button on her car remote without looking back.

As the elevator door opened, she realized she had

picked up the wrong briefcase. She needed the older one, containing the new documents plus art show information and real estate brochures just in case she decided to make a permanent move to DC. She turned to head away from the elevator and ran straight into a tall, heavyset man dressed in dark jogging clothes, his hood pulled up over a ski mask. Angela screamed, but before she knew what was happening he had shoved her into the back of the elevator hard, knocking her to the floor.

"What the…?" She struggled to get up, but the man had knocked her back so hard she found herself stretched out on her back. Instinctively, she covered her face with her arm for protection.

"Stay there, and I won't hurt you." The man spoke in a gravelly voice hard to understand. His knee was planted firmly on her midsection, and she reached up, trying to push him away; all she could reach was his stomach, and she was only able to give him a slight push.

Ignoring her feeble attempts, the man jumped up, grabbed her briefcase and her purse, and sprinted from the elevator. By the time she got to her feet, her assailant was out of sight—and so were her briefcase and purse. But that, she realized, was the briefcase from work, not the one where she had placed the documents. She was too shaken to breathe a sigh of relief at this moment.

Thank God she still had her keys in her pocket! Angela ran to her car, punching in the door code as she went, and retrieved the older briefcase from the floor of the front seat. She sprinted back to the elevator, her heart pounding as she fumbled at the board to punch in the code only the residents of the condos knew. As she pushed the last button, she screamed for the door to close.

When she reached her floor, heart rate still accelerated, she rushed to the door. Her spare door key was in her purse, traveling to destinations unknown, but she had put a combination key box, like realtors use, on her doorknob. She'd lost two keys since moving into the condo; this was a precaution so she would never find herself without access again. Hands shaking out of control, she had to start the combination over a second time before she could retrieve the key and open the door.

After entering, she double-locked the door and then remembered to look around before feeling comfortable, even though the building was located in one of the most secure areas of the city, or what had been considered so up until now. After retrieving her handgun from the coat closet, she turned on all the lights and went room by room, SWAT style, like the CIA field agent she was not. Being an intelligence analyst was not usually a dangerous job for the agency. She figured this frightening incident probably had more to do with living in DC than with her job, but she was involved in a personal caper not sanctioned by the CIA.

The "not sanctioned" label kept her from calling the police to report the attack and the robbery. Besides, she couldn't give a description of her assailant, and there was nothing of any value or importance in her briefcase. However, her purse was quite expensive in its own right, though it held nothing she couldn't easily replace. She never even kept her wallet in her purse—just in case.

After checking out the condo, Angela tried to put the night's frightening event out of her mind. Rummaging through her drawers, she pulled out her flannel pajamas, even though it was spring, and put on thick socks, an attempt to stop the chills and shaking that came in the aftermath of the attack.

After downing a glass of wine, she opened her briefcase, ready to spread out the packet of information left in the beige Ford. She knew she could lose her job if anyone found out she possessed classified documents, even though she had not solicited the information. Losing her job was not a concern at this point. She had inherited enough money from her father and her grandparents to never have to work, if she so chose, and could still live a comfortable, even a luxurious lifestyle.

The real estate brochures were a moot point now. She wasn't sure she even wanted to continue working, but she wouldn't leave the city until she had the information she needed to find her father. Someone wanted her to have this information and was handing it to her on a silver platter. She laughed as she spoke the cliché in her mind, remembering how her dad, whose real name she now knew was Jon Shockey, had hated clichés.

After only a few minutes, she was speed-reading through the files, the same files she had seen at work, and she found herself replaying the events from that horrible two days, a lifetime ago, when she lost her father. Page shuffling ensued as Angela searched, hoping something would leap out at her. She knew sleep would not be possible after the harrowing incident in the elevator.

The one night I need you with me, Randal, you are

gone to no-telling-where, and I can't even reach you by phone. Yes, it is time for you to propose, and it is time for my loneliness to end. You would have to leave just when I had decided to share my information with you. Maybe you could have helped me.

Angela poured herself another glass of red wine and returned to the table covered with pages all stamped SECRET, indicating she should not be snooping. But someone thought the information was for her eyes, even though she had no clue as to why that someone had given her the documents, or why they had them in the first place. But there was no way she would turn them over to the CIA. She needed to know about her father, but especially she needed to know if there was any way he could have survived the plunge into the Tekooni River in Alaska.

An hour rolled by, and the wine began to do its job of relaxing her, and she could no longer hold her eyes open. She looked like a bobble head, and no amount of jerking herself back to consciousness helped as her head landed on the pile of papers in front of her. Summoning her mind back to life, she jerked her body upright and knocked over her glass. Wine saturated the papers, and Angela ran to the kitchen, grabbed a dishtowel, and began sopping up the wine.

"Damn! What a mess!"

She picked up the papers that had soaked up the most red liquid and began fanning them through the air, trying to keep the ink from running. As she did, several pages flew out of her hand.

"Double damn! What next?" she yelled, tense with anger and frustration.

Now down on her hands and knees, she tried to

gather up the papers, but one sheet escaped, turning face down on the hardwood floor, red wine threatening the print on the typed side. Quickly, she grabbed it and turned it over, hoping to read anything on it before it was ruined. One emboldened line jumped from the red creases to her eyes huge with excitement:

Where is Jon Shockey and who might know?

An hour later, Angela Shockey sat at her desk, typing out her resignation.

Chapter Five

Montana

"You have a letter from D.C., Sue Ann. Might want to take a look at it. It doesn't have a return address, but from the fancy handwriting, I'd say it's personal." Custer took the wooden spoon from Sue Ann, swapping it for the letter. "I'll take over here for you."

Custer had not seen correspondence from D.C. in decades, the last time being a summons for an urgent assignment in Alaska, the rescue mission that still haunted him.

"Just turn it off. It's simmered long enough." Sue Ann wiped her hands on a dishtowel and sat down at the table, where she reached for her reading glasses. "I wonder who sent this." She continued staring at the envelope without opening it.

Custer reached in the drawer and pulled out a steak knife. "Here, let me open it for you." Sue Ann passed the envelope to Custer and watched as he made a quick, clean opening. "Here you go."

Sue Ann peered over her glasses at the first page, reading it slowly, absorbing every word. After finishing the first page, she put it face down on the table and began reading the second with her lips moving in sync with her eyes. The third and final page was placed on top of the other two before she took off her glasses and looked back at Custer, who was pretending to fuss over the stew with no interest in the mysterious letter.

"Well, now! What a surprise! After twenty years..." Sue Ann picked up the stack of pages and began reading them again but this time aloud for Custer.

Dear Sue Ann,

I am sure you thought you would never hear from me again after so many years without so much as a note, but I am at a place in my life where I need family, and you and Betsy are the only family I have left. Thoughts of you have always remained with me, but I knew our worlds were too far apart with me in Philadelphia, or wherever, and you in your mountains with, I'm guessing, your old friend Custer. And Betsy has a wonderful life with her hero husband Hawk. Yes, I've read all of your books and Betsy's, with the exception of the last one. Hopefully, I will get to hear your life story from you in person, told over many cups of coffee as I gaze at the Beartooths with you on that porch you talked about the last time we spoke on the phone so many years ago, years I am embarrassed to try to recalculate.

It is time, Sue Ann! It is time for me to talk about Dad again even though the pain is still severe, and it is time to be with my second, or more accurately third mother and the only sister figure I have ever known.

For the past ten years, I have worked with the CIA as an Intelligence Analyst. No, I have not given up my love of art, my father's contribution to the best part of me, but the art was pushed back for the past few years while I pursued what I thought would be my career.

Lately, I have grown weary of my job and need time to regroup. As always when undergoing stressful periods, my mind diverts to the happiest time of my life—those wonderful few months in Alaska with you, Betsy, and Dad. Now I am what some consider middle-aged, and what I have to show for it is a wonderful collection of artwork, my dad's, and memories fading because of not being able to include them in conversation with people who would understand. I am sure I sound destitute, and in an emotional sense I have never been needier.

I know you have recently fought a battle with breast cancer, but by the time I read about it, you had won the fight, and I am so thankful. I should have called you then, but I just did not take the time and was not sure I wanted to begin remembering all I had lost. For the last few years I have been able to put the past behind me, but recently the nightmares have returned. In my sleep, I replay over and over Betsy and me holding to each other as we watched Dad disappear beneath the murky waters of the Tekooni River in Alaska, taking with him the monster who wanted all of us dead.

By the time you get this, I will be on my trip driving across the United States, on my way to Montana. No one knows where I am going, and for now, I want to keep it that way. If anyone calls, please say you don't know where I am. I have never mentioned you to anyone, but my friends all work for the CIA. Need I say more? I left in a hurry after turning in my resignation, no time for goodbyes or a discussion of logical thinking or wasted years that could count toward retirement.

No, I am not waiting for an answer from you. I can get a place in Red Lodge, but I need to be close to you for a while. Thoughts of seeing you and Betsy and meeting Custer, Hawk, and Betsy's little cowboy Trapper are making me happier than I have been in a long time. Please tell Betsy I am coming, and I fully expect her to teach me to fly fish and ride a horse.

All my love,

Angel

"Can you beat that?" Sue Ann smiled as she placed the letter back in the envelope. She looked across the table at Custer, who sat expressionless. "I wonder what has stressed her out to the point she needs to be with Betsy and me? But it doesn't matter. I'm going to see Angel again, and that does my heart good."

Custer picked up the envelope and looked at the postmark. "This was mailed a week ago. I should check the mail more often maybe. I think you'll be finding out pretty soon what she has on her mind."

Sue Ann took the envelope from Custer and stared at the postmark. "Oh, my goodness! She could be in Red Lodge checking into a hotel as we sit here. We have to get busy, and I need to tell Betsy—and Tobi." Sue Ann jumped up and grabbed her jacket as she headed out the door. "Aren't you coming with me?"

"No. I'll just get in your way when you're in 'hurry up' mode. I'll make sure we have plenty of wood for evening fires and get the spare room ready for her. I'm guessing she will be staying right here with you."

After Sue Ann pulled away, Custer headed down the path to the old cabin. He needed to check if Raven had gotten his message.

Angel's been thinking about her dad lately and needs to spend time with Sue Ann and Betsy. Resigned from her job—with the CIA—and she's headed here to

Montana. And she does not want anyone to know where she is. Hmm! Makes me nervous.

Custer put his thoughts aside as he entered his cabin. He reached for the hidden cell phone and turned it on, but the message signal showed nothing. Either Raven did not get his earlier call, or he was ignoring it.

Raven, it's me again. You need to know Angel is on her way to Montana after twenty years of silence. Don't know if it means anything or not, but am thinking you need to know.

Custer moved to the rope bed and sat down, putting his hand to his chest. Feeling the heavy palpitation, he cut his conversation short.

My heart says you need a good prodding—you need to be alert! Boots by the door? I question leaving the old code, not really knowing the reason for Angel's visit, but my gut answers for me: "Yes—by the door!"

Knowing his cabin might be visited by a CIA agent, even though she was not a field agent, Custer decided he had to find a better hiding place for the phone. Considering the old flip phone was almost obsolete since it was sent to him so long ago by Raven, he considered tossing it. But he did not know Raven's main cell number. In the old days, he would have just handed it over to an operative, and they could have accessed the number and its location, but those days were long gone. The best he could do was to hang on to the phone—just in case—and hope Raven would respond to his message.

Chapter Six

Tobi headed his truck out Beartooth Highway, glad his favorite road had opened early after the mild but snow-packed winter. His idea was to drive to Cooke City, stopping along the way to take pictures as the Beartooths did their metamorphosis from winter white to green meadows pitted with snow patches while stems of wildflowers peeked through the cool soil, lured upward by the sun's warmth. Tobi knew he could still see extreme skiers on the summit taking advantage of the last vestiges of deep snow as they made their too-quick ski runs, followed by an arduous climb back to the highway. Here they would thumb their way to the top, just to do it all again. Tobi would stop and watch as the athletes zigzagged down the mountain, and he would enjoy talking to them on their way back up, taking him up on his offer for a ride to the top in his truck.

Tobi needed something to keep his mind off Star, and on this dangerously curving highway that climbed to almost 11,000 feet in elevation, there was no way he could let his mind wander, especially as he neared the top. He was sure to hit snow and ice at the Top of the World, the name of the gift shop where he always stopped for coffee.

As he approached the first pull-off heading up, he noticed only one car, not a good sign for Red Lodge business, but it would get better as the school year ended and vacation season formally started. Usually, when the highway opened for the season, the pull-offs were full of tourists snapping pictures. Tobi pulled in beside the small but sleek black SUV.

Mercedes! Tourist for sure. And not a spot of dirt on it.

Tobi reached into the back seat for his camera, something he never left home without. His daughter Carrie begged for pictures every time he called her, and he had promised to send her some mountain shots with the aspens just coming into their shimmering green stage as if fertilized by the leftover snow still clinging to the shade of the stately groves. The school year would soon start winding down in Denver, and Tobi was anxious for his daughter's long summer stay with him. Carrie loved Montana as much as he did, and he knew when she was old enough to make her own decision she would be living here with him.

As Tobi moved toward the edge of the overlook, he noticed a petite woman sitting on a large rock with a flat surface. Her knees were drawn up, with her camera balanced precariously on top of them as she took shot after shot.

"Wow!" She muttered without looking at him.

"Yep. Wow!" Tobi stood a few feet away and began focusing his own camera. He moved to the other side and snapped several pictures before moving back toward his truck. As he passed her, he heard her fidgeting with something and realized she had replaced her camera with a sketchpad. In just seconds, the Beartooths in all their glory appeared, and even though they were penciled, he could tell the finished product

41

with color added would be awesome. Without knowing why, he aimed his camera at her as she sketched and took a couple of shots before turning back to the mountains.

"You know that's invasion of privacy?" She never looked toward Tobi as she made the remark and continued to sketch as if not concerned by his actions.

"I'm sorry. I should have asked first. Guess I was overtaken by how fast the snowcapped mountains appeared on your sketchpad. That's another 'Wow!'" As he spoke, he could not help but notice how pixie-like she was. He couldn't see her face, but her black hair was cut short, frayed around the edges close to the line of her face and jagged but a little less than spiked on top. With the sun hitting it, her thick black hair glistened like black silk, as if in competition with her Mercedes. She looked like a child sitting there, and he noticed her black boots had a tall heel on them, probably an effort to add height to her petite stature. Tobi knew something about this, since he was on the short side, something unavoidable since his mom and his dad were both short. But what he lacked in height, he made up for in physique, and that was his doing.

"You are an amazing artist. What now? Will you take this home and turn it into a painting? I can just imagine how that would be, with the aspen leaves just opening—and if you look closely, you can add patches of wildflowers sticking their heads up like they're reaching for the sun." Tobi moved closer, hoping she would allow him to continue to watch as she sketched.

"Maybe. But right now I'm homeless. It will be a while before the easels come out and it is transformed into a real piece of art." Shading her eyes to block the sun, she looked up at Tobi.

"Homeless maybe, but not destitute, judging by that rig you're driving." Tobi looked into the young woman's face and could not help but smile. She was for sure a pixie, the cutest he had ever seen, or perhaps she was a china doll, with her slightly slanted eyes. There was something about her that was different, even rare. He expected to see dark brown eyes hinting at her Asian ancestry, but instead the most tantalizing blue eyes he had ever seen stared up at him.

Tobi shook his head, and before he could stop himself, another "Wow" escaped his lips. "I'm sorry. It's just..."

"I know. I get that a lot. You were expecting dark eyes, and you got freak blue instead." With this said, she resumed sketching while continuing the conversation. "I could say the same about your eyes, you know. Such a bright green I can see them from here. I've only seen eyes that color green once, or rather twice, in my life. Guess we are both a couple of freaks."

"Freak? Not you! Your eyes are amazing—like they're mimicking the sky in color and effect." Afraid he was embarrassing her with the compliments, Tobi cleared his throat and directed his gaze back to the scene below as he aimed his camera again. "I'm sorry about the intrusion." Tobi clicked several pictures. "My name is Tobi. I live just out of Red Lodge—in those mountains back there." This drew another "Wow" just as Tobi figured it would, so he felt more conversation was okay.

"So you're just passing through?" Tobi lowered his camera and directed his eyes back to the woman.

"Yes. I guess you could say that. But I really want

to go over the pass. They told me at the hotel Beartooth Pass might have to close again at the end of the week if the predicted bad weather gets here." Again she blocked the sun from her eyes and looked up at Tobi. "Angela...my name is Angela." She smiled, giving Tobi a wholesome grin as she held her hand out. "Help me up?"

"Sure!" Tobi took her hand and pulled her up. She kept her sketchpad tucked tightly under her arm and reached for her camera bag after standing.

"Here! I'll help you with that." Tobi took the camera bag and followed her to her vehicle. "This is a really nice rig. Gives new meaning to the term 'SUV.' " Tobi eyed the full length of the luxurious vehicle.

"Yeah. Maybe a bit much for Montana, but it was great for Washington." Angela opened the back door and stuffed her sketchpad into a briefcase. "Here. I'll take that." She took the camera bag from Tobi and placed it on the seat. "I guess I'll be going. I want to make it to Cooke City before dark. I think I'll stay there tonight and come back Chief Joseph Highway tomorrow. Might as well see as much as I can, since the highway is open, although I hear from the shopkeepers in Red Lodge that everything can be covered in a few feet of snow regardless of the season."

"You do know there is still ice and snow at the pass? Are you okay driving in that?" Tobi eyed her tires. "This is four-wheel drive, isn't it? I guess if you live in Washington, you can drive in ice and snow."

"It's all-wheel drive, but I'm from D.C., not Washington state. We get snow and ice in D.C., but I've never driven over a mountain pass in it. I'm sure I'll be fine, though." Angela took a seat under the steering wheel and noticed Tobi staring at how close she had to be to the wheel in order to reach the pedals. "One of the drawbacks to being short!" Angela answered Tobi's thoughts as she closed the door. After rolling the window down, she added, "Nice to meet you, Tobi."

He watched as she pulled away and hoped she was prepared for what lay ahead. After taking a few more pictures and doing a video panorama, he packed up his camera and jumped in his truck, prepared for the climb upward.

He stopped at Top of the World and got a large coffee, expecting to see Angela there, but she was nowhere to be seen. As he checked out, he asked the girl at the register if she had seen a petite woman with short black hair in the last few minutes. She told him she had not, and Tobi headed on his way.

When he got to Cooke City, he watched for the black Mercedes but saw it nowhere. He made a loop by every motel but to no avail. As he made his way back down the main drag, he noticed a couple of men, part of a road work crew, and decided he would stop and ask if the Mercedes had passed through.

"Hi. Did you by chance see a black Mercedes SUV pass by? A pretty woman, very petite with short black hair, would have been driving it." Tobi watched as the two men talked it over before telling him no such vehicle had passed by.

Tobi pulled in at a café but did not get out of the truck. He sat beating his thumbs against the steering wheel, wondering what he should do. It had started snowing halfway to the pass, so he had not stopped at anymore turnoffs to get season-end shots, but he had not really looked for off-road skid marks since Angela was so far ahead of him.

Without further thinking, Tobi backed up and headed back the way he had come. He had to know Angela was not in any trouble.

All the way back, he looked for tracks in the snow that might indicate she had gone off the road, but it was useless since fresh snow was falling fast. He did another quick stop at Top of the World to make sure they had not seen her since he was there earlier, but again, Angela had not been seen. Tobi headed back down, promising himself to stop at each pull-off on the way down the mountain.

The snow had stopped when he approached the first turn-off. As he parked, he saw one of the barricades was down. Tobi left the truck and hurried to where the barricade was knocked down. Peering down through the snowy mist, he could see a black vehicle part way down the side of the mountain, stopped from its deathly descent to the bottom by a clump of small pines. Halfway between the vehicle and the top, he saw a small person pulling herself slowly up the steep, slippery terrain, her high-heeled boots more hindrance than help. She even succumbed to crawling on all fours at one point, trying to gain distance.

"Angela!" Tobi cupped his hands over his mouth and called to her and then headed as fast as he could toward her, digging the heels of his hiking boots in as he descended, sometimes doing a sideways hop that seemed faster and surer. Angela looked up and waved. Then as if she could climb no more and knew she was about to be rescued, she sat down, wrapping her arms around her body and rocking back and forth in an attempt to stave off the temperature growing colder by the second.

The steep decline demanded Tobi be cautious, and it took several minutes for him to reach her.

"Oh, my God! Are you all right, Angela?" Tobi sat on the ground as newly falling snow pummeled them, and he hugged her to him. She was shaking out of control.

"Can you finish this climb?" Tobi held to her shoulders and looked in her face, trying to judge if she was hurt or not.

"Yes, I'm…just shaken…a little. When I hit the trees, it knocked me out." Angela reached to her head to feel the lump where her head had hit the side window. "But I'm okay. I can walk if you help me."

With his arm around her waist, Tobi began the slow maneuvering up to the parking area. When he got to his truck, he opened the passenger door, picked Angela up and placed her on the seat, and fastened her seatbelt around her. Reaching into the back, he took a down sleeping bag out of his emergency gear, unzipped it, and wrapped it around her, tucking it tight on each side. Then he hurried around and crawled in under the wheel and started the motor, turning the heater on high and making sure all vents were aimed at Angela.

"I stayed in the car for a long time hoping someone would find me, and hoping my head would clear, but I decided if I was going to get help before dark and before the temperature dropped too far below freezing, I needed to get back to the road. I'm afraid my light ski jacket was not enough when the temperature began dropping." Angela's teeth had stopped chattering, but she pulled the sleeping bag up closer around her ears.

"Thank goodness I had a wool cap in the car, or my ears would be frostbitten."

"I need to take you to Red Lodge, to the hospital emergency room. You might have a concussion. I'll call the highway patrol and report your accident as soon as I have cell service." Tobi put his hand in front of the vent to make sure the warm air was directed toward Angela as he headed back down the highway.

"Please! Don't…drive fast!" Angela spoke through teeth that had begun to chatter again, more out of fear than from cold. Tobi slowed considerably while casting glances at his passenger. Within minutes, Angela was asleep.

****

"She was extremely lucky!" The ER doctor sat down across from Tobi in the waiting room and gave him the report, assuming he was close friend or family to the patient. "She will be sore for a few days and has a slight concussion but no fracture. It wouldn't hurt for her to stay here overnight for observation, but she insists she is fine and will be close if she needs medical attention. My suggestion is you make sure she gets plenty of rest and doesn't overexert herself."

"Thank you, Dr. Henderson. I'll take care of her." Tobi smiled, knowing he would be assuming the role of friend to this complete stranger.

"She said she was stopped from going all the way down to the bottom by a clump of small trees. Talk about a brush with death! I can't imagine how frightened she must have been. I've only been in Red Lodge for ten months, and that highway scares me to death every time I go on it, even if it is a beautiful drive." The doctor rose from his seat. "She'll be out in a minute. You might want to bring your vehicle to the side door there. Call if you need anything, or just bring her back to the ER if she starts getting nauseated or acting irrational."

****

Tobi parked outside the ER door, waiting for Angela to appear.

What the hell have I gotten myself into? I don't even know this woman—but she is awfully cute! In fact, she's so little and cute, I feel like I should call her a girl instead of a woman.

Tobi questioned his actions, but he knew going back to search for Angela had been the right thing to do. His mind hit replay as Custer's words rang in his ear.

"You have a strong, innate sense of protection. A man's highest calling is the protection of a woman. Do not put barriers across the pathway to your heart opened by Star, Tobi, for that path leads to your soul."

Chapter Seven

"Just take me to the Pollard Hotel, Tobi. That was where I had planned to stay when I got back from Cooke City—that is if I had ever reached Cooke City." Angela leaned her head back on the truck seat.

"No. You don't need to be alone. Dr. Henderson said for you to take it easy. He really thought it best if you stayed at the hospital overnight." Tobi kept his eyes on the street, wondering if Angela would go for what he had planned.

"I'll be fine. I'm used to taking care of myself, with no family or husband." Angela sat up straight. "Oh—but I no longer have a vehicle! Is there a place in Red Lodge to rent a car?"

"The wrecker service said it would be tomorrow before they can rescue your rig, but don't worry. I have a plan." Tobi passed the Pollard Hotel and knew this would raise questions.

"There's my hotel! Where are you going, Tobi?" Angela turned her head, looking at the hotel as they passed. "Oh! That hurt! My neck is a little sore."

"And that is why I'm taking you to my sister's house. I called her while I was waiting for them to bring you out. She said to bring you right over, and you can stay for as long as it takes you to recuperate."

"But I don't have clothes or anything. My suitcases are still in my car, sitting in a clump of trees down the mountainside." Angela looked around and felt in her coat pockets. "Dang! I lost my cell phone! Well, I guess I can change my service provider now. Been meaning to do that anyway, since I left my old job."

Angel thought about Randal, but he had not bothered to call in two weeks, so there was obviously no need to worry about him. The only person she might want to keep as a contact was Herb Feller, but she could easily get his number from the Agency. It was then she remembered the briefcase that held the classified documents.

"Stop, Tobi! We have to go back to my car! I left my briefcase in it, and it has important documents in it!"

"I'm sorry, Angela, but it's almost dark. That would not be a good idea. I'm sure the briefcase will be safe. The wrecker will have the rig and its contents in Red Lodge tomorrow morning."

"I can't believe I didn't grab it when I crawled out of the SUV. Damn!" Angela beat the sleeping bag with her fist.

"If it makes you feel any better, I'll go first thing in the morning and get your briefcase and your luggage before the wrecker gets there."

"You would do that for me, a complete stranger? I am so sorry for you to have to go to all that trouble, but the briefcase is super important. If someone got to it before me, it could really be bad."

"I promise I'll be there at first daylight, so don't worry." Tobi saw Angela relax and wondered what could be so important she was ready to turn around and go back to the crash site. "You'll be fine without your suitcase until morning. My sister is petite, too. You might have to roll up her jeans an inch or two, but otherwise, they will be a good fit. And you'll have my six-year-old nephew for entertainment." Tobi glanced at Angela to see how she was taking the news. "Trust me. You will be in good hands. Tomorrow, after you've had a good night's rest, I'll help you get a rental car while we see if your car can be repaired."

They pulled in at Betsy and Hawk's cabin just after dark. Tobi noticed his mom's Jeep parked by the hitching post.

"This is your lucky day, Angela. You will have both my mom and my sister to make a fuss over you."

Tobi jumped out and hurried to the passenger side to help Angela out, knowing it was a long drop for such a short, frail person. Her door was already open, and she was balancing her pointed heels precariously on the chrome bar that served as a running board, while eyeing the distance to the ground. Tobi reached up and gently lifted Angela down.

"Thank you, Tobi, but I feel like this is such an imposition. I'm a stranger and don't even know my rescuer's last name." Angela took her first step and stopped, grimacing as the soreness in her ribcage grabbed her. "Oh! This is not good."

Without hesitation, Tobi picked her up and started to the front door. Before he could knock, the door opened and Hawk stepped out on the porch.

"I don't guess you need any help, Tobi. Looks like you've got everything under control. Come in, Angela, and welcome."

Tobi stepped through and carried Angela to the sofa, gingerly placing her on it and fluffing the cushions at her back.

"Thank you, Tobi. You are kind, but I'm not an invalid—just a little sore in spots." Angela stretched her shoulders and moved her head slowly, side to side.

"Where is everybody?" Tobi looked around for Betsy and his mom.

"We're back here." Betsy called from the back of the cabin. "Getting the guest room ready for Angela. Be right up."

"And where is my nephew? Thought sure he'd be here ready to make a new friend." Tobi turned back to Angela. "Just wait 'til you meet him. Trapper is the cutest little cowboy gentleman you'll ever meet. He'll tip his cowboy hat, which he wears inside the house, too, and give you a smile that'll melt your heart."

"Trapper? Did you say Trapper?" Angela pulled herself up on the edge of the sofa, staring at Tobi and trying to turn her head in the direction where she had heard the woman's voice.

"Trapper is with Custer at the grocery store. He took my rig. Your mother sent him for ingredients for that chicken soup she feels is the cure-all for whatever ails—even soreness from a wreck." Hawk smiled at Angela. "You're in good hands with Betsy and Sue Ann, Angela. And by the way…I'm Hawk."

As steps were heard coming from the back of the cabin, Angela forced herself to stand, grimacing a little in the process. Her eyes, glued to the hall, were already filling with tears, knowing she was about to be in the loving care of Sue Ann and Betsy.

"Well, Angela, we have your room all ready and…" Betsy stopped as she entered the great room. She stared at the girl—the almost-sister she had thought she would never see again. Sue Ann entered behind

Betsy and stopped when her daughter stopped, her gaze following in the same direction. Both women broke into huge grins and hurried across the room, grabbing Angela in a threefold bear hug.

"Angel…Angel…is it really you?" Betsy released the girl whose smile tried to hide the pain caused by the hugs, but Sue Ann could not let go.

"You're here—you're really here, Angel! I just got your letter today and haven't even had a chance to tell Betsy yet." Sue Ann loosened her hug but took Angel's hand in hers. "Oh, my! You are Angela, the girl in the accident… Tobi said he was bringing someone for us to help recuperate—you're the girl who was almost killed on Beartooth Highway!" Sue Ann wiped her eyes on her shirtsleeve. "Are you all right, sweetie?" She rubbed her hand over Angel's shoulder and down her arm, being as careful as possible. "We never connected his 'Angela' with you."

"I started going by Angela after my grandparents died. It just sounded more professional than Angel. And I don't think I could have gotten a job with the CIA if I was Tulen Dubois."

"Angel? Tulen? What's going on, Mom…Betsy?" Tobi's eyes darted from his mother to his sister and then to Hawk, who just shook his head and held his hands up to show he was as perplexed as Tobi was.

"It's a long story, Tobi." Sue Ann walked to the window. "Custer and Trapper are back. Let's make a pot of coffee. It's story time."

Chapter Eight

Custer had never met Raven's daughter, but there was no doubt she was his. He almost told her how her eyes were exactly like her father's but caught himself. Not even Sue Ann knew he had a past with Shade Dubois, and because of oaths, promises, and signed contracts, he would have to keep it that way.

"You should see the sketch she drew when I saw her at the first turn-off. It's amazing!" Tobi glanced at Angel, who gave him a thank-you smile.

"It comes natural, Tobi. Her father, Shade, was the most amazing artist I've ever known. He painted the picture of Betsy and me under the Northern Lights, the painting that hangs over the mantel in the cabin."

"Shade was your father?" Tobi asked. Betsy had told him all about his mother's greatest love, Shade Dubois, and about his tragic death.

"Dad finished the painting? Really?" Angel ignored Tobi's question and put her coffee cup down without taking a sip. "How did you get it? You told me his cabin and studio had burned to the ground by the time you and Betsy got back to Moose Springs after taking me to my grandparents in New York."

"Actually, Custer played a big part in that, didn't you, dear?" Sue Ann directed the question to Custer, who was being uncannily quiet.

"Well, not really. I just rescued the big package

from the deliveryman who was having a hard time getting up the trail to Sue Ann's cabin. And I helped them hang it over the fireplace. That's all." Custer headed for the coffeepot. "Anybody else want coffee?"

"So you still have the cabin Dad left you?" Angel looked at Sue Ann and then cast a glance at Custer, who was taking his time at the coffeepot.

"Yes. It's my favorite place in the whole world. And it's where I met Custer, even though it took a few years for me to admit I loved him and to agree to marry him. Custer's old cabin is down the trail from my cabin." Sue Ann patted Custer's hand after he took his seat beside her again.

"So did you know my dad, Custer? I mean, since he bought the cabin so close to yours?" Angel watched, waiting for Custer to answer.

"I actually was not at my cabin when Sue Ann's place was sold. I was out of state at the time, but I was glad to see Sue Ann and Betsy were going to be my neighbors when I got back and met them. Guess it never entered my mind I'd be living in the cabin some day with Sue Ann as my wife." Custer reached for Sue Ann's hand. "It was a tragic turn of events, Angel, for all of you, including Sue Ann, but out of tragedy was born a different union of two people, but one also based on love. Please don't fault me for that. Fate can sometimes deal a hand hard to accept."

"Oh, no, Custer! Please don't misunderstand me. I am so glad Sue Ann has you, since my dad is no longer around." Angel's attention was drawn away from the conversation when Trapper brought his own sketchpad over to show Angel.

"Oh, my, Trapper! Is this a picture of your pony?

It's quite good." Angel smiled at Trapper.

"Thanks. I take art classes at school. I'm finishing first grade but I can still take art next year." Trapper leaned in for Angel to scoot to one side so he could sit on her chair with her. "I have trouble with his head. Can you show me how, Angel?"

"Sure I can. You watch what I do. I'm going to draw dotted lines and you can trace over them." Angel began making dots, and Trapper leaned in as close as possible to see the artist at work.

"Now watch this! Does Dakota smile like this?" Angel drew a happy face on the pony and Trapper laughed and laughed.

"Yep. That's Dakota all right!" Trapper took the sketchpad around the table to show each family member.

****

Betsy insisted Angel stay with her and Hawk, since they were closer to Red Lodge, just in case she needed to go back to the hospital. With only a little arguing, Sue Ann agreed but with the stipulation that Angel come to her cabin in the mountains as soon as she was up to it.

"I'll be back by lunchtime tomorrow with a pot of chicken soup." Sue Ann gave Angel one more careful hug before she and Custer left. "Yes, it's good for the soul, but it's also good for what ails a person physically."

Angel went to bed as soon as Sue Ann and Custer left, needing to sleep but knowing she would worry about her briefcase, sitting in a clump of pines, just waiting for the wrong hands to get hold of it. But after what she had endured that afternoon, she found her body too much in need of rest to protest, and she slept. Little did she know that, as soon as her eyes closed, Tobi and Hawk were on their way to Beartooth Highway with heavy duty flashlights and all gear necessary to retrieve the briefcase and her luggage, so she would awake to find it in her bedroom the next morning.

****

On the trip back to their cabin, Custer remained quiet, adding little to Sue Ann's conversation and excitement over Angel being in Red Lodge.

"She looks just the same as she did the last time I saw her, with the exception of a little aging around the eyes, and believe it or not, she is much bigger. Isn't she just a little doll? My, how Shade loved her!"

Custer's mind was filled with questions about Angel, questions he could not share with Sue Ann. Why did she show up now after twenty years? *Since my dad is no longer around.* He said Angel's words over and over in his mind, wondering why she did not say, "Since my dad is dead."

"Custer, I asked you twice what you think about Angel. You seem so distant. Is anything wrong?" Sue Ann placed her hand on his arm.

"No. Nothing is wrong. Angel is a beautiful young woman and is a talented artist like her father. I just wonder why she chose to show up now after what—twenty years? Does she have some problem we need to be concerned about? And she worked for the CIA, certainly not a dead end job, but she resigned." He kept his eyes on the trail. The bumpy road required his full attention, and he was glad to have a reason to go silent again.

"You sound so suspicious, Custer. That isn't like you." Sue Ann turned her gaze back to the trail.

"I don't mean to be, Sue Ann. I was just wondering. I'm sure everything is fine. If not, Angel will confide in you when she comes to stay with us." He slowed the vehicle as they came into the yard of the cabin. "I look forward to getting to know Angel."

Custer built a fire while Sue Ann changed into her lounging pajamas. By the time he got his boots off, she was curled up on the sofa, wrapped in a quilt, staring at the painting of her and Betsy.

"Mind if I sit with you?" He broke her gaze, and she smiled at him.

"Do you have to ask?" She opened the quilt for him, and he took her in his arms. She cuddled against him, forcing her attention from the painting. "Don't worry, Custer. Angel being here will not come between us. You are my husband, and I love you more than life itself."

Custer held her tighter but could not help looking at the painting. Would Sue Ann still feel this way about him if she knew he had a past with Shade Dubois? Would she still love him if she knew Shade was alive?

As if giving him a warning, Custer felt a pain shoot across his chest. He could feel his face redden and soon sweat popped out on his forehead. Pulling his arm from around Sue Ann, he threw the quilt off as he grabbed his chest and leaned over. His breathing was strained, more panting than breathing. She knelt in front of him, her face full of panic.

"Custer! Darling, are you all right?"

He laid his head back on the sofa and closed his eyes, willing the pain away. "I'll...be...okay. Give...

minute. Pills in kitchen…cabinet…"

She hurried into the kitchen and in seconds was back with a pill bottle already open.

"Here, Custer! Open your mouth and put this under your tongue." Sue Ann knew this was serious when he asked for his Nitrostat and did as he was told without making a fuss.

Piling the cushions on one end of the sofa, she directed his head onto the cushions, put his feet up on the sofa, and covered him with the quilt. Sitting beside him, she pushed his hair away from his face and caressed his cheek.

"Thank you, Sue Ann." He opened his eyes and smiled up at his wife. "I'll be fine. Don't worry. It's better already. Just give me a minute."

"How long have you been having these pains, Custer? I need to call an ambulance and get you to the hospital." Her face showed fear.

He reached for her hand and pulled it to his heart.

"Sue Ann, Doc knows all about my pains. I went to see him earlier this week. There is nothing more that can be done, and you and I both know it. I'll live as long as I am supposed to…no more…no less." He sat up and rubbed his hand through his long hair. "I am not afraid, and you should not be either. You and I both know my old ticker is playing out. The Creator has been generous, allowing me three wonderful years with you as my wife, and I am grateful. Now, let's not talk about it anymore." He drew her to him again and held her.

With her head on his chest, Sue Ann could not contain her tears as her ear felt the irregular beat of her husband's heart. In her mind, she prayed for more time but knew this decision was not hers to make. She, too, would be grateful for every second they had left together, and she vowed not to show her worry in front of him.

****

Angel sat on the porch with Sue Ann, drinking coffee and looking at the Beartooths.

"It is so beautiful here. I know now why Dad bought this place for you. It is every bit as pretty as the mountains in Alaska—a different kind of beauty, but spectacular like Alaska. The Healing Mountains!"

"Yes, they are healing." Sue Ann rested her head against the back of the rocker. "Your dad knew the possibility of our getting to share a long life together was slim—maybe even nonexistent—and he bought this cabin for me. According to the deed, he purchased the cabin and land a couple of months before he died. Shade was so terrified for us, and I guess he had every right to be. He kept saying he should leave, but I just could not imagine life without him." Sue Ann turned her head toward Angel without raising it from the back of the rocker. "See where that got me."

The two sat quiet, rocking and looking upward. After a couple of minutes, Angel stopped rocking and sat up.

"Sue Ann, when the agent with the CIA came to tell you Dad's body had been recovered from the river, did he offer to bring him back to Moose Springs for burial?"

Sue Ann stopped rocking and gave Angel a questioning look.

"No. I asked about it, but he said the agency would do an autopsy, a long process, and then his body would be offered to your grandparents for burial. Legally, I had no claim to it—to him. The only thing I was offered to show Shade's body had been recovered was my father's wedding ring I had given him as a token of my love." Sue Ann paused, gathering her thoughts. "I hate to discuss this with you, Angel, but the agent said his body had been in the water so long, cremation would be the only way. Did your grandparents have him cremated?"

"No. I asked them, but they said the CIA never offered them Dad's body. My grandfather said he did not pursue it, feeling it would add more suffering for my grandmother. They had lost Dad a long time before he…you know." Angel leaned back in her chair, keeping her eyes on the mountains.

"That makes sense, I guess, but I never really had closure, and I'm sure you and your grandparents didn't either. I think that is why it took so long for me to fall in love with Custer. I know it sounds silly, but I'd look at the mountain, at the trail leading up to the high mountain lakes, and I'd imagine seeing him on the trail, striding toward me. It was no different when I'd go back to Moose Springs, especially if the Northern Lights were dancing. I'd sit outside the cabin we shared and imagine he was there with me. I could almost hear him saying, "Shh! Listen, Sue Ann, to the Sélamiut…the Sky Dwellers; they will communicate with you if you believe."

"I wish Dad had taken us and left Alaska before— you know. We could have just disappeared. I overheard him tell you one time he had places we could hide." Angel kept her eyes on the mountain but could feel Sue Ann's gaze shift toward her.

"You heard him talking about Costa Rica? I had no idea you knew about that. I think that is where we would have gone if we had made it to Fairbanks the day..." Sue Ann did not finish and cast her eyes down to her lap where she fidgeted with the hem of her shirt.

"The day Betsy and I went to the river landing instead of being ready to leave for Fairbanks when Dad got back—like we were told to do?" Angel spoke in an angry tone. "Don't think I haven't kicked myself a million times for being disobedient that day. If only..."

Custer's Jeep pulled into the yard, putting a halt to the guilt session.

"Well, I see you got yourself a real Montana rig, Angel. Good thing, since I heard your Mercedes met an untimely demise. You'll be happy with the Yukon. Good rig for the mountains." Custer stepped up on the porch and stopped to give Sue Ann a kiss on the cheek. "So how are you, Angel? Soreness 'bout gone?" Custer leaned against the porch post beside Sue Ann.

"Yep. Good as new. In fact, Tobi is coming over after lunch, and we're going hiking. He says he's bringing a fly rod to start my fly fishing lessons, since Betsy has a deadline to meet on her new novel. Is Tobi as good a fly fisher as Betsy?" Angel smiled at Custer, knowing the answer already.

"Depends on who you ask. If you ask Hawk, he'll tell you real quick Betsy is the best caster in this part of Montana, even better than he is, and Hawk's guided for years."

"And what would you tell me, Sue Ann?" Angel cut her eyes at Sue Ann and smiled.

"Now, Angel, you know I could never give you an honest opinion on that one. Suffice it to say both of my children are excellent fly fishers—like their mother, their father, and their stepfather." Sue Ann smiled up at Custer. "But you'll see. Tobi will have you doing a long haul in no time, and if he misses anything, Betsy will take up the slack when she takes you. Hopefully, I'll be going with you soon. I'll give myself a little time to build up to a hike, and then I'll show you both how it's done."

"I hope you came to stay, Angel. Sue Ann has been hoping every day since she got your letter that you'd show up with your bags." Custer put his hands on the porch rail and let his gaze follow Sue Ann's to the mountain peak.

"My bags are in the Yukon. I just hope I don't wear my welcome out."

"I don't think that's possible. If Sue Ann has her way, you might not ever leave Montana or stay anywhere except this cabin."

****

Tobi slowed his pace so Angel would not overexert herself on the hike to Keyser Brown Lake. Angel assured him her soreness from the wreck was gone, but he was not convinced, having seen her grimace a couple of times when making a long-stretch jump from one rock to another while crossing a stream. His legs were longer than hers, so he knew she would be taking several steps to every one of his. They stopped when they got to the trailhead that led down to the lake, and Tobi took off his backpack and handed Angel a bottle of water.

"A little over a mile to go, and it isn't a bad hike." Tobi helped Angel get her daypack off. "To have never hiked before, not to mention still recovering from a bout with Beartooth Highway, you're doing great."

"I've never hiked, but I do work out several times a week at the gym, and I'm an avid runner—treadmill runner, that is. The gym is the safest place in D.C. for running. I'm actually pretty fit for a city girl." Angel took several gulps of water before screwing the top back on her bottle. After putting the water in the side pocket of her daypack, she put the pack on and turned to Tobi. "Ready? I'm anxious to get this lesson started. Who knows—I might even catch a trout!"

Tobi grabbed his pack, putting it on as he led the way down the trail to Keyser Brown.

****

After an hour of "ten o'clock, two o'clock" repeated over and over by Tobi, a "metronome for casting" as Betsy called it, Angel felt she had the basic cast under control. When she was finally rewarded with a small cutthroat trout, a trout indigenous to these high mountain lakes, she felt like a pro.

What she did not have under control was the sensation she felt when Tobi put his arm around her, placing his hand over hers to show her exactly what he meant by proper wrist action and body movement.

"It's all in the timing, Angel. And the wait on your back cast is just as important as the forward cast."

A couple of hours later, she watched as he bent over the big flat rock in the meadow, packing up the fly rods.

Nice butt—but only one part of a complete package! And he doesn't tower over me like Randal and most men. I'm thinking I won't be missing Randal after all, and I'm glad I'm not married or engaged.

She saw his smile and figured he had read her

mind. When she realized she was staring, she began fidgeting with her pack.

Rescuer syndrome. She made quick glances at her fishing instructor. *Tobi is my guardian angel. And what a fine-looking guardian angel, with a body that could only be heaven sent!*

Chapter Nine

Tobi noticed Angel smiling as they rested, sitting side by side in the meadow grass looking at the perfect image of the mountain peaks reflected in the clear lake water below.

"What are you smiling about, Angel Shockey?" He matched her smile with his own.

"Oh, nothing. Just feeling really lucky to be out here in the wilderness with such a handsome fly fishing instructor." She lay back in the grass, putting her hands behind her head, and noticed he had gone silent as he pulled a blade of grass from beside him and stuck it between his teeth.

"You think I'm making a pass at you, don't you?" She looked at him and waited for a response.

Tobi stretched out beside her and propped on one elbow, looking down at her.

"I don't know." He arched his eyebrows and grinned at his student. "But a man can always hope. Got no ties binding me at the moment. What about you? Did you leave anyone behind in D.C.?"

"I had someone I thought I was serious about, but he was away when I decided to leave for Montana. He hasn't called in over two weeks, the whole time I've been gone, and I did not bother to say goodbye. Instead of becoming engaged, like I thought would have happened by now, Randal and I have become estranged.

He just doesn't know it yet." She pulled her cap over her eyes but continued to talk. "What about you? Betsy told me you're divorced, but you're bound to have someone you are interested in, with those amazing eyes. And those muscles!"

He reached over and pulled the bill of her cap up so he could see her eyes. Just as he'd suspected, her bright eyes twinkled, full of mischief.

"I don't have anyone—but things are looking up." He pulled her cap back over her eyes. "Well—are you?"

"Am I what?" Sky blue met mountain meadow emerald as Angel pushed her cap back and met Tobi's stare.

"Making a pass at me?" He maintained a serious look but with a smile threatening the corners of his mouth.

"Yes, Tobi Parish." Angel pulled the cap down over her eyes again. "I am most definitely making a pass at you." She paused for a few seconds. "So what are you going to do about it?"

With no hint of what he was about to do, he maneuvered under the cap bill that hit just above her mouth, and pressed his lips to hers. He pulled away a few inches and waited. He was rewarded by Angel running her tongue sensually over her bottom lip as if savoring the kiss.

Pulling her to him, he kissed her, but this kiss was filled with newfound passion and desire.

****

Angel lay still, enjoying the impromptu show of affection from this man she had only known for a few days.

Rescuing me has to count for a lot. Her thoughts took control as she smiled at Tobi.

He was so much like Betsy, making Angel feel she had known him forever. Tobi could easily make her forget Randal ever existed—if in fact he had ever existed.

Randal's loss!

She cleared her mind of any guilt as she sat up, propping on an elbow like Tobi. *His eyes are so tantalizing I want to leap right in and never resurface.*

"So—what's next, Tobi Parish?"

"How about this?" He grabbed her and pulled her on top of him, their lips meeting again. Wrapping his arms around her, he pulled her tight against him. Strong hands moved to her hips, pressing her tight against his masculine parts. She wrapped her legs around his, locking her hiking boots under his thighs and straddling him. Even with their clothes on, their bodies gave more than a hint of what was about to happen. Both were hungry—passion long overdue.

He rolled her over onto her back, pinning her hands over her head while holding his weight off her with his knees. Their lips met, dancing with passion as if the two had known each other longer than the time confirmed.

With lips seeking permission, his eyes became lighter and brighter, forming backup for what he was about to say.

"Like I said—timing is everything, but sometimes, there just is no need to wait."

Tobi pulled his T-shirt over his head and then started on Angel's clothing. First he removed her shirt, hoping there would be nothing underneath. He was not disappointed. As his hands began working at her shorts, she reached through, unsnapping his. When she unzipped his shorts, she let her hand linger over the bulk beneath, causing him to stop in his effort to remove her shorts.

Soon, they lay locked in each other's arms, naked and unashamed, as they began the lovemaking foreplay that had been in his mind since the day he met her.

"Did you read *The Hawk and the Deer*?" Angel asked as Tobi's mouth found her small breasts.

"I did, and my favorite part was the waterfall scene, although sometimes it is hard to put those words with the faces I know so well. What was yours?" He straddled her, again keeping his weight off her small body with his knees as his lips found pleasure in her breasts.

She circled her hips beneath him as if urging him to move lower. As she circled, she began to quote from the book:

"She lay naked on the rock, unashamed, and watched propped on one elbow as her beautiful lover undressed and exposed for her again—this time knowingly—the beauty of his exquisite stature. Leaning over her, he kissed her again even more sensually than before, his tongue searching until it found a partner and began its erotic dance in her mouth."

Hearing the words, Tobi moved up and began a replay of Betsy and Hawk's waterfall scene. He kissed her and let his tongue search and begin its own erotic dance in her mouth.

"Their tongues played like trout fingerlings in a wild current." It was Tobi's turn to recite from the scene at the waterfall where Betsy and Hawk first made love.

The replay of the scene released a fierce craving in Angel as she left herself open to wild lovemaking. Panting, she finished the scene.

"Running his rough, cowboy hands the full length of her body, he absorbed every inch, every hidden detail, savoring the hidden wet spots he uncovered. As he moved lower, he continued kissing her in all the secret places his hands had discovered."

"I can't believe you memorized that whole scene. You must really love that book." Taking her recitation as a demand for more, Tobi moved lower, "searching and savoring the hidden wet spots he uncovered."

"So what came next, Angel?" Tobi's heart was racing, his erection hard and searching for her. Barely able to speak, he whispered, "I have to get this right!" Through his panting, he smiled down at her, knowing full well what came next. She moved under him, teasing first and then directing him with her hand, demanding he take the plunge and catapult them both over the edge. Her voice quivered as she spoke.

"Hawk—no, I mean Tobi—held tightly as she moaned and writhed in hot, painful pleasure, compressing his body into hers..." Angel's voice caught as exhilaration swept through her. He was in her, and she found it difficult to speak. All she wanted to do was to allow passion and wanting to fill her to overflowing. With one final gasp and with her body shivering beneath him, her voice screamed the next line. "Overflowing it with the liquid passion he had saved for weeks."

Tobi knew what came next even before Angel began reciting, and by the time she said, "liquid passion," he was driving, thrusting hard to make sure he did this passionate love scene justice.

He made his final plunge, taking them both to the journey's end, both lovers' cravings filled. Her shrill cry of pleasure reverberated through the meadow until her breath caught in her throat. He held taut, letting the feeling, and the liquid passion, ripple through her until the last mini-pulse was gone and he began slipping naturally from her.

He rolled onto his side, propped on one elbow as he had been before they made love, and smiled at her. Returning the smile, she reached up and caressed his cheek as she began reciting again:

"Waves of exhilaration rippled through their bodies, leaving the lovers drained and exhausted."

To Angel's surprise, Tobi joined her in the last line: "The rapture temporarily over, the ecstasy complete."

****

The two men watched through binoculars, from behind the boulders high up on the trail to a higher lake, September Morn. The lovemaking scene below left them both hot, sweaty, and extremely horny. The smaller, not so handsome man expressed his desire to be back in D.C. with his mistress…not his cold wife. The other man, the handsome one, reacted with a deep-throated laugh.

"I think you know where I want to be."

The watchers had known every move Angel made since leaving D.C. The GPS tracking devices they had placed in her cell phone and on her Mercedes did not lie, and by the time the tracking devices died in her wreck on Beartooth Highway, they already were heading for Red Lodge. Tracking her using the old-fashioned devices of questions and common sense had not been a problem once they reached the town where locals were friendly and only too happy to share information about the people the "pretty little woman" was staying with, and the two men began learning everything about the location, including the Beartooth Mountains that surrounded the cabin of Sue Ann and Custer. Angela's Yukon, as well as Tobi's truck, were both now being tracked via satellite with the newest software and tracking devices.

It won't be long before we'll be trailing our little lady right up to her daddy's front porch.

The watcher chuckled to himself as he packed away the binoculars for another day of watching as the handsome couple left their lovemaking site and headed back down the trail.

Dr. Sue Clifton

Chapter Ten

That night, in her bedroom upstairs in Sue Ann's cabin, Angel opened her briefcase and took out the classified document still stained with red wine. She did not need to look at the pages to know what the report said. She had almost a photographic memory and had memorized the most important passages just as she had memorized the scene from *The Hawk and the Deer*. When she finished looking it over, she put the document away.

But where is my father now, and who left me the documents and for what reason?

Angel had tricked Sue Ann into telling how her dad had talked about the jungles and rainforests of Costa Rica as a hiding place for his family, but where in Costa Rica should Angel begin searching after his more than twenty years in hiding? And what if he wasn't in Costa Rica? Surely he had many hiding places all over the world. Maybe she should have stayed longer with the CIA to get more information. Or even better, she could have confessed her identity and given the information she had discovered to her old friend Herb Feller, and perhaps he would have helped her find her dad. But deep down she knew Herb would never violate rules of confidentiality, not even for her. He was too honest, too dedicated, too CIA.

The rest of the report had given specifics on how

74

her father had been rescued, something about Eagle carrying her father's bleeding, limp body for miles to rendezvous with a chopper sent by the CIA. The information concerning Eagle grabbed her attention and made her think it could be Custer.

Angel had re-read *Heart of the Beartooths* before coming to Montana. In it, Sue Ann admitted to her love for Custer after he saved Betsy and Hawk from a hired killer. Angel had thought nothing about this except to feel a little jealous, knowing Custer had replaced her father in Sue Ann's heart, even though they all believed her father was dead. But it was in *Mountain Mists* that Sue Ann had written: "An eagle circled overhead, and Custer watched, consumed by the giant wingspread of what was, in past visions, his own animal spirit."

And Custer had shot the would-be killer of Betsy and Hawk with a high-powered rifle from an unfathomable distance like a trained sniper—and while suffering a heart attack. Angel read the lines from *Heart of the Beartooths* she had written in the margin of the document: "Custer had not shot the rifle in years but had not lost his aim. There was no time to think about his sights being on a woman. His only consideration was Betsy and Hawk and the peril they were in. As his shot hit its target, he felt a burning in his chest that forced him down on a nearby rock."

Is Eagle Custer's code name? And if so, does he know where my father is? Yes, I wanted to be reunited with Sue Ann and Betsy, but I also need to know if Custer is my link to finding my father.

Angel stared at the papers and knew there was still much information she had to find, and she needed to start with Sue Ann and Custer.

I feel like a traitor. But there is no way I can tell Sue Ann what I'm really doing here. Dad is alive! That is what is important, and I have to find him—to be with him, even if it means disappearing into his hidden world. If Sue Ann knew Dad was alive, I think she would be just like me and would have to find him even though she is married to Custer. Dad died once for us, and he would do it again if he thought we might still be threatened by his resurrection, even though ONE died in that river for sure. I have to do this alone, but I don't know where to start.

Angel left the room and tiptoed down the stairs, trying not to disturb Sue Ann and Custer. She had waited an hour after they retired to their bedroom, hoping she could look for information. Sue Ann had told her she had some things of her dad's she would share with her, personal items that Jake had found in the mineshaft on the property where Shade's cabin was located before it burned. Angel needed to see if she could find anything that might provide her with clues to where her dad was hiding.

****

Custer lay in bed with Sue Ann cuddled close beside, sleeping soundly. But sleep eluded him, and he knew it was because Angel was in the room down the hall. He liked the girl, even though every time he looked at her he was reminded of her father. But he was uncomfortable with more than the stare from her surreal blue eyes. She had asked him if he knew Shade since the cabin given to Sue Ann was so close to his own. He tried to convince himself it was a reasonable question, but something told him to be wary.

She was with the CIA. I can't forget that.

He turned to face Sue Ann and was about to put his arm around her when he heard a creak in the hall. He listened intently but did not hear any other noises for several seconds. Then he heard another low creak, this time on the stairs. He left the bed, pulled on his sweats, and put his ear to the door. The bottom step on the stairs had a loose board, and he knew if anyone was on the stairs, the bottom step would tell the story.

A loud creak gave him the information he needed. Angel was downstairs.

He decided to wait a few minutes before going down to check if she was okay. Perhaps she needed more covers. He and Sue Ann kept their house cooler than most people. He decided to get another of Sue Ann's grandmother's quilts for her, just in case.

He was almost to the bottom of the stairs but stopped when he heard Angel rummaging around in Sue Ann's desk drawers. Not knowing whether he should continue down or not, he went no further. When the rustling noises stopped, he decided maybe it was in Sue Ann's best interest for him to confront Angel.

Custer stepped over the last step, being as quiet as possible. As he turned the corner, he saw her sitting at Sue Ann's desk with a book open in front of her, on top of a stack of papers.

"Having trouble sleeping?" he spoke softly, trying not to startle her, but his effort failed. She gasped, slammed the book shut, and jumped up, casting a frightened look in Custer's direction.

"Didn't mean to scare you. Heard you coming down the stairs. That bottom step is a little loose and creaks. Gotta fix it before someone gets hurt." He walked toward the desk. "I thought you might have gotten cold and needed another quilt on your bed. We have extras in the closet here." Custer moved to the closet under the stairs and put his hand on the doorknob.

"No. I am very comfortable, thank you. I just couldn't sleep." Angel picked up the book and turned it around so he could see it. "It's *The Gully Path*, Sue Ann's biography. I've wanted to read it for a while. This copy was on the desk." Angel moved around the desk blocking his view, but he knew she had stuffed the papers into the long drawer.

"Betsy told me about her dad, Tate Douglas, and how he and Sue Ann met and—you know." Angel left the desk and headed toward Custer.

"Yes, I know." He smiled. "I'm sure Sue Ann will be thrilled you are reading it. That's the author's copy her publisher sent before the book was released." He turned to go back upstairs.

"I really miss my dad, Custer—even more after being with Sue Ann and Betsy again. I thought it would help, but I'm not sure coming here was the right thing to do." Angel took the book and moved to the sofa, but she did not open the biography. She stared up over the fireplace at the portrait her dad had painted.

Custer moved to the fireplace, matching her gaze. "Give it some time, Angel, and don't hurry off. Sue Ann needs you to stay for a while." He took a seat in one of the fireside chairs. "So you inherited your dad's artistic ability as well as his blue eyes?"

"I thought you didn't know my dad?" With eyebrows pulled tight, Angel questioned his remark.

"Sue Ann used to talk about Shade's eyes. I am reminded every day when I look at the blue diamond in the nugget ring he gave her." Custer looked from the portrait back to Angel.

"Oh! Of course!" Angel relaxed and opened the book again.

"Well...I'll leave you to your reading." He left the chair and turned toward the stairs, and this time Angel did not stop him.

****

Sue Ann listened through a crack in the door but knew not all of what Angel had told Custer was true. The book, Sue Ann's biography, had not been on the desk but at the bottom of a stack of papers and manuscripts in the back of one of the deep side drawers. Angel would have had to dig through this stack in order to find it. What was really strange was that the bookshelves in the opposite end of the great room were filled with all of Sue Ann's and Betsy's books, including *The Gully Path*. In fact, just that morning, she had showed Angel where she could find a copy of the biography when she was ready to read it.

Sue Ann made her way back to the bed and returned to her sleeping position when she heard Custer coming back up the stairs.

****

Custer tried not to disturb Sue Ann as he crawled in and lay as he had been before, on his back, staring at the ceiling. His suspicions about Angel's surprise visit were coming to fruition, and he hoped Sue Ann would not be hurt in the process. She did not need stress in her life.

"So—do you think Angel found what she was looking for?" Sue Ann whispered the question without turning to face Custer.

"No." Custer's answer was terse, true to his nature, saying only what he believed necessary for the situation at hand.

Chapter Eleven

Tobi sat at his computer after face-timing with Carrie. June and July would drag as he anticipated his daughter's summer visit, the whole month of August. He had not seen Carrie in three months, longer than he had promised he would ever go without seeing her. But at least he was no longer suffering emotionally over Star's decision to remarry. Thoughts of that day at Keyser Brown returned, and Tobi pulled out his cell phone, hoping Angel would come for a visit—an overnight visit. Since she had showed up in Red Lodge, he had not gone more than a day without being with her and making love.

This relationship, if that was what it was, was infringing on valuable study time for the online classes he was taking through Montana State. His new ambition was to get a masters in law enforcement, something that would either increase his efforts to be a private investigator or give him the credentials he needed to be a CIA agent. As long as his inheritance was keeping him comfortable, he would continue to work on his education and his credentials. His old boss with Denver Police Department still called him, begging him to come back, and the shcriff in Red Lodge had asked if he was interested in working for his office, something that could be in his future but not feasible right now.

When Tobi did not get an answer from Angel, he called his mother's cell, with the same result. Next up was his sister, who answered on the first ring.

"Well, I guess that makes your twin third choice, since I am holding Mom's and Angel's purses with their phones. They are in the fitting room at Whispering Pines, trying on western jackets. Angel has already found a darling little outfit that I'm sure will knock your eyes out. Next stop is Paris Montana and a visit with Heidi for a pair of her custom-designed vintage-look chaps to go with the boots we bought. I'm thinking you need to take this girl to the Griz and teach her to boot scoot." Betsy paused to take a breath. "Let me guess—you're looking for Angel." Betsy smiled into the phone. She had been so worried after Star dumped her brother, but with Angel in Red Lodge, all her worries were over, or so she hoped. The way Angel smiled every time Tobi walked in made it pretty obvious she was as enamored with him as he was with her.

"And what is the shopping occasion? Are you three planning a trip without me?" he asked, making his way to his deck to finish the conversation.

"You know, Tobi, you don't get to consume all of Angel's time. We knew and loved her first."

"I know. You and mom remind me all the time." As he took a seat, he heard Custer's Jeep motor winding as it climbed to where the cabin was. "Got to go, Sis. Custer is here. Tell Angel to come by when she finishes her shopping trip." He started to hang up but stopped. "Uh, Betsy, would you do something for me?"

"Maybe—depends." Betsy knew what was coming next.

"When Mom is not around, convince Angel to stay with me tonight. I need some uninterrupted time with her if we are ever going to get this relationship going in the right direction. Mom is really hogging her lately."

****

Custer left the Jeep door open and stopped, holding to the door before heading toward Tobi's cabin. When he did begin, his walk was wobbly and slow. Holding tight to the rail, he put one foot beside the other ascending the two steps as if it required great effort. His breathing was heavy, and he placed his hand over his heart and began coughing.

Tobi took one look and fear seized him.

"Are you okay, Custer? You don't look so good." Tobi stood, ready to catch his stepfather if he fell, but Custer made it to the chair. "Can I get you some water?"

"No." Custer wheezed before taking a long breath. "Just let me sit a minute." More silence followed as Tobi kept his eyes on him.

"I think I better call Mom. You're awfully pale. And you're scaring me." Tobi stood and leaned over Custer, who had his head back with his eyes closed.

"No. Just don't have much energy. No need to worry your mother. Not yet." Custer opened his eyes and looked at Tobi. "But soon maybe."

"What do you mean by 'soon maybe?'" Tobi stood. "I'm calling Hawk."

Tobi left his chair and walked to the other end of the deck, dialing his cell phone while he walked. He spoke in a low voice, a quick conversation, before taking his seat by Custer again.

"My time is approaching, Tobi. Nothing Doc or

anyone can do." Custer coughed again, holding his chest, and again attempted to take a deep breath that did not come.

"I'm getting you some water. Do you have your pills, Custer? Are your pills in the Jeep?" Tobi leaned close and spoke louder than was needed out of nervousness.

"I'm dying, Tobi—but I'm not deaf." Custer gave a low chuckle as he fumbled in his pocket with a shaking hand. Tobi decided he was taking too long and reached into the pocket, pulled out the bottle, unscrewed the cap, poured a pill into his hand, all in one quick move, and handed it to him. "Here. Put this under your tongue while I get you a glass of water."

Twenty minutes later, Hawk's rig came to an abrupt stop in the yard and continued gyrating even after he got out and hurried to the deck, bypassing the steps, from ground to deck in one long bound. Hawk pulled his chair over right beside Custer and stared at him but didn't say anything, seeing his uncle had his pill bottle in his hand.

Custer opened his eyes and looked from Hawk to Tobi.

"What's the matter? Haven't either of you ever seen a man die?" Custer gave a hint of a smile, and Tobi and Hawk sighed with relief simultaneously.

"Unk, why didn't you tell me you were having problems? And—I watched my dad die. Remember? I'm not ready to replicate that experience." Hawk's face was filled with concern. "What can we do, Custer?"

Custer remained silent for a minute before speaking.

"Doc wants me to sign up for a transplant. Know

anybody with a spare pump?" Custer gave a low laugh as he pulled himself to the edge of the chair. "I need you two to help me, but there is nothing you can do for my medical condition other than promise you won't tell Sue Ann about this little episode. And promise me you won't do a bunch of emotional carrying on when I do go. You two have to be strong for Sue Ann."

"Okay, Custer." Tobi stood, ran his fingers through his hair, leaned back against the rail, and folded his arms. "I'm not going anywhere, so don't worry about Mom. And you know Hawk and Betsy will always be here for her. What else? You have something more on your mind." Tobi kept his eyes on Custer.

Hawk continued to sit on the edge of his seat, but he, too, kept his eyes and ears focused on his uncle. He knew whatever Custer asked of them, he and Tobi would do. He also knew what Custer wanted would be important to him, not only as the husband of Sue Ann but as a Crow elder who believed in the old ways, the traditional ways of his ancestors. Hawk had a feeling he knew what Custer's request would be, something Custer had shared with him a few weeks ago when they took Trapper to Keyser Brown to fish.

"The Sacred Wheel." Custer said the words without explanation. He knew Tobi would not understand but Hawk would and could explain it to Tobi. Besides, Custer did not have the breath it would take to give Tobi the details.

"What is the Sacred Wheel, Hawk?" Tobi turned to Hawk and waited for an explanation.

"It's the Bighorn Medicine Wheel over by Lovell, Wyoming. It's a sacred place to the Crow and to other Native peoples. A lot of rich history and culture there, as well as deep religious and spiritual meaning."

"I need to go there one more time, but you two will need to help me. Considering I almost didn't make it up the two steps to Tobi's deck, I'm thinking I'll need a horse to get me the one and a half miles to the top. I can call in a favor and get permission for us to go up on horseback." Custer tried to stand but was forced to sit back in his chair. Without waiting to be asked for help, Tobi took one arm and Hawk the other, and they helped Custer to stand.

"Thank you. I think I can make it from here. I need to get back home before Sue Ann gets back from shopping with Betsy and Angel. She watches me now. I had a little spell the other night, and it scared her pretty bad."

"Oh, no! You're not driving yourself home. I'll drive you, and Tobi can bring your Jeep. We were all asked to dinner tonight anyway, but I don't think you are in any shape for company." Hawk held Custer's arm until he got his balance and then let go, knowing his uncle took great pride in his independence.

"I'll let you drive me if you were coming anyway. I'll be better in a few more minutes. These spells are coming more often, but I usually get over them pretty quickly. And yes, company would be nice. It gets the attention off me." Custer stopped before descending the steps and looked back toward Tobi.

"Are you coming, Tobi?"

"Yep. Just got to grab my hat. I'll be right behind you in my rig."

****

On the way to Custer and Sue Ann's cabin, Custer became very quiet. His thoughts were not of his demise itself but of his dying without confessing his secrets to someone. Custer thought about telling Hawk but changed his mind. Perhaps he would write a letter to Sue Ann and leave it in his cabin. He knew she would go there often to surround herself with memories, just as she had done when he took himself out of the picture to let her make her decision between him and Tate.

Tate! Here I've done nothing but worry about leaving Sue Ann with no one to care for her, and I completely forgot about Tate. Maybe it won't be necessary for Shade to come out of his self-imposed exile after all. Custer smiled without realizing it as he looked straight ahead, relaxing a little in the passenger seat.

"What are you smiling about, Unk? You must be feeling better." Hawk smiled, more out of relief than pleasure.

"Do you have Tate's cell number, Hawk? I bet if he knew my time was short, he'd hightail it back here so Sue Ann would not be alone. Guess I should have talked to him about this last year when he came for his dad's funeral, but it just didn't seem the time. He was having a hard time with the fact his dad chose to be buried in a cemetery beneath the Beartooths and not back in Philadelphia beside his mom. And I guess it was hard seeing Sue Ann and me together as husband and wife, even though he performed the ceremony." Custer pulled out his cell phone, ready to enter Tate's number as a contact.

"I hate to tell you this, but Tate has found someone, a new psychologist who works at the mission. Frankly, Betsy and I are thrilled. She was planning on telling Sue Ann today when they were in town. Tate has

87

been alone for so long. He needs someone to love." Hawk kept his eyes on the road.

Custer's smile faded. "Well, that's both good and bad. Never thought I'd hear myself say I didn't want Tate to find someone else."

Hawk turned onto the forestry trail, and Custer became quiet again.

****

The meal was ready when the three guys got to the cabin, and even though Custer was very quiet, he had no more chest pains. Tobi and Angel left first, and it wasn't long before Betsy was ready to go, claiming to be overly tired from their girls' day out. Trapper had fallen asleep on the sofa and never knew when Hawk picked him up.

After everyone left, Sue Ann brought Custer a cup of decaf coffee, and together they sat in front of the fireplace.

Custer broke the silence.

"So I hear Tate has found himself a mate. I'm glad. He's a good man and deserves someone after all he went through fighting for his country and now helping our wounded warriors, especially those with PTSD." Custer took a sip of his coffee while keeping his eyes on the glowing embers of the fire. "It's not good for anyone to be left alone at our age."

Sue Ann placed her cup on the side table, put her feet under her and her arm on the back of the sofa, and glared at Custer.

"And who do you think is going to be left alone? Are you worried about me?" Sue Ann's voice became animated and louder than usual. "You can cut the act, Custer. I know your heart is giving you problems, but

I'm not ready for you to leave me, so get it out of your head!"

"I wish I could, Sue Ann, and I am worried about leaving you alone. I kind of thought Tate might come back around, but I guess I waited too long."

Sue Ann jumped to her feet, grabbed her cup, and walked fast toward the kitchen.

"I have a husband; I don't need a guardian. I'm going to bed. No more discussion!"

Custer continued to sit and gaze at the fire, ignoring Sue Ann's heavy footsteps on the stairs.

I never thought dying could be so hard.

Chapter Twelve

The Sacred Medicine Wheel
Wyoming

Hawk and Tobi saddled up the horses while Custer stood looking up the steep path to where the Medicine Wheel was located. For this pilgrimage, he had meant to wear traditional clothing, moose hide pants and shirt, but Sue Ann was afraid he would get chilled and convinced him to wear his warmest clothing with only his lace-up moccasins representative of his Crow people.

"Your horse is ready, Unk. Walk back here, and I'll help you mount."

"No, Hawk. I can manage." Custer looked at the tall gelding. "I have to manage, in case Grandfather is watching, or even worse, Grandmother." Custer stood with his left foot in the stirrup, willing himself to mount, and after several attempts his persistence was rewarded. He reined the horse around with its head pointed toward the trail.

"Did you bring the fruit for the little people, Hawk? I hope so, because I completely forgot. It's not good to forget the little people."

"Little people?" Tobi mounted his horse and moved up by Custer so he could hear the story.

"The Medicine Wheel has been here for over a

thousand years, even before the Crow, and they were the first Plains People." Custer sat straight and tall in his saddle, proud to be sharing his history and religious beliefs with Tobi. "One of our great leaders, Red Cloud, came here in the 1800s for his vision quest. While he was on his quest, the little people came to him and took him down into the earth's core beneath the wheel. The little people take care of this sacred place, and they gave Red Cloud powerful medicine to enable his soul to return to the Medicine Wheel after his death. His people—my people—can come to the Medicine Wheel even today and talk to Red Cloud."

"Wow! What a wonderful story! I want Carrie to hear that one when she comes out. In fact, I'd love for her to see this and to feel part of it, since her grandpa is Crow." Tobi could feel Custer's smile and the pride it held that his stepson identified with Custer, as both a father figure and a grandfather to Carrie. Tobi realized Custer may have never really known where he stood with him, Sue Ann's lost son, even though it had been three years since he had resurfaced and his mother and Custer had married. And then there had been his biological father Tate showing up. But through it all, both Betsy and Tobi had remained loyal to Custer while also loving their father.

Hawk handed the bag of grapes and strawberries up to Custer and then mounted his horse.

"Oh, wait! Trapper insisted I bring this for the little people—a gift from him. He said to apologize for the gum being sugar free, but it's the only kind his mom lets him chew." Hawk and Custer had a good laugh with this one, but Tobi just smiled, remaining lost in the conversation.

"Okay, Unk. Lead us up. The little people and Red Cloud are waiting for you," Hawk said.

"So are you going to keep me in the dark about Trapper and the little people?" Tobi directed his remark to Hawk, who rode beside him.

"It is good for you to learn about Crow culture, Tobi, even though you are not Crow. You and Betsy, as well as Trapper, are Crow in spirit." Custer had decided he should answer Tobi's question. "I believe being Indian comes from the heart and does not always have to be by blood. I hope I am here when you bring Carrie to the Sacred Wheel. I'd love to tell her about the little people."

"We brought Trapper up here when he was three, and he swears to this day he saw the little people." Hawk took up the story, smiling, remembering the day. "You should ask him about it, Tobi. He's dead serious and can describe them like he spent a long time looking at them and talking with them. Who knows? Maybe he did. A lot of people, even those in the field of psychology, believe children have a connection with those past and can see things adults can't."

"You mean like believing in and experiencing the paranormal?" Tobi clarified.

"Yes. That's exactly what I mean. Native Americans don't have a problem with believing, since we practice spirituality. My son Trapper, even though he is not my flesh and blood, is more Crow in this respect than many of my blood relatives. Trapper believes, and I believe in my son."

"I can still see him, on his little hands and knees, peering down into the cracks." Custer chuckled. "He lined up jellybeans along the top for them. We could hear him divvying them out, saying, 'One for you, little man, and one for you, little lady.' We brought the camping gear and camped below that night. When we came back up the next morning, Trapper ran to where he had left the jellybeans, and they were all gone. I can still hear him giggling—better than when he leaves cookies and milk for Santa Claus, and the little people don't leave gifts, at least not tangible gifts. What a memory to treasure!"

As they approached a bench along the trail, Custer stopped his horse.

"This is the first mandatory stop. We stop four times before getting to the top. I suggest you pray, but that must come from your heart, not my mouth." Custer looked to the sky and spoke. "Forgive me, Great One, for not dismounting. My bones are old, and I'm afraid I can't dismount and remount four times and still have the energy to pray when I get to the Sacred Wheel."

Hawk and Tobi dismounted, hearing Custer's prayer. Each bowed their heads. They were about to remount when they noticed Custer looking up, his hand cupped over his eyes to keep the sun from his vision as an eagle soared above the Sacred Wheel. Then, as if recognizing Custer, it flew down the trail, calling as it circled over the three horsemen.

"I hear you, Dúuptakoische, and I thank you." After making his acknowledgement to his animal spirit, Custer dismounted, stood beside his horse, and bowed his head.

Tobi looked at Hawk, and Hawk read his mind and nodded toward Custer. Then he put his hands to his lips and pointed to his eyes and Tobi's, the universal sign telling a person to watch.

Custer took the saddle horn with his left hand as he balanced in the stirrup with his left foot. Then with no noticeable effort, he mounted his horse and continued up the trail. Two more times Custer dismounted, remounted, and continued the ride, but when he got to the final stop, he gave his reins to Hawk and continued up on foot. Hawk and Tobi trailed behind, giving Custer distance and showing him the respect he deserved as a Crow elder. Several times, Custer leaned over and picked something up off the ground.

"I need to go alone from here. If you two would keep an eye on my horse, I'll be about my business. If you want to pray, think, or just talk, you can stay on this side. I'll be over at the cracks with the little people." Custer started to walk toward the wheel and stopped, turning to face Hawk and Tobi. "I could be here a while. Got a lot on my mind to talk out. If you get tired of waiting for me, just sit on one of the benches we passed on the way up."

Custer approached the sacred wheel slowly, not because of physical weakness but out of respect, longing for spiritual answers, seeking solace, and to know for sure he had atoned for his sins, and most of all needing assurance of Sue Ann's well-being after he would join his ancestors and was no longer present to care for and protect her. He knew seeking atonement for his transgressions was really no longer necessary, since the Creator had forgiven him decades ago when he had first ended his bad days with Tiger's Eye, but it would never hurt to ask again for forgiveness for these and all transgressions. At that time, Custer had come home to humble himself and regain his cultural dignity. His greatest regret was not going directly to the Sacred

Wheel to seek forgiveness and redirection when he first got back to Montana, rather than attempting to drown his nightmares and guilt in alcohol. In Indochina, he had hidden his real identity just as Raven had, both living the insanity of youth gone awry in an attempt to gain wealth and fame without regard for those they were being paid to kill.

I need to admit my past and let someone know Shade is alive. But who do I tell? Tobi? Hawk? Sue Ann? This, too, is an answer I seek.

****

When Tobi and Hawk reached the plateau, they dismounted and ground-tied the horses. They could see Custer on the far side, kneeling as he offered the fruit to the little people.

"What an awe-inspiring place!" Tobi stood still, soaking in the sight of the large circular expanse, surrounded by ancient mountains, each with generations of their own stories to tell. "I feel like I want to stop, drop to my knees, and pour my heart out to God!"

"There's nothing stopping you, Tobi. God, Creator of All Things, First Maker—my mother and I believe they are all One-And-The-Same. When Betsy comes here, she takes a long time meditating and praying. She says it is the most spiritual place she has ever experienced, and she grew up in the Bible Belt, going to church every time the doors opened." Hawk walked away from Tobi and took a spot on the far side of the circle, where he kneeled. He took the bandana from around his neck, placed some objects in it, and tied it to the rope railing.

The railing around the wheel was covered in

scarves, handkerchiefs, and medicine bags filled with all kinds of personal objects. Hawk had told him on the way up how people leave prayer scarves that usually encase tobacco, something sacred to the Crow and many Native peoples, as well as personal objects belonging to the person, or the subject of the prayer. Tobi had brought nothing and wished he had googled the Medicine Wheel so he would have known what to expect and what to bring. He certainly had many things he could pray about, but he came empty-handed.

After about fifteen minutes, Hawk walked back to Tobi. As if sensing Tobi was lost on what to do, Hawk picked up a stone from the path.

"Custer always comes to the wheel empty-handed except for the fruit for the little people. With his philosophical way with words, he told me once, 'An empty hand does not signify an empty heart; sometimes a vacuum is the best spiritual medicine, since it leaves so much room for spontaneous reflection and prayer.' He would come and meditate for days at a time, and all he brought was five stones he picked up on the path up the mountain."

Tobi began looking around and picked up five smooth stones.

"Okay. Now what do I do?" He opened his hand to show Hawk the stones.

"This is what Custer told me. You take a stone, rub it in your hands, and tell it exactly what you are thinking and praying about." Hawk took a stone from Tobi's hand to demonstrate. "A stone, like everything in nature, is alive and will live forever, so your thoughts and prayers live forever. You take the first stone and place it on the south corner; the next one goes on the west; the next one north; then east. The fifth stone is placed in the middle and goes down four times for heaven." Hawk demonstrated each placement with an invisible stone.

"Okay. Makes sense. But you put out a prayer scarf." Tobi directed his gaze to where Hawk had tied his scarf to the rope.

"That's just what I like to do." Hawk looked back at the wheel with its rope railing almost completely covered in prayer scarves and other objects, significant only to each giver. The ground, too, was covered in objects and prayer scarves. "In a way, this can be viewed as environmental effluence." Hawk made a sweeping motion with his hand to encompass the whole Sacred Wheel area. "This will all deteriorate, and eventually all of these, when they become too numerous, will be taken down and destroyed, buried, or whatever. But that doesn't bother me. Once my prayer leaves my heart, it is on its way. The scarf becomes a symbol of thanks—nothing more."

Hawk and Tobi took a seat on the bench closest to the top to wait for Custer. They both sat silent, reveling in the beauty of the mountain terrain. Each knew what the other was thinking but said nothing for several minutes until Tobi broke the silence.

"What will Mom do without Custer, Hawk? I worry about how stressful life will be for her without him."

"I don't know, Tobi. I wish she would come and live with Betsy, Trapper, and me, but she won't even talk about the possibility of Custer dying, much less leaving the cabin Shade left her. Maybe, when the time comes, you and Betsy can convince her. I know that is one of the answers Custer is praying to receive, but we will never know the answer he gets."

The two became silent again until they saw Custer treading down the hill toward them. Both stood, retrieved the horses that had hobbled their way to the grass beside the trail, and then headed to meet Custer.

The ride back to Red Lodge was long and silent. Custer stretched out on the back seat and took a nap, or pretended to, most likely not wanting to open himself up to a repeat conversation about his health problems.

He had indeed received answers to his prayers, but one answer was implied. When he placed the smooth stone on the ground with the pointed side facing south, he repeated what lay heavy on his mind. Who should he tell about Shade being alive? The reply was not an answer but was the promise of an answer to be presented to him shortly.

As for his health and looming death, Custer had received a vision while standing, searching the heavens at the Sacred Wheel, but though invigorating to his heart and soul, it seemed like an impossible dream. In his vision, horses symbolized the most important people in his life.

Standing on the precipice of the ten-thousand-foot cliff overlooking the vast western plains, Custer closed his eyes and lifted his arms, praising the turquoise and vermillion sky. The vibrations of a thousand horses thundering across the vast grasslands beneath him forced him to open his eyes and receive answers. His brown-and-white Appaloosa stallion raced across the pink cloud, coming directly toward him. Custer reached to grab the reins flying beside his beloved horse but missed them by inches and had to right himself before tumbling over the ragged red-dirt edge.

More horses appeared as the mottled stallion circled. First, a golden palomino, her curly mane flowing as her tail billowed behind her, cantered through the haze, her hoofbeats as light as a young Crow girl performing her first dance. Storm, the black stallion of the Pryor Mountains, reared, his front feet pawing at the sky as he beckoned for the mares to come to him. The sound of the free and glorious horses filled Custer with a longing to ride unrestrained, as he had in his early days. The brilliant sky and brown plains graced his heart with the power he felt only when riding bareback with his arms stretched to the sky, man and horse as one.

Fearing his vision, a gift from the Creator, was but a temporary reprieve from his earthly longing, Custer opened his eyes and looked down. Wearing the buckskins from his young manhood before his bad days, he touched his long black braid where it lay across a sun-darkened chest that rippled in sinews as strong and tight as a young buffalo's. The braid, held firm by the beaded headband, a gift from Grandmother, reminded him of his first vision quest.

Once again he felt the power of youth, and he smiled, knowing his time was near to ride with the sky riders but not quite yet, as signified by the reins just out of his grasp. His great stallion, the Appaloosa, with his brown and white colors running together, symbolic of the two races Custer represented, remained close but elusive, giving Custer again the idea that his time had not yet come. The beauty and grace of the palomino mare could only represent Sue Ann, and the black stallion, Storm, could be no one but Raven, his dark effervescent mane moving in sync with his hoofbeats, animated in vibrant splendor while seeking his place in this long-awaited finale.

****

When they got back to the cabin, it was dark, but Sue Ann, Betsy, Angel, and Trapper were waiting on the porch. Betsy and Trapper stepped off and headed for the Suburban. Each stopped to kiss Custer as he made his way to the cabin. Hawk checked the horses in the trailer before taking his place back in the driver's seat.

"It's getting late. We should head home and get Trapper to bed." Betsy reminded Trapper to buckle up and then took her place in the front. Giving one last wave to her mom, Custer, and Angel, she stared out the front window without saying anything more. Her heart was heavy.

Tobi made it to the front porch and gave his mom a kiss, but Angel rose to her feet, kissed Tobi on the cheek, and announced she was ready to go. Tobi, thrilled to know Angel was coming with him, was pleased with their fast retreat. He had so much to share with Angel.

****

Sue Ann placed a bowl of homemade vegetable and elk meat soup with a bran muffin in front of Custer and took a seat across from him.

"So how was the Medicine Wheel? All the snowdrifts gone for the summer?" She placed her hands on the table, clasping her fingers.

"Yes. Pathway was clear—in many ways; the sight serene and awe-inspiring as always." Custer did not look up as he took his first spoonful of soup. "Ah! This is good. Warms my heart..." He reached across with his left hand and took her hand in his. "Like my loving wife, whose hands prepared it."

They sat in silence until he pushed his bowl to the side. Reaching across the table, he took Sue Ann's hands in both of his and smiled.

"Did I ever tell you what a wonderful wife you are?" He looked into her eyes, waiting for an answer that did not come. "I was an old man when you married me—not so much in years, but in health—old before my time, my braids too soon silver. When I had that second, bad heart attack, you never left my side in the hospital and read to me for hours. You brought me back, and miracle of miracles, you chose me to be your husband. The Creator rewarded me more than I deserve."

Sue Ann looked away from him, feeling tears forming. When she looked back, his eyes glistened with moisture, and she knew.

"How long?" she asked, trying not to lose control.

"My sunset fades. Soon my feather will fall. Grandfather speaks it, but it is not immediate. Another mission blocks the path to the hereafter, but I do not know what it is."

Sue Ann released Custer's hands and moved to stand behind him. With her arms wrapped tightly around her husband's neck, she kissed his cheek and then held her face tightly to his.

"Then we will cherish every bright, beautiful sunrise and sunset and speak no more of their fading; nor will we speak of fallen feathers."

Chapter Thirteen

Custer drove up just in time to see Angel's head disappear around the aspen trees on the trail leading to his old cabin.

What is she doing? She has to be going to my old cabin, since that is all there is down that trail, but why?

He had just dropped Sue Ann off at Betsy's so she could keep Trapper entertained while his author mom completed her last read-through for her latest novel before sending it off to her editor. Custer had said he would help with Trapper, but he was feeling really good today, with more energy than usual, and decided he'd go check on the cabin. Besides, Trapper wanted his grandmother to teach him to make Indian fry bread, something Custer thought better left to the grandmother. Sue Ann had asked Angel to go with her, but Angel said she thought she would just stay at the cabin and read. Also, she was hoping Tobi might come by later. Yet here she was headed toward Custer's cabin.

Custer gave Angel time to get there. He planned to walk slowly, hoping to conserve this newfound energy.

I'd think she was just curious to see the cabin, but Tobi took her there the other day. He even took her inside to see where he lived when he first came to Red Lodge as Timothy Harden.

Custer went upstairs and put on his lace-up

moccasins before heading down the trail. He was surprised not to be out of breath when he reached the cabin and felt it had something to do with the last mission he was to accomplish. He stopped just out of sight and listened. Inside, Angel was moving furniture, obviously looking for something. Making no noise, Custer made his way to the porch and took a seat in his favorite straight chair, leaning back against the wall like he always did, letting his gaze rest on distant mountain peaks.

"Damn! I know there is something here somewhere. I just have to find it." Angel was talking to herself. In the next few minutes, Custer heard cabinet doors open and close, with Angel moving everything around in her search.

Custer continued to sit quietly and wait.

After another fifteen minutes of rummaging through everything in the cabin, Angel backed through the door, carefully relocking it, not leaving the tiniest clue the old cabin had been broken into using the credit card trick. She turned away from Custer and headed down the steps, but sensing something, or someone, she stopped at the foot of the steps and, with obvious dread, turned around.

"Find what you were looking for?" Custer kept his chair leaned back as he spoke.

"Custer!" Startled, Angel yelled his name. "I was just…" Angel could think of nothing to say.

"Come and sit. It's time we talk." Custer put his chair down on the floor and moved it closer to the other straight chair.

"I'll just stand." Angel did not understand what was happening but knew she would have to explain herself.

"Suit yourself." Custer sat back down and began. "Tell me what you think you know about your father."

Angel sat down on the edge of the porch but kept her back to Custer. Several long seconds passed.

"You'll tell me if it's true?" Angel kept her eyes focused on the trail at the edge of the aspens.

"Yes. But I'll determine when and what if anything is to be told to Sue Ann and the rest of the family. If you can't agree to that, this conversation is over." Custer became quiet...waiting for Angel's answer. Again, a long silence followed.

"Your code name when you took assignments with the CIA, after leaving Tiger's Eye, was Eagle. My dad's code name, after he left Tiger's Eye, was Raven."

Custer remained silent.

"Are you going to answer?" Angel asked, sounding irritated.

"You have not agreed to my terms as yet." Custer repeated the terms.

"I agree to your terms. Now will you answer my first question?"

"Yes. My code name was Eagle, and Shade's code name was Raven."

"Your last job with the CIA was a special assignment. Your job was to track my dad down in Alaska and bring him to the CIA agents waiting for him—by force if necessary."

"Yes, that is true." Custer offered no additional information.

"You saved my dad by diving into the Tekooni River and dragging him to the bank the day Betsy and I thought we saw Dad drown along with the monster who kidnapped us."

"Yes." Again Custer answered tersely.

"My dad is alive even as we speak." Angel looked at Custer now, waiting for the answer to the most important question of all.

"That I cannot say for sure." Custer knew this answer would not suffice.

"What do you mean you 'cannot say for sure'?" Angel stood and put her hands on her hips. "You have contact with him. I know you do."

"No. I have not been in contact with your father in three years. I've tried but failed." Custer rose from his chair and walked to the edge of the porch.

"How do you contact him?"

"He sent me a cell phone, but I don't know where he is. It is preset for dialing only his number, one I cannot access on my own. He does not answer or return my calls."

"Is that what was mounted under your table? A charger for the phone?"

"Good detective work. Yes, it was there, but I moved it. Afraid the CIA might find it." Custer smiled at his attempt to lighten the situation, but his attempt failed.

"Is Dad in Costa Rica?"

"It is one possibility, but like I said, he does not answer or return my calls." Custer set his chair back down on all four legs, clasping his hands with his elbows on his knees. "Now it's my turn for questions. If you refuse to answer, this discussion is over. Understood?"

"An informant, someone I don't know, provided classified documents." Angel knew the question before

Custer asked. "He, or she, made two separate drops of information. I'm not sure who or why, but I knew the answers to where Dad is hiding would be here in Montana." Angel turned to face Custer again. "Why, Custer? Why is my dad in hiding? Why did he not let me know he is alive?" Angel's voice cracked with pent-up emotion.

Custer took his time, staring at the mountains as if seeking help, and calculated his answer carefully before speaking.

"The same reason he was shot that day, and the same reason he went into that river with the 'monster' who kidnapped you and Betsy—to save you, Sue Ann, and Betsy. He had every intention of dying in the river that day, the only thing that would stop any efforts by Tiger's Eye operatives remaining loyal to ONE. This would be the same operatives wanting to cash in on several million dollars in blood money left in ONE's special account in Switzerland still today. He left it for whoever was to kill Jon Shockey, alias Shade Dubois, alias Raven…just in case he survived. Shade was unpredictable and considered invincible; to ONE, he was a never-ending curse that refused to die, and Shade knew his loved ones would never be safe unless he remained dead. ONE did not trust Shade even in death, so the blood money continues as an offer for anyone who finds Shade and proves he is dead."

"And you really don't know where my father is?" Angel looked Custer in the eyes.

"No, I do not, and I don't think you should try to find him. If you try, you'll have a trail of hardcore thugs in your wake, trying to cash in on the big prize." Custer moved to the ground and stood beside Angel, placing his hand on Angel's shoulder. "I know you want to find your father, Angel, but think of what you'll be doing if you try, even if you don't succeed. You will be risking the lives of Sue Ann, Betsy, Hawk, and Trapper, not to mention yourself and Tobi. And they will kill your father, or attempt to, and if they don't succeed, he will run again to new locations. What kind of life will that be for Shade?"

Angel sat in silence, her bright eyes dimmed by tears she wiped away with the back of her hand.

"If I find my dad, I'll stay with him. I'll hide with him. I need to be with him, Custer. Please help me find him. Besides, I need to warn him that people know he's alive."

"And what about Tobi? Sue Ann was hoping something would come of the two of you. Tobi loves you. He has suffered a world of hurt in the last few years. Are you willing to add to it?" Custer kept his eyes on Angel, watching for any sign of concern for Tobi.

Angel cast her eyes to the ground and took her time in answering.

"Tobi is my greatest concern. I am in love with him, but I still need to find my father. My life has been so pieccmeal without family. If things work out, I can still have a life with Tobi, if he wants—a life that will include my dad. That is my hope and my prayer."

Custer left Angel and walked to the back of the cabin. When he returned, he was holding a cell phone.

"It's all charged up. All you have to do is punch the numbers that correspond with the letters R-A-V-E-N-E-A-G-L-E, but don't expect him to answer. Think about what you are going to say before you dial the numbers. And think about the repercussions for opening up this can of worms, the deadliest imaginable. In other words, are you willing to risk the lives of this part of your family, the ones here for you in Montana?" Custer held out the phone to Angel. After she took it, he turned and headed for the trail without looking back. He had one answer to his prayers at the Medicine Wheel.

Chapter Fourteen

Angel could not bring herself to stay with Sue Ann and Custer. Even though she knew Custer would try to make her feel at ease, she felt too guilty, torn between wanting to find her father and knowing she was putting the others she loved at risk.

I should break off my relationship with Tobi. It will hurt him, and Lord knows I don't want to do anything but love him, maybe even spend the rest of my life with him, but I need to find my dad. It would be better for everyone if I just left without a word, but that would really hurt the only family I have at the moment—the only family I've really ever had.

Angel left the suitcase on the bed half packed and walked to the window of her bedroom in Sue Ann's cabin. She gazed at the mountains, hoping they would speak to her, console her the way they did Sue Ann and Betsy, but no consolation came.

I'm on my own.

After finishing her packing, she made her way downstairs, stopping to put the letters she had written on Sue Ann's desk. Then she headed to the fireplace to gaze at her dad's masterpiece one more time. Standing on the hearth so she could reach the painting, Angel rubbed her fingers over his signature in the bottom right corner.

"Raven, I need you! This is going to be so difficult.

I don't know what to say to you, and I don't know where to start looking for you, but I have to try. Please hear me, Dad! Help me to find you!"

Angel realized she was offering prayers to her father, not the one who would be in control of this endeavor, and probably not the one to help her if it turned into a dangerous situation. She stepped off the hearth and rolled her suitcase behind her as she made her way to the porch, where she stopped, giving one more deep, longing look to the mountains. She spoke aloud.

"You live in these mountains, God. I know you do, and I am counting on you to help me. Protect my family—all of my family, and please don't let Tobi hurt too long."

****

Angel headed through Red Lodge, hoping she would not see Tobi or any of her family. She wouldn't have been able to tell any of them where she was going, since she didn't know either, but she had to be alone, away from the ones who mattered most to her, in order to decide what to do. Perhaps she had been wrong to leave D.C. so soon. If she had waited, maybe she would have received another drop from the Postman, something to help her in her quest. She even considered calling Herb Feller and confiding in him. He would know what to do and could either offer her help or refuse her. Either way, it would be more of a possibility of help than she had now. Custer was certainly not able to help her, his health was so bad. She knew he would help if he could, but for now all he could do was give her his one link to her father, the cell phone, a lifeline if Custer ever needed him.

As she turned onto the road leading to Columbus and Interstate 90, she glanced in her rearview mirror and saw two men in a black SUV. Feeling uneasy, she decided to make a quick left turn and go back through town. Seeing the car go on past, she breathed a sigh of relief before turning around.

****

Tobi pulled up in front of his mother's cabin, surprised not to see Angel's Yukon parked at the hitching post. She should be expecting him to arrive so they could go for a hike and possibly replay the waterfall scene from *The Hawk and the Deer*, something they had talked about since the day they first made love at Keyser Brown.

"Where is she?" He left his truck door open and ran inside to see if she might have left a note for him. This was so unlike her.

He was about to leave when he saw two envelopes on his mother's desk. Walking hurriedly to the desk, he tore into the envelope with his name on it, anxious to see why Angel had stood him up. As he read aloud, he stumbled over to the sofa and fell back as his heart began replaying the same hurt he thought was over.

Dear Tobi,

My mind is a wreck, my heart full of turmoil and longing for something beyond my reach! I was never destined to have you. I cannot stay in Montana. My past has crept back in and has overtaken all that I thought was to be permanent joy with the one man I have found that I could love, and that is you. If I stay, you will be hurt along with the rest of my family, and I cannot let this happen.

My life will always be incomplete if I do not carry

out the one assignment left for me, and it cannot include you, my darling. Perhaps, some day, I can return, but if love, a more durable and honest love, finds you, rush to it and be happy. I will never forget you.

Angel

With no hesitation, Tobi jumped into his truck and headed off to try to catch her. He knew which way she would head, the most feasible route for someone who did not know her way around Montana, and he knew if he hurried he could beat her to I-90. She could not have been gone long. He had seen Custer in town, and Custer had told him Angel was at the cabin.

As he headed through Red Lodge, he prayed traffic would be at a minimum and that no law enforcement would stop him. But just to make sure no one stopped him, he took out the red blinking emergency light, something he used as a volunteer firefighter, and placed it on top of his truck, even though he knew this was an illegal use of the light.

People stared at him as he plowed through Main Street, but no one tried to stop him.

Now for the homestretch!

Ten miles out of Red Lodge, he met Custer and Sue Ann on their way home from Betsy's. He did not wave but knew what would happen next. Within seconds, his cell phone was ringing.

"Where's the fire?" Custer spoke into his cell phone.

"No fire, Custer, except in my heart. Angel is gone. She left me a letter, and one for Mom, as well. I don't know what Mom's says, but it seems Angel has some assignment she has to finish that can't include me."

"So what do you propose to do, Tobi? You can't force her to stay if she doesn't want to." Custer felt guilt and worry at Angel's leaving but knew there was nothing he could have done to stop her.

"I don't know, but I have to try. I'll call you later, Custer. Need two hands for the steering wheel." Tobi hung up his cell as his foot became even heavier on the accelerator.

****

Custer relayed Tobi's words to Sue Ann, who immediately told Custer to speed up. She had to see what Angel's letter said.

Custer sped up, but he was not in a hurry to see Sue Ann's heart broken. He was also concerned with what Angel was going to try to do.

What if she heads out to Costa Rica in search of Shade? What if this whole anonymous source of information has set her up, knowing she has the best chance of finding her father, and it's all to kill Shade for the millions left in the Swiss bank account?

The more Custer thought about it all, the more he knew what he had to do. Just before turning onto the forestry road that led to the cabin, Custer turned the truck around and headed back the way he had just come.

"What are you doing, Custer? Have you lost your mind? I need to read Angel's letter and see what's wrong, why she is leaving us."

"I'm taking you back to Betsy and Hawk's place and then I'm going to catch up with Tobi and Angel. I cannot explain, Sue Ann. I promised. You will just have to trust me. I know what I am doing."

****

Tobi pulled in at the service station by the interstate when he saw Angel about to leave the gas pumps. He pulled in front of her, blocking her route, and got out, heading for her car door.

"Back up and park over by the motel, Angel. You are not going anywhere until we talk."

She knew it would do her no good to head for the interstate. Tobi would follow her to Costa Rica if he had to, and she could do nothing to stop him.

He parked beside her car, got out, and slid in on the passenger side. He looked at her but said nothing and then stared out the front window.

Angel didn't know what to say, so she remained silent, looking straight ahead at the service station. She had counted on being far away by the time Tobi found her letter, but he had reached the cabin much earlier than scheduled.

"You need to explain, Angel. What is so pressing that you would leave me? You said you love me, yet you are willing to leave me to wallow in self pity, without knowing what I did, or did not do, to make it so easy for you to run away from me." He kept his eyes focused on the window, hoping this would help her to open up.

"I can't tell you, Tobi. I told you in the letter…it's an assignment only I can complete, and it is something I have to do alone. You have to trust me."

Again, silence filled the SUV. After almost a minute, he spoke.

"No!" Vehemently, he shook his head. "No!" he exclaimed, louder. "Whatever this assignment is, you are not completing it alone. If it's CIA old business, so be it, but I'm going with you. I'm a trained detective, and I know what confidential means." When she started to protest, he held his hands up to stop her.

"No! I won't leave this car. I'm not losing you, Angel. And that's a fact!"

"This does not concern the CIA, Tobi." She pulled her knees up on the seat, facing him. "And I promised not to include you."

"Promised who? What the hell are you talking about, Angel?" His voice raised again. "I love you, Angel. We were meant to be together. Custer as much as predicted it before you ever came to Montana. If it concerns you, it concerns me! Don't you see that?" He reached for her hand and squeezed it hard.

"Tobi, I have no control over this. I gave my word. You have to let me go." She put her other hand on top of his. Her eyes pierced through the short distance between them like a bright blue laser, begging for understanding, for release from the love that was preventing her quest to search for her father.

"No!" Again, Tobi refused to release her.

With his arms outstretched, she fell into them and wept against his chest. He cradled her with no intention of letting go and tried his best to kiss away her tears and fears. She knew she would not be able to leave without him. She also knew only one person could release her from the oath she had taken that morning.

Tobi wiped the tears from Angel's eyes and told her to get out and follow him.

After getting a room at the motel, he made love to her like there was no tomorrow. Exhausted, they both fell asleep. He awoke when he felt her blue gaze boring a hole through him.

He opened his eyes and smiled at her, pulling her

into his arms, hoping to make her feel comfortable, safe, and trusting. Before either could prevent it, they were making love again, but this time when the ecstasy ended, they did not sleep.

"Marry me, Angel. I know we've only known each other for a few weeks, but I can't imagine life without you. Besides, we've spent every day and almost every night together since your first fly fishing lesson. Neither of us is getting any younger, and I don't want to ever come close to losing you again." He kissed her, a deep kiss signifying forever in the way he felt about her.

"I love you, Tobi, but…"

He put his fingers over her lips.

"No buts…"

****

When Tobi and Angel left the motel room, they were surprised to see Custer in his Jeep, waiting for them. With a sheepish grin, Tobi spoke.

"I caught her. Told you I would." Tobi reached for Angel's hand.

She walked to Custer and gave him a hug.

"I'm really glad Tobi stopped you, Angel. I would never forgive myself if…" Custer did not finish what he was about to say. "We need to talk, but not when Sue Ann is around. Let's go to the casino and have dinner. We can talk there."

An hour later, Tobi knew everything about Custer's past and how he had saved Shade's life. Angel reached across the table and gave Custer's hand a squeeze, a gesture that said, "Thank you for letting me include Tobi."

"Well…that is quite an assignment, darling. So you were going to the jungles of Costa Rica in search of your father, all based on some anonymous information you received." Tobi shook his head, not believing the danger this tiny woman was willing to put herself in all alone.

"Yes, and it would have been all my fault." Custer shook his head, not believing what he had almost let happen. "I'm sorry, Angel. I just never thought you'd go through with trying to search for your dad. And I'm sorry for making you take that oath not to tell anyone in the family. I'm glad Tobi knows, but that being said, I still do not want Sue Ann to know. She will undergo undue stress knowing her husband has been dishonest with her all these years in letting her think Shade was dead. She will probably hate me for it, but I promised Shade."

"Nothing could make Mom hate you, Custer. She loves you too much, and from what she has told me, she would understand Shade pretending to be dead to protect his loved ones." Tobi reached for Angel's hand again. "Question is…what do we do now?"

"First thing, I have to go pick up your mother. I whisked her away to Betsy's without so much as even a lie for an explanation. If you two go with me, it will be much better. What did you say in the letter, Angel?"

"I just told her things were moving too fast and I needed time to think things through. I implied it was something between Tobi and me, but I didn't say it outright."

"Good! Let's leave it at that, but don't you go running off to Costa Rica! Do we understand each other, Angel?"

"Yes, Custer. Besides, I'll have to consult my fiancé before I go running off to the jungles." Angel turned her face to Tobi's. "Yes, Tobi Parish. I'll marry you."

Chapter Fifteen

An impromptu engagement party was held at Sue Ann and Custer's home that night, and a scene that could have been covered with an aura of doom and gloom was instead filled with happiness. Tobi had found love just as Custer had promised, but Tobi also knew this new relationship would be his greatest trial.

"You have a strong, innate sense of protection." Custer had stated that day so long ago when Custer was consoling his stepson. "A man's highest calling is the protection of a woman." Tobi knew, when he asked Angel to marry him, he was promising to love and honor her, but he was also swearing to protect her against all harm.

As the couple raised their champagne glasses in a toast proposed by Custer, Tobi added a remark at the end.

"I am so thankful my Angel said 'yes,' and I promise to cherish, love, and protect her as long as I have breath in me. You were so worth the wait, sweetheart. I just wish I had an engagement ring to give you. But now we can pick it out together."

"When can we start planning the wedding, Angel? I hope it's soon." Betsy hugged her soon-to-be sister-in-law.

"Tobi and I are waiting until Carrie comes. It's not that long, and we want her to get to know me, and to be

119

in our wedding. To think I'll be a wife and a mom at the same time! I could not be happier." Angel hugged Tobi, who bent down and kissed her.

Sue Ann had slipped out of the room while Tobi and Angel were telling of their wedding plans. As she came back in, Betsy repeated what Angel had just said.

"Oh, how wonderful! I am so ready to see my granddaughter. It is just too long between visits. And Carrie will love you, Angel, just as we all do." Sue Ann hugged Angel and then her son. "About that engagement ring, Tobi. I have a solution, if you both agree to it." Sue Ann reached into her pocket and pulled out a ring box. "I would be very pleased if you two would consider these your wedding rings."

Sue Ann handed the ring box to Tobi.

"Open this, Tobi. This was your grandfather Zeke's wedding ring. It was bought for him by my mother many years after their marriage, and she had the emerald stone mounted in the middle of the diamonds because my dad always loved my mother's green eyes. If you two, especially Angel, agree, I'd love for you to wear it."

"Is this the ring my dad wore, Sue Ann?"

"Yes, Angel. To my knowledge, it is the only ring Shade ever wore as an adult. I'll understand if that's a problem for you."

"No! I think Dad would be honored for Tobi to wear this ring, and it is part of the family history Tobi never knew. We both had gaps in our family histories, but not anymore. Are you okay with it, Tobi?"

"I love the idea of wearing my grandfather's wedding ring, Angel, even if it's my color eyes rather than your blue. Let's just say, when I have it on my finger, you will know my eyes are always looking at you with love." Tobi put the ring on his finger, and it was a perfect fit. "How about you keep it 'til the wedding, Mom."

"Of course I will, Tobi. And now for you, Miss Angel. There is only one ring that will do for my future daughter-in-law." Sue Ann turned away from the group and slipped the blue nugget ring off her right hand, and when she turned back, she smiled and placed it in Tobi's hand, curling his fingers around it. "Shade can't be here to give his little girl away, but this ring will always be a reminder of his love for his Angel."

Tobi opened his hand, and the large blue diamond sparkled, just like Angel's blues had dazzled him on their first meeting on Beartooth Highway.

"No, Sue Ann! Dad gave the blue diamond to you. It wouldn't be right!" Angel protested Sue Ann's action. "Besides, it's worth a fortune!"

"Custer, Betsy, and I talked about this not long ago, hoping you and Tobi would marry. It is so right that you have this, Angel. Your dad would be thrilled. If Shade had lived, and if he were standing here right now, it would be exactly what I would do. Betsy will inherit my beautiful brown diamond that Custer placed on my left hand when we were married. The blue diamond is yours, Angel."

Seeing Angel's tears rolling down her cheeks, forming little pools of joy in her smile lines, Tobi knew he had his fiancée's approval. Reaching for her left hand, he placed the blue diamond on her ring finger as an engagement ring first and wedding ring after the ceremony.

Betsy ran to Angel and gave her a big, tearful hug

and was soon joined in a group hug, with Trapper squeezing his way to the middle of the group and grabbing Angel around the waist.

"So where do you want your wedding, Angel? Do you want it at the waterfall like Betsy and Hawk, or the little chapel on the outskirts of Red Lodge like Custer and me? Or do you have another place in mind?" Sue Ann asked the question with visions of planning running through her head.

"Oh, I know already where I want my wedding. Right here in this cabin. We can stand here in front of the big fireplace with Dad's painting over us. We will all be together *Under Northern Lights*, just like the book you said you would write about that year in Alaska."

Angel looked at Custer as she made the remark and noticed his face had become somber. She knew he was wondering if he would be among the "all." To let him know she understood his feelings, she moved over and hugged him.

"Thank you, Custer. For everything."

Chapter Sixteen

Tobi let Angel off in front of the café while he parked the truck. Angel was still reeling over being an engaged woman and could be caught smiling almost constantly. Just as she was about to push the door open to the café, she heard brakes squealing on the street. She turned and saw a black SUV backing up fast. In seconds, a man jumped out of the car and headed in her direction.

"Angela! Angela!"

Angel watched as the tall man approached. He had on a sports cap, zip-off nylon pants, and a fishing shirt not tucked in and open in the front, disclosing a white T-shirt beneath. Something was familiar about him, but it wasn't until he stepped up on the curb in front of her that she recognized him.

"Randal?"

Before Angel knew what was happening, Randal scooped her up and swung her around. Holding her close to his body, he locked his lips to hers without letting her feet touch the ground.

Angel was caught off guard and did not know how to get herself out of his bear hug. She tried to push away, but there was no releasing her until he was ready.

"I can't believe I found you. What do you mean, leaving without calling me? I've been worried sick!" He stood back, eyeing her up and down. "You look wonderful, darling!" When he grabbed her hand, she tried to jerk away from him.

"Kiss her again, and I'll deck you." Tobi walked up to the scene, took Angel's hand, and pulled her away from the man. "I don't know who the hell you are, but this is my fiancée!" Even though he was much shorter, Tobi bowed up like he was ready to hit the man. The absence of height did not preclude the absence of strength, nor the ability to use muscle if necessary, where Tobi was concerned.

"Fiancée? What the hell is going on, Angela? Tell him who I am." The man stood back but glared at Angel, waiting for her to explain.

"Tobi, this is Randal Davison. We dated some before I left D.C. Randal, this is Tobi Parish, my fiancé." Angel moved her other hand and wrapped it around Tobi's arm.

"I'd shake your hand, but I'd rather knock the hell out of you." Tobi directed Angel toward the café door and away from Randal.

"Wait a minute, Angela! You can't just..." Randal looked hurt by the information. "I've called everybody you were friends with at work and called your phone constantly for weeks. I finally used unauthorized sources, if you know what I mean, and followed your credit card trail to Red Lodge. Why didn't you answer my calls?"

"She doesn't need to answer your questions." Tobi lowered his voice and moved closer to Randal when he saw passersby staring. "You need to leave by the same highway you came in on—now!" Tobi was yelling again by the time he got the last word out.

"Just give me a minute, Tobi." Angela took Randal

by the arm and moved a few feet away from Tobi. "You did not call me for at least two weeks after you left. I have good friends here, and I needed a change, so I resigned my job and came here. Meeting Tobi was the best thing that could ever have happened to me. We are in love and we are engaged. End of story." Angel turned to leave, but Randal caught her arm and turned her back around to face him.

Tobi flew into a rage, thrusting his whole body into Randal, knocking him off his feet. As he lay on the pavement, Tobi straddled him, hitting him with his fist again and again.

"Tobi, stop!" Angel took Tobi's arm and stopped his next punch. "Come on. Let's go before you get in trouble." Angel led Tobi away from Randal, who was rising to his feet wondering what had just happened. When Tobi tried to go back, Angel told him to keep walking.

"Who is that guy, Angel? What the hell does he mean to you? Is he another of your secrets?"

"No, Tobi. He is nothing to me...never was, but I didn't know it at the time. I'm sorry. I told you about him but didn't make a big deal out of it. I really thought it was over when he left on an assignment and didn't call for two weeks. Then I lost my phone in the accident, so any calls he made never reached me. I didn't think there was any reason to care." Angel and Tobi got in the truck and headed out of town.

"Assignment? What kind of assignment, Angela? Is he with the CIA, too?"

"Yes. Randal is CIA. An old friend of mine, Herb Feller, introduced us a few months ago. I thought the relationship was going somewhere, but it never did."

Angel reached for Tobi's hand. "And I am so glad it didn't, because now I have you."

Tobi pulled the truck over at the next turnoff and pulled Angel to him, kissing her long and hard.

"I'm sorry, sweetheart. I guess I shouldn't have hit him, but it's not easy walking up and seeing some stranger kissing my future wife. I guess you know now I'm the jealous kind." Tobi pulled the truck back onto the road and headed for his cabin.

"Yes, and I know you are a lot stronger than I thought. Randal is a big man. But what if he doesn't leave town, Tobi? I don't want you fighting him. He could press charges against you."

Angel got her answer the next day when she looked out Tobi's window and saw a black SUV pulling into the front yard with Randal behind the wheel.

"Tobi, Randal Davison just pulled into your yard." Angel watched as Tobi huffed his way to the door. "Take it easy and let him talk this time. I don't know why he's here, but we need to find out." Angel stopped Tobi, putting her hands on his cheeks. "Promise?"

"Okay, but he better be quick, and if he touches you..." Tobi did not finish as he stepped out on the deck, followed by Angel.

"I'm not here to fight you, Tobi. This is business. And I'm sorry about what happened yesterday. I had no idea Angela had found someone else, and that's the truth."

"What kind of business?" Tobi asked.

"CIA business. Herb Feller sent me." Randal made no effort to approach the deck until Tobi nodded his head for him to enter the cabin. Randal reached into the back seat of the SUV and pulled out a briefcase.

"How did Herb know where I was?" Angel asked as she sat at the table.

"He didn't until I told him. I told him I used CIA resources to track down your travels. So how did you total the Mercedes? We saw the wrecker bill."

"It's a long story, but it had a happy ending. Tobi rescued me." Angel reached across the table for Tobi's hand. "So why is Herb looking for me?"

"It seems a briefcase of yours was found and turned in to the Agency. It had some classified documents in it that you were not supposed to have. Herb wanted me to find you and ask you about them." Randal stood, lined up the code numbers to unlock the briefcase and opened it on the table.

"Briefcase of mine? What kind of classified documents? I don't know what you're talking about." Angel moved to the coffeepot and got the three of them each a cup of coffee. "One sugar, right?" Angel noticed how pissed Tobi looked that she remembered how Randal took his coffee.

"I have copies of what was in the documents. Ordinarily, I'd not be showing you these, but Herb said if it was in your briefcase, you had already seen them and needed to explain. He said to tell you, your ID badge was also inside, and your fingerprints are all over the briefcase, so there's no denying it's yours."

Angel took the documents and scanned them. She knew without looking at them that they were the documents about her father, the last drop made giving her the information about Custer, but she also knew they were not in the briefcase taken, but she was not about to disclose this. After she perused the pages, she handed them to Tobi.

"Wait! Sorry, but this is classified information." Randal intercepted the documents, taking them from Angel. "You don't have clearance, Tobi. And that's not me trying to get back at you for that punch yesterday." Randal rubbed his sore jaw. "Angela can tell you it's CIA policy."

"Sorry, Tobi, but he's right." Angel smiled at Tobi, and when Randal wasn't looking, she winked at Tobi, reminding him that she had her own copy of the documents.

"Can you explain how these were in your briefcase, Angela, and can you explain how the police were able to retrieve them? Herb says you could be in a world of trouble unless your explanation is a good one." Randal put the documents back in his briefcase and locked it by twirling the code numbers.

"I have an explanation, but I want time to process all of this and to talk it over with Tobi. Can you come back tomorrow, about the same time?" Angel stood, giving Randal his cue to leave.

"Well, I don't guess you're running off again. Herb didn't say for me to put you under arrest, so I guess if he trusts you, I should, too." Randal stood, picked up the briefcase, and headed to the front door. "I'll see you tomorrow, then."

After Randal left, Tobi pulled Angel into a hug. When he released her, he held her back and looked her in the eyes.

"Time to see those documents, but I'd like Custer here. He is a big part of this and might offer some advice on how to proceed. I'm sure you still want to try to find Shade."

Angel nodded her head in agreement and headed

for her Suburban, with Tobi on her heels. She pulled up the carpet in the back of the rig and opened the compartment holding the jack and spare tire. A packet of papers with red stains across the back peered out at them. Tobi was already on his cell phone calling Custer.

****

Custer, Tobi, and Angel sat at Tobi's kitchen table and listened as Angel read the documents aloud. She knew exactly what was in them, with her photographic memory, and it was a good thing, since the red wine she had spilled on the pages had distorted some of the words.

"So everything about me and Shade is given in this document except for actually identifying Eagle. How did the police come up with your briefcase with another copy of the documents in it?" Custer asked the question.

Angel sighed, knowing she was about to get a stern reprimand from both Tobi and Custer for her negligence in not telling about the night she was attacked in the elevator inside the garage at her condo.

Angel told about the incident in as matter-of-fact a way as possible, but Tobi did not buy it.

"You mean you were attacked in the elevator, your purse and briefcase were stolen, and you never even called the police? Angel, do you realize you could have been killed, and I would have never gotten to know you or to love you? Damn!" Tobi left the table and paced, making his way to the front deck.

"Well, that didn't go too well, did it?" Angel cast a glance at Custer.

"No, but since Tobi said what I was thinking, I'll

go easy on you." Custer picked up one of the sheets, put on his reading glasses and began looking over the document. "And you are sure there were no classified documents in the briefcase stolen?"

"I am positive, Custer. I got the packet from the beige Ford parked right beside my parking spot, just like the informant told me in the message I received on my phone. I stuffed it in my old briefcase. When I got to the condo garage, I reached across the console for my purse, got out, and went to the back seat and picked up my briefcase, the wrong one. The two cases are just alike but one is newer, the one I picked up by mistake. My attacker knocked me down in the elevator and took my purse and the briefcase that contained the usual from work, a few notepads, a CIA handbook for employees, my badge, and that kind of stuff, but no documents."

"When did you realize the thief had made off with the insignificant briefcase?" Custer asked as he removed his glasses and laid them beside the documents.

"Almost immediately. I was more concerned with retrieving the new documents than about my own safety. I ran back to the car and grabbed the briefcase that had the classified documents in it. You could say my picking up the wrong briefcase was a freak of luck—or more like a godsend."

Tobi reentered the cabin, gave Angel a quick peck on the cheek, and returned to his seat to look over the documents one more time.

"So this one is all about Eagle on special assignment to save Raven. But it does not disclose who Eagle is. How did you connect Eagle with Custer,

Angel? Is this something blatant that anyone could find?" Tobi looked across at Custer and then to Angel.

"No. I figured it out from Sue Ann's book *Heart of the Beartooths*, where the eagle is the animal spirit of Custer, coupled with his ability to shoot a high-powered rifle from a long distance and hit the woman, the would-be assassin, at Devil's Canyon. To me this identified Custer as a sniper, very important to Tiger's Eye. I just put it together, and I was right."

"You said there were two drops by this anonymous guy...what did you call him?" Tobi asked.

"The Postman. This person contacted me through a letter the first time and a text message the second, but since I never heard the voice or saw the person, I have no idea if the Postman is male or female."

Tobi rubbed his chin. "So what did the first documents tell you about your father, and where are they?"

"They're here." Angel reached over beside Custer and picked up the document. "But I can give you a quick synopsis. These told about Dad's time with Tiger's Eye as an assassin, something I could hardly read. And it told about how he quit and did a complete turnaround, putting his life on the line sneaking into Vietcong prisoner-of-war camps and saving captured American soldiers. At first, he took pay for the soldiers he saved, paid for by rich entrepreneurs, but then when families started contacting him and offering to sell everything they owned to pay for his services, he began rescuing the soldiers and refusing pay. That is what got attention from the CIA. The Agency found out about ONE's huge reward to have Dad killed after ONE escaped from prison, and the CIA started trying to find

Dad, to protect him."

"Raven never wanted their help. He was a loner—still is, if he's alive." Custer kept his eyes on the documents and did not look up to see Angel's reaction.

"You think he is alive, don't you, Custer." Angel reached across and put her hand on top of Custer's.

"What I think does not matter, my dear. It is what your dad thinks that matters. Does he want you to find him? No, but only because he fears for your life, along with Sue Ann's and Betsy's, and now there are others to consider, like Trapper. That little boy has been traumatized once already, when he was kidnapped. We cannot let that happen again." Custer looked at Angel with a face covered in concern. "I wish we knew if Shade keeps up with what is happening here. He did until three years ago, when I called him to tell him Sue Ann had chosen me to marry, but I think he is trying to forget now. I don't want to scare you, Angel, but I think your father was contemplating taking his own life at that time."

"What makes you think that, Custer?" Angel showed alarm at Custer's disclosure.

"I've never heard or felt a more dejected, downtrodden voice, and this from a man I felt was invincible. Shade was relieved Sue Ann and I were married. He knew I would protect her with my life just as he had, but in his relief, great sorrow and depression enveloped him. He loved Sue Ann more than any man has ever loved a woman. Yes…probably even more than I love Sue Ann, although that is hard to comprehend. She was all he talked about when I would visit him in physical rehab. And he talked about you, Angel. He called you his pixie Angel. He had a picture you had drawn of him when you saw him once by accident in the Space Needle in Seattle when you were just a young girl. How he got it, I don't know. Someone, a good friend, must have saved it from his cabin in Alaska. He had it framed and looked at it constantly, along with a picture of you with Sue Ann and Betsy."

"So what do we tell Randal when he comes tomorrow?" Tobi asked. "Any ideas, Custer? I don't want him to know who you are. No one should ever associate you with Eagle, for the sake of all of us. Somehow, I just don't trust this guy, and I don't think it's because I caught him kissing my fiancée." Tobi reached over and pulled Angel to him, putting his arm around her. "Do you trust him, Angel?"

"I don't know, Tobi. Herb seemed to think a lot of him, but someone knows too much about my dad, and I don't know why he, or she, chose to share the information with me. Since the documents are classified with the CIA, it has to be someone within the Agency."

"Do you want my thoughts?" Custer sat waiting, gauging the reaction of both Tobi and Angel. When they both looked at him but kept silent, he took this to be silence with consent and began.

"I think you were given the documents because someone knew you would start your own investigation to find your father. I'm not so sure you should trust anyone from the CIA, not with several million dollars riding on your father's head in a basket. Let's say someone in the CIA found these classified documents, someone who could never dream of getting the kind of payoff that killing Shade would bring. Suppose they put this chain of events in motion intentionally to get you headed toward the truth so they can follow you to Shade."

"But for what purpose, Custer? I was an intelligence analyst, not a field agent. The only classified documents I ever saw were the ones I was trying to review or create. Analysts are taught the intelligence cycle, how to brief and write for executive management, and how to write the 'Agency' way, which is more succinct, like a scientific research paper rather than a long and arduous academic paper. And they know every document I have accessed, none of which were concerning Jon Shockey or Shade Dubois."

"Randal Davison is coming tomorrow, and we have to be ready. What will you tell him, Angel? What *can* you tell him?" Tobi's voice revealed his fear and concern for Angel.

"The truth, or at least part of it." Angel picked up her cell phone. "I won't tell him I have the document that was supposedly stolen. He's CIA and can figure that out for himself, if he doesn't already know. Perhaps I should call Herb just to make sure he sent Randal looking for me." She glanced at Tobi and then Custer and waited for their nod of agreement. Then she punched in the number she had gotten from the agency after losing her first phone.

After two minutes of listening to Herb rant about her leaving without saying goodbye, Angel asked the question.

"Did you send Randal to question me about some classified documents and my briefcase? It's important, Herb. I need to know if you sent him."

Tobi and Custer could hear the deep male voice on the other end and knew he was reprimanding Angel, not only for not telling about the briefcase being stolen from her car, but for not telling him who her father was. Herb said he knew Randal was looking for her but she needed to head back to D.C., ASAP, and be debriefed on the documents. He also said there could be repercussions since she could not prove she did not get the classified documents in some illicit way.

"The briefcase was stolen from my car, Herb. And I know nothing about the documents, certainly not how they were obtained or who found them, since they were not in my briefcase when it was stolen. Do you believe me?"

"All I know is your briefcase was turned over to the police with documents illicitly received from someone. It is not up to me to believe you, Angel, but it is up to you to come up with a reasonable explanation."

Angel, tired of the preachy way her old friend was speaking, told him she would call him later and suggested he get some control between this phone call and the next. She also told him she was hurt by his accusations. With this, she hung up the phone.

****

"So are you going to tell Randal you have the classified documents?" Tobi asked the question after he and Angel made love that night. It was a question she had not answered point blank.

"No. I'm going to tell him my car was broken into in the garage at the condo and that the briefcase was stolen. That's all I'm telling him. I'll tell him I believe it is a setup, but I have no clue why someone is trying to set me up; nor do I know for what they are trying to set me up. I will admit to my identity as Jon Shockey's daughter since he knows this already. I should have to explain nothing more."

"And then?" Tobi caressed Angel's breasts as he held her in his arms.

"You better make sure your passport is up to date."

Chapter Seventeen

Randal's meeting was short the next day. Angel told her story about the briefcase being taken at her condo in D.C., and she told Randal who her father was. The agent did not act surprised by the information. Just before he got ready to leave, Angel's phone rang.

Angel answered the phone and was surprised to hear Herb Feller's voice on the other end. He apologized for "acting like an asshole" the day before but then excused his actions as being his job. His real reason for calling was to speak to Randal, who it seemed did not have his phone with him, since he had not answered three missed calls.

"It's for you, Randal. Herb Fellers, and where the hell is your phone? In your shoe?" Angel stared at Randal, who immediately began searching his pockets as he took the phone from Angel.

"Yeah, Herb. It must have fallen out of my pocket in the car. What do you need?" Randal turned to Angel, whispering, "Excuse me," and holding up a finger as he took the phone to the deck.

Angel and Tobi tried to eavesdrop but could not make out the muffled conversation, especially after Randal walked to his car, obviously to look for his cell phone. When Randal came back into Tobi's cabin, he asked to speak to Angel alone on the porch. Tobi balked at the idea, but Angel told him it would be all right.

"Angela, I think you should come back to D.C. Something is not right here in Montana, but I can't quite put my finger on what is making me feel this way, other than you are leaving me for another man, one you hardly know. If you had just waited, I planned to offer you a ring."

"You can stop lying now, Randal. I don't believe that for one second. A man who is in love does not stop calling for two weeks. Anyway, I'm glad we didn't work out. I love Tobi, and I am going to marry him, and that is that. Take your reports and go back to D.C. There is nothing here for you." With that, Angel turned and walked back to the door of the cabin but stopped before going inside. "Oh, and tell Herb I appreciate the vote of confidence." With that, she stepped inside and slammed the door.

****

That afternoon, Tobi finished his last assignment for his classes and looked for his fiancée to announce he was ready for whatever she wanted to do, be it looking like tourists in Costa Rica or getting married ahead of their scheduled wedding date even though he knew Carrie would be disappointed not to be a bridesmaid. Carrie had talked to Angel on the phone several times and was excited about the wedding and about having her as a stepmother.

Tobi found Angel in deep thought, sitting under the aspen trees to the side of the cabin, staring at the mountains. When he sat down beside her, he noticed she was holding the cell phone, Custer's link to her dad.

"Ready to make your call?"

Angel turned to face Tobi. "What do I say, Tobi?

138

'Hi, Dad, this is Angel—you know, the daughter you left behind. Well, just checking to see if you really are alive. Later'?"

"That's your decision, Angel. But I bet if you just go ahead and make the call, you will feel much better. Chances are he won't answer, since he never answered Custer's calls, but you will never know until you try, and at least your voice will be on his messages."

"What if I go to Costa Rica and lead someone to Dad who is after the money for killing him? Then I'll have Dad's blood on my hands again." She buried her head in her hands on top of her knees.

"What do you mean 'again'? You had nothing to do with your dad being shot and ending up in the Tekooni River." Tobi pulled her head up, holding her by the chin. "Tell me what you're most afraid of, Angel."

"If Betsy and I had gone home like we were supposed to, that day in Moose Springs, if we had not gone to the landing to watch the breakup, Dad would still be alive...really alive, and here with me. He'd be walking me down the aisle instead of Custer walking me. I want to see my dad again and feel him hug me, but I'm afraid to look for him for fear of someone following me."

"Make the call, Angel. Right here. Right now! We can wait and see if he calls you back before we head for Costa Rica—if you want, that is."

She flipped open the phone before she had more time to think and dialed the numbers corresponding to RAVENEAGLE. The phone began to ring on the other end. When she heard a click, she began talking.

"Dad...Dad...It's me, Angel. I know you're alive,

and other people know you're alive, too. I need you, Dad. Call me back, or I'll come looking for you in Costa Rica. I love…" The click on the other end told her either someone hung up or the answering machine had cut her off.

"Now we wait." Tobi stood and held out his hand to her. Hand in hand, they walked back to their cabin in the mountains.

****

Custer was having a hard time sleeping and quietly left the bed, not wanting to wake Sue Ann. He had the gnawing feeling that he was missing something important, something Raven had said to him a long time ago about places where it was easy for a man to disappear. Angel had heard her dad tell Sue Ann about hiding the family in Costa Rica, and perhaps that was where he was, but even though Costa Rica was half the size of Mississippi, it had twice as many people, and the landscape encompassed jungles, rainforests, volcanoes, and overpopulated cities. Probably the easiest place would be the cities, if a man wanted to lose himself, but that wasn't a likely choice for Shade, a diehard survivalist.

Custer remembered the last day he talked to Shade in person. Shade knew he had to remain dead or his loved ones would be at risk of being used just as Betsy and Angel had been that day in Alaska—bait for ruthless, money-hungry bastards to lure him out. He had talked incessantly about Sue Ann and how he wished he had died that day. He said he would rather be dead than know he could never be with her again. At first, he had been angry at Custer for saving him and refused to talk to him. Finally, he gave in. Custer was

140

his link to seeing that Sue Ann and Betsy would be okay. Custer had told him about the cabin in the Beartooths and had overseen the purchase for Shade months before ONE found him.

Never did I dream I would fall in love with Sue Ann—something else Shade pretended he wanted to happen so she would be protected, but deep down, he died all over again the day Sue Ann and I married. Oh, Raven! It's time to put all of this to rest before I leave Sue Ann for good.

Custer turned his eyes to the painting he no longer hated, and Shade's words came back to his mind. Shade had prepared to disappear from protective custody, the temporary physical rehabilitation facility set up for him where he had rebuilt his strength, a place where he was hidden from society and those who would attempt to kill him.

I remember asking him, "Raven, what if Sue Ann needs you some day? What then?"

Raven replied, "Sue Ann will always know where I am if she seeks the information. She only has to look to Aurora—to the lights that brought us together."

I figured he was being poetic, something he did quite often. That was the last time I saw Raven. When I came a few weeks later, he had escaped from his protective prison and disappeared.

****

At the end of the week, Sue Ann called Tobi's cell phone over and over but got no answer. She began to get concerned when she could not get Angel to answer either.

"Custer, would you go over and check on Tobi and Angel? I can't get either of them to answer. You know I have a sixth sense where my children are concerned, and I just feel uneasy for some reason."

When Custer drove up to Tobi's cabin, he noticed the truck was gone but Angel's Suburban was still there. He knocked on the door but got no answer. Turning the doorknob, he found it unlocked and cracked the door.

"Angel? Tobi?" No answer came, so Custer went inside. What he found made his heart palpitate. Every cupboard door was open, with the insides strewn as if someone had frantically searched for something of importance. The bedroom downstairs was the same way. Custer knew he could not call the sheriff on this one. As he was about to leave, he heard someone running across the back deck. He opened the door and saw a man dressed in black, with a ski mask over his face, running through the woods. Custer knew he could never catch him, but he hurried to his Jeep and tried to follow him as far as the Jeep could go. Just down the forestry road on the other side of Tobi's place, he saw a black SUV speeding away with no regard for bumps or ditches.

"Damn! Where are Tobi and Angel?" Just as their names left his lips, his cell phone rang. Custer looked and saw it was Tobi's number.

"Tobi, where are you? Is Angel with you?"

"I'm on an airplane and Angel is right beside me. We are going to Costa Rica to look for Shade. Is anything wrong? You sound shaken, Custer."

"Thank goodness. Someone has done a number on your place, pulled everything out like they were hunting for something. I'm not glad you're going to Costa Rica, but I am glad to know you are together and both of you are safe. Tobi, you have to be careful. I think someone, maybe several people, are on the trail for Shade. Did Angel use the phone?"

"Yes, she did. She left a message and told him she was coming to Costa Rica to look for him, but he never called back. I don't know if we can find him, but we have to try, for Angel's sake." Tobi hesitated and the sound of a recording announcing preparation for takeoff could be heard in the background.

"Gotta go, Custer. Give Mom and Betsy a hug for me and tell them I'll call from Central America. Wait, you can't do that, since neither of them know about Shade. Just tell them we have gone on a trip, a pre-honeymoon. Yeah, that will do. Later, Custer."

"Be careful, Tobi, and keep your phone handy." The click on the other end made Custer shudder with fear for the young couple.

"Damn it, Raven! Listen to your messages and call your daughter. She needs you."

****

The two men packed their luggage into the black SUV and headed for Billings Airport. The cabin had yielded no information, but a quick glance in Angel's car had led them to a copy of an itinerary dropped on the floorboard.

"Costa Rica. I'd bet my sorry-ass little salary that's where he is." The man showed the itinerary to his partner.

"Not much to bet on, but if we find Jon Shockey, you won't need your sorry-ass little salary. We'll both be sitting pretty." The man pulled off his black shirt and put on a white knit pullover. "How long do we have to kill Shockey and get the picture of his corpse and fingerprints to that organization in Switzerland?"

"About six weeks, according to the boss. Angela better know where she's going. Regardless, it's the only lead we've got. I wish we knew who Eagle was. It would give us one more option."

"But we don't. So where are they landing in Costa Rica?" asked the driver.

"San Jose, the capital. Prepare to swim through a myriad of sweaty tourists."

"We won't find Shockey in a city. That's not his scene. I'd say maybe on some isolated island in the Pacific, or close to the top of a volcano, or in the middle of a jungle full of weird-looking critters and poisonous snakes."

"And spiders…" The man in the passenger seat chimed in, openly shivering as images flooded his brain—long-legged monstrous arachnids, dangling in front of his face, bringing back nightmares of a childhood spent in a ghostly old spider-infested house.

"I hear those damn spiders can spin their webs faster than hikers can knock them off the trail." This time full-fledged shaking seized his body, and muted verbal shrieks followed in the quake, maximizing his phobic response.

"You've been in some of the worst battles in your career with the CIA, had bullets zipping by so close they could rip your face off, and you suffer from arachnophobia? Just doesn't make sense." The driver shook his head in disbelief. "Ought to be a pill for that."

The other man, still shivering at the thought of traipsing through Costa Rican jungles notorious for huge spiders, put his head back on the seat and closed his eyes. "It better be worth it is all I've got to say."

Part II

Raven Wings

Beware of the Winds

Oral tribal lore tells us of whispering winds,
Winds of sorts that tell of omens good or bad.
~
Whispering wind words from gone grandparents
warning many people to be aware of all winds.
~
Of blowing winds before Grandfather Sun's
appearance;
they warn us be cautious when in morning darkness.
~
Of whirling winds, you should hit at, or spit at these;
welcome good evening winds coming to sweat lodge
fires.
~
Beware of ghost wind causing many facial paralyses;
outside, beware of the winds that twist mouths.
~
Listen to whispering winds in fast at Bear Butte;
Listen to elders in dreams when they whisper.
~
Of songs learned from wind against tree branches,
listen to the cedar and pine trees as they whistle songs.

~Two Man Seminole/Glenmore,
Northern Cheyenne of Busby, Montana;
Also known by Cheyenne Names:
White Antelope, Vo'kaa'e Ohvokomaestse
or Two Man, Hetane Ohnesestse

Chapter One

Whiteman crawled on his belly through the floor of the dark African jungle as flat as he could get on the ground and yet still be able to move with his knees and elbows inching him forward. This was nothing new to him, but he was beginning to feel the years, years when most men were already retired.

Free time? For what? To spend lonely days thinking about a past I wish had never happened? To think about all I've lost and can never regain? Hell, I'd rather crawl my way through a viper's den and die on the spot. Brave! Yeah, that's me. I have more courage than I need when it comes to dying, but none when it comes to living.

He glanced ahead at the three young soldiers in his charge and wondered if they had any idea what lay ahead for them. These three had been handpicked, the best of the best, meaning they were the ones who had the natural skills to take out the ruthless head of a ragtag though lethal army of rebel soldiers. This army was made up mostly of boys stolen from their villages as children, or given away by parents misguided enough to think they could save themselves or other family members by handing over their young sons. The boys were then reared by the rebel commander to be masochistic monsters, brutalizing, raping, and dismembering women, children, or any villager of their choosing, or of the choosing of their commanders. The worst case of Stockholm Syndrome ever known was attached to these boys. Their childhoods had been ripped from their undernourished bodies, forced into adulthood as mini versions of the man who led the army, known only as Kamanda, Swahili for Commander.

Whiteman had spent months training the three recruits, but only two would make the cut, the two already chosen in Whiteman's mind. Either of these two could take out Kamanda, each with the stealth and prowess of a tiger; each with a personal reason for wanting this kill. Their young sisters had been kidnapped before their tiny wombs had time to develop, and now both girls served as bush wives of Kamanda. Each girl, now in her teens, had a brood of her own children, future killers and bush wives fathered by Kamanda and the others.

Whiteman had listened as Haji, one of the trainees, told stories of watching, as a boy, hidden in the edge of the jungle, as his mother and grandmother were tied up and raped repeatedly before having their breasts and limbs cut off their bodies while still alive. He still could hear his ten-year-old sister screaming his name as she was carted off through the jungle by Kamanda's army.

Saka and Jelandi had similar stories, just as brutal. One had seen his father and grandfather tied to trees and sliced repeatedly with machetes until no flesh remained for the ropes to hold.

Whiteman had trained them well and knew if one of the two chosen could not put a bullet between Kamanda's eyes, it was probably not possible, which meant what many believed was true: Kamanda was the devil himself.

Only a few yards remained to the target, to the enemy officer who stood in proxy for Kamanda on this trial run. Whiteman followed the three, watching through binoculars but giving no commands or advice. It was the ultimate exercise to determine who was ready and who was not. Then he saw it.

There, only a few feet in front of the first sniper, was a major highway—a driver ant colony in the process of moving, and more deadly than the vipers' den Whiteman had so flippantly dismissed only minutes before. The ants poured down the path by the millions, following a trickle of water left over from the drenching rain of days prior.

Whiteman could see them without binoculars, even from his position in the back, and he could only hope the young snipers saw them, too, but he knew their vision in the dark was not as good as his. Some said it was Whiteman's light blue eyes that made him better able to see in the dark, but whatever the reason, he saw the insect army and knew they were more fearsome than the Vietcong he had confronted in his younger days.

Damn driver ants! No, that is not the way I want to die—a death worse than a real inferno, a slow, agonizing burning and biting, holding on with tiny locked jaws bearing down on raw flesh. Avoiding those little brown bastards is worth the delay.

Whiteman stopped, watching to see if Haji, the leader, would change the course from what they had gone over and over before beginning the mission. To his good fortune, Haji veered right of the course, going around the driver ants. Saka, the hunter, followed Haji when he saw the reason for his change of course. Now only Jelandi was left to change his course.

Whiteman had drilled "Follow the plan," but adjusting to surroundings was also necessary for any sniper worth his salt. The only one of the three Whiteman was not sure of was Jelandi, "the Mighty Warrior," as the haughty young rebel called himself. He would be the rebel, the one not to follow, given the chance, and he always brought up the rear.

Whiteman crawled past Jelandi, who had stalled, watching his two comrades as they continued off course. He seemed confused by their action.

Haji and Saka welcomed the ditch that would take them within rifle range of the target. Each one dug in, inching forward while walking their rifles in front of them but holding them close to the ground. The rifles were wrapped in ghillie camouflage like the uniforms they wore.

Whiteman crawled a distance behind the two and could see the target sitting in a chair just outside the tent set up as a makeshift camp. It would be an easy shot for Whiteman, but he was not the one who needed experience.

Haji was in position, ready to set up for the shot. But before he could free his rifle from its ghillie cover, shrill screams cut through the jungle night, causing the encamped enemy soldiers to bolt to action.

Jelandi! The little son-of-a-bitch did not follow the group and is under attack by the driver ant platoon!

Whiteman remained still, watching to see how Haji and Saka would handle this unplanned event.

Whiteman could hear Jelandi thrashing through the dense jungle vegetation, ripping his ghillie suit off and throwing his helmet. Whiteman knew he'd probably also thrown his rifle down in his attempt to rake the fire devils off his skin, but he would have little success.

The bastard ants can cover a man in seconds, acting like stinging, biting machines and emitting more venom as a group than poisonous snakes. Jelandi will need a shot of anti-venom as quickly as possible or his death, a real death, will be by driver ants and not by the enemy.

Shots rang out, but Jelandi's screams did not cease. His laser sensors, all in the uniform and helmet he had shed, were of no use when driver ants took precedence over the human enemy. Jelandi was tackled by two enemy soldiers, who carried the bucking, screaming warrior to the tent. Then the spotlights began spreading across the ground as the enemy searched for Jelandi's accomplices.

Aborting the mission was not something in Whiteman's repertoire as a soldier of fortune—or commander of fortune, since he demanded total control for these operations or he was "not available." He had taken the job only because the CIA agent who had aided him in his escape from protective custody years ago had asked him to do this as a favor. The friend was a humanitarian who had sworn to help save the "forgotten children" of Africa, children like the sisters of the three trainees and the boys forced into Kamanda's army. Whiteman was not paid by the government, and the money he was paid was returned to the organization anonymously. These training operations were top secret, just the way Whiteman liked it. "No publicity!" In fact, the foundation behind this current effort did not have "an official relationship with the U.S. government," as one highly placed government official had stated in a newscast.

The target was still there by the tent, and he was standing now, following the light trail left by the spotlight as it jumped across the dense jungle vegetation. Whiteman watched, wondering if Haji would take his shot. Without hesitation the sharpshooter removed the cover from his rifle barrel, spread his body, firmly grounding himself in his position, and balanced his rifle on the small tripod.

The blank bullet left the rifle sounding like a loaded bullet, adding an adrenaline rush but nothing more, for the young sniper's efforts. It would not be ruled a kill until the alarm sounded indicating the laser had hit a sensor on the target's body. Almost instantly, the alarm sounded, and the target fell to the ground. The young soldier had his first kill!

Child's play!

Whiteman grumbled in his mind, a little hungry for the old days when training was not simulated with lasers but with hard-core action. Some days now he felt he was playing video games, or Laser Tag as it was dubbed, not real training of soldiers on how to shoot and kill. But deep down, he had no desire to replay the adrenaline rush of his youth that had taken away everything he loved. MILES, standing for Multiple Integrated Laser Equipment System, would suffice, and he no longer was expected to take human life—only to train the young ones how to approach a target unnoticed with the stealth of a tiger, to aim, fire, and hope like hell they never had to be at the receiving end of the same tactics used by an enemy using live ammunition.

Haji and Saka began backing out of the ditch. As

they passed Whiteman at the end, Whiteman gave a slight salute. The two separated, taking different routes back to camp. Whiteman knew they had one more engagement and wondered if they would realize it.

Jelandi was tied to a chair in the enemy camp, his head dangling down onto the vest loaded with laser sensors and covering his chest that heaved as venom from the ant bites raced through his body already swelling and covered in large bumps. His captors poured buckets of water over him and slapped him again and again, demanding he tell how far away and where his friends and their camp were located.

Whiteman knew it was a long shot but doable, and it was necessary, but would the young snipers kill their comrade in training?

Saka stopped and quickly got in position to shoot. The shot left the soldier's rifle and hit the target. The alarm announced Jelandi was dead.

When the two reached the safe zone, marked by a rope tied between two trees, they leapt to their feet and made their way to the training headquarters. The enemy part of the training would meet them there shortly, and all hell would break loose as Whiteman reprimanded each trainee, friend or enemy, telling them what they did wrong and how they should have done it. Jelandi had to be carried to debriefing on a stretcher after suffering from the poison injected by the driver ants, but his physical state would not deter Whiteman from coming down hard on him and informing him he was no longer a choice for the mission each was hoping to complete. This reprimand was followed by an order to take him to the medics for an anti-venom shot to stop the swelling fast doubling his skin area.

Saka was treated differently. Whiteman gave him a big slap on the back, with words of approval for his quick thinking and praise for having no second guessing in killing his peer in training.

"Cap'n Whiteman, you say, 'Never leave man,' but you like Saka kill Jelandi." The young soldier did not understand the conflicting rules of engagement.

"Never leave your own if you can rescue him, but if you can't, kill him or he might disclose information that will jeopardize the other men in your unit, and to save him from being tortured." An interpreter restated the explanation, but Whiteman had already turned away from the two snipers and headed for his tent.

He peeled off his gear and the uniform sticking to him in the jungle heat and humidity, and moved under the makeshift shower outside his tent, allowing the cold water to run over his body. Once he finished, he entered his quarters and crawled onto his cot, lying naked and wet in an attempt to remain cool for as long as possible under the slow-moving battery-operated fan overhead. His bones ached, and he knew sleep would come instantly once he took a pain pill.

Reaching under his mattress, he pulled out the picture he carried with him everywhere, even to the jungles of darkest, most dangerous Africa.

The beautiful woman with long blonde curls cascading around her face looked at him and smiled. On each side of her stood a teenage girl, one with blonde curly hair and green eyes like her mother, and the other a pixie with a slight slant to her pale blue eyes peeking from under short black hair. Above them, the sky opened in green and yellow curtains. He could almost feel the waves of the curtains as they opened and provided a stage for the three loves of his life—three loves unfulfilled.

Whiteman put the picture under his pillow and willed himself to put them out of his mind, out of his heart, at least until the next night.

Not mine to have and hold...not mine.

He closed his eyes and dropped into the bottomless pit of sleep and void.

Chapter Two

Custer headed back to the cabin after dropping off Sue Ann. He figured she and Betsy would have a crying session over Tobi and Angel leaving on a long trip without a hint of their plan, or a goodbye. Custer had tried to convince them it was just young love with no ties that bind, but he didn't think they bought it for a minute.

Just before he turned onto the forestry road to the cabin, his cell phone rang. He looked at the caller ID and saw it was blocked. Thinking it was another telemarketer, he answered and then hung up without saying anything. As he stepped up on the porch, the phone rang again. This time he answered it, ready to give the telemarketer a piece of his mind and to demand he take his number off his caller list. But when he said "hello" using his irritated tone, the voice on the other end surprised him.

"Custer Larson, or should I call you Eagle…" The voice was spoken through a synthesizer, giving the speaker the sound and demeanor of a robot with an unidentifiable accent.

Custer remained silent for a few seconds.

"Who is this, and what do you want?" Custer stopped on the porch, giving the caller his full attention.

"I have a warning for you to deliver to Raven's daughter. She is in great danger in Costa Rica. Many are looking for Raven and would not hesitate to use her for bait just like was done in Alaska."

"Keep talking," Custer said, not willing to acknowledge or deny any of what the voice had said concerning Raven or Eagle but knowing he needed to hear more.

"There is nothing more to say. I just needed to tell you, Eagle. I know you know where Raven is and so does his daughter. Give the message to her and her future husband and pray they live long enough to marry."

"How do I know you are telling me the truth?"

"You don't. But you could always call Herb Feller with the CIA…if you trust him, that is. I'll let you figure that out, but be very careful." With this, the caller hung up.

As Custer entered the cabin, he scrolled through his contacts, stopping on Herb Feller's cell number.

Angel is not the only one who can play detective. She should be more careful where and when she leaves her phone unattended. Someone might copy her contact list.

Herb Feller answered on the fifth ring and sounded irritated, probably because he did not recognize the caller number, or so Custer thought.

"Well…Eagle. To what do I owe the honor of your call?"

"So you have my number in your contacts as I do yours? I'm not surprised."

"Yes. It wasn't hard to figure out who Eagle was after reading your stepdaughter's and your wife's books. Of course, without the classified documents mysteriously showing up in Angela's briefcase, and

Angela running off to Montana, there would have been less need to read Dr. Parish's books or Elizabeth Larson's."

"I'm not calling you to chat about my wife's or Betsy's books. I need to make sure Angel is safe. I had an anonymous call from someone warning she is in danger. I assume you know where she is."

"I am CIA, Eagle. Of course I know she and Tobi are about to land in Costa Rica. I hope she has better luck finding her father there than we have."

"Why exactly is the CIA trying to find Raven? He was in protective custody the last time I saw him— protective custody with the CIA means he is not a wanted criminal." Custer walked to the fireplace and looked up at the portrait signed by Raven.

"I'm afraid that is classified information, Eagle. You know how it works."

"I know I don't trust any of you, especially the CIA. That's why I never signed a contract and refused to take any more special assignments."

"But you did go on special assignments if they involved Jon Shockey. That tells me you two were much closer than you indicate." Silence followed. "I can't help you, Larson, but I can tell you Angela could be in danger. There are those who still would like to cash in on the money left for killing Shockey, should he have survived that day in Alaska, and we both know he did." More silence followed. "I have a meeting to attend. Tell Angela, or is it Angel now, to watch her back."

Feller hung up before Custer could chide him about why the CIA could not confiscate the blood money, but he knew already the money was secure in another country, most likely a Swiss bank, and no one could stop the chain of events set in motion by ONE, who was as relentless in death as he was in life and had made sure there would always be someone waiting to assassinate Shade.

Custer put his phone away and sat on the sofa, still staring at the masterpiece of Shade Dubois. Once again, he replayed the last conversation he had with him.

"Sue Ann will always know where I am. She only has to look to Aurora, and I'll be there." Custer repeated the words aloud several times.

Look to Aurora! How the hell can Sue Ann see the northern lights in Montana? Did he mean she needed to go back to Alaska? She did that plenty of times before marrying me, and Shade never showed up.

Custer replayed in his mind the day he had his big heart attack and how Sue Ann stayed right beside him the whole time he was convalescing. And later, she picked him over Tate to marry.

Look to Aurora!

Custer jumped to his feet.

The portrait of Sue Ann and Betsy under the northern lights! The northern lights...of course!

Custer balanced himself on the hearth as he reached up over the mantel and carefully took down the painting. Holding it firmly on each side, he carried it to the table by the big windows where the light was best, and laid it face down on the table. Plastic-coated thick cardboard was stapled to the back of the frame, held on by what looked like fifty or more heavy staples. Custer took his knife out of his sheath and began prying the staples out one at a time. He knew it would take time, since he had to be meticulous and save each staple to be hammered back in place so no one could tell the backing had been removed. He hoped this would pay off with information on the place, or places, Shade used for hiding.

When Custer had enough staples out, he lifted the cardboard away from the frame so he could see the back of the painting. Nothing could be seen written on the back of the canvas. Still, he continued taking all the staples out so he could get a good look. When the last staple came out, he lifted the stiff cardboard off, but as he attempted to lay it beside the painting, it slipped through his fingers and hit the chair closest to the table and bounced onto the floor.

Custer ignored the cardboard and inspected every inch of the back of the canvas, hoping to find some clue, or better still, an address or phone number for Shade. He was disappointed to find nothing.

As he reached to pick up the cardboard, there it was…on the underside that now lay facing up.

The clues were not behind the canvas but were painted on the front of the cardboard. None of Shade's artistic talent was wasted, not even on this cardboard backing. Each of the four scenes displayed the artistic talent of a master. Four safe havens had been painted so realistically it would be impossible not to locate each.

The scene in the top left quadrant depicted a monastery hanging from the side of a mountain in the Himalayas. Sway-backed ornate roofs ended in pointed peaks and covered adjoining mini palaces. Built low to the ground, they looked as if they had been built by fairies. In the corner was written "Shokhai Gompa" with the translation under it "Morning Monastery," aptly named as it faced due east.

The top right quadrant was so realistic it could have fooled anyone into thinking they could dive right into this deep blue lagoon on one of Thailand's remote islands. The lagoon, smothered by forested mountains on its shoreline, showed little habitation, with only two thatch-roofed huts standing on stilts along a pristine white sand beach. In the corner of the bluest water imaginable was written in Thai "Taang Naam" with the words interpreted beneath as "Lost Water."

The scene on the bottom right side was smaller than the others, but it was a scene Custer had been forced to look at since the day he delivered the painting to the new owner of this cabin, Dr. Sue Ann Parish. But in this scene, Shade stood under the northern lights with his arms around a younger Sue Ann. No sign was needed to give the name of this location with the snow-covered mountains behind a cabin identical to the one burned after Shade's supposed death.

The fourth scene, in the bottom left quadrant, depicted a tropical paradise, a jungle filled with macaws and all kinds of colorful birds as well as different species of monkeys sitting happily on tree branches. Through the middle of the jungle paradise, a dirt road wound, stopping at a huge wooden gate. A large sign covered the gate with the words "Mono Paraiso." On the sign, "Wildlife Preserve" followed in English. In bold red letters across the top of the sign was written "Private Property, No Trespassing" in both English and Spanish. Pulling out his phone, Custer googled the Spanish words "Mono Paraiso" and found they meant Monkey Paradise, a fitting title for Shade's Costa Rican sanctuary as he had painted it on the backboard.

Custer dialed Hawk and told him to bring his phone, since it had a better camera than his, and his computer. Hawk wanted to know what was up, but Custer told him he needed to come and to hurry and to be discreet. He did not want Betsy or Sue Ann to know what was happening.

It's time to tell Hawk. I need him, and, more importantly, Tobi and Angel need him.

****

Hawk had many questions after his uncle told him his life story, mostly about his bad days as a paid assassin, and then how he got off the hook by helping the CIA on some special assignments. But when he told him about saving Shade, Hawk jumped to his feet, angry that his uncle had kept this information from his mother-in-law.

"How could you, Uncle Custer? And you married Sue Ann! Don't you think that's a bit underhanded? Damn!" Hawk walked out on the porch, and Custer did not follow him. In a few minutes he came back in.

"I'm sorry, Uncle Custer. I shouldn't have been so disrespectful. It was just such a blow. I guess Shade couldn't come back to life for fear of Sue Ann, Betsy, or Angel being kidnapped. Makes sense, since Betsy and Angel *were* kidnapped in Alaska."

"Well, now Angel and Tobi could be in danger, and we are the ones to help them. Good thing we updated our passports last fall, even though Sue Ann and I decided not to go to Japan with you and Betsy and to take Trapper to Mississippi instead. Never thought I'd have another passport, especially a legal one, after my bad times in Indochina. Guess it was the Creator leaving stepping stones, preparing me for what I've got

16

to do." Custer shook his head, thinking back and then stood. "We have business before we take off to Costa Rica."

Custer showed Tobi the painted scenes on the cardboard and told him he was sure Shade had left this as information about his international sanctuaries—just in case.

Hawk took pictures of each quadrant, downloaded them to his computer, and printed them off scene by scene. He made sure he got perfect details, especially in the Costa Rican scene since it was the best clue as to where Shade might be.

Meanwhile, his uncle tried to call Tobi and Angel, but their phones were turned off while they were still flying. It would be late tonight before they could tell Tobi and Angel about the warning.

While he waited, Custer became quiet and contemplative as he stared at the scene in Costa Rica.

"Shade needs to call Angel. But I'm not sure he still has that phone. He said for me to throw mine away and forget him. Maybe that is what he did and he won't even get Angel's message."

"Let me see the copies again, Custer. Maybe we're missing something."

"Like a working cell phone number?" Custer asked.

"Yes. My eyes are better than yours."

While Hawk looked at the copies, Custer rummaged in the kitchen drawer until he found the magnifying glass he often used.

Hawk took the glass and scrutinized every inch of the scenes.

"Here!" Hawk held the glass firmly in place and moved

17

it to the table so Custer could see it without risk of moving it.

"You're right! It's ten numbers. It has to be his cell number." Custer and Hawk both added the number to their contact lists.

"Now what, Unk?"

"Get your passport, pack your bag—or rather, a backpack—and think up a lie to tell your wife and mother-in-law. Let's get on the Internet and purchase plane tickets to Costa Rica."

After Hawk left, Custer dialed the number he thought was Shade's. It rang several times before voice mail picked up. The direction was succinct and to the point, and Custer recognized Raven's voice: "Leave a message. Be brief."

Custer waited for the beep and then stated his business in the quickest, most precise words he could use.

"Angel is in Costa Rica looking for you and could be in danger. She knows you're alive and so do others who want to collect on your hide. I'm going after her. Call me. Not negotiable!"

****

Hawk and Custer did not take time to sit down and have coffee and pie at Betsy and Hawk's cabin. Custer could not believe the lie Hawk came up with, but neither Sue Ann nor Betsy feigned disbelief. The two women sat attentive as Hawk spun his yarn.

"This is quite an honor for Uncle Custer to be chosen by the Tribal Council to represent them in forming a new alliance for the preservation of Native American sacred places in the West. The conference is in Washington, D.C. Since his heart has been giving him a little problem, I'm going with him. Do you think you and Sue Ann can manage while we're gone, Betsy?"

"This is awfully quick, don't you think, Hawk?" Betsy asked, but a few minutes later, she began helping Hawk pack the minimum into his backpack.

"Well, actually, the guy who was supposed to go cancelled at the last minute, so they picked Unk as a replacement." Hawk could not face Betsy when he was lying.

"Let's see now." Betsy opened up her laptop. "Now what is the title of this conference in Washington, D.C.?" Betsy cut her eyes sideways, adding exaggeration to her puckered lips and tightly pulled jawline. Hawk took one look at her and knew he was trapped.

Hawk walked over and turned the lock on the bedroom door.

"Okay, sly little fox. Tobi and Angel are in Costa Rica because of some unfinished fed business Angel's involved in. Custer found Tobi's cabin ransacked after they left, and he's afraid for Angel and Tobi. You know Unk when he's in his protector role, but I need to go to protect not only Tobi and Angel but Uncle Custer, who is determined to go. He claims he feels like he did before his heart attacks, a sign he is meant to go. He does not want Sue Ann to know, afraid she'll worry too much and stress herself out."

Betsy moved to Hawk and put her arms around his waist.

"I'm scared for you to go, Hawk, but I know you protect our family. Will you call me often? I have to hear your voice to know you're okay."

Hawk reassured Betsy, and she began taking out what he had in the backpack and repacking.

"Costa Rica is tropical. Take your zip-off fishing pants, breathable angler shirts, and your hiking boots…not your jeans and cowboy boots." Betsy moved to Hawk's closet and began taking shirts and pants off hangers and handing them to Hawk. The last item she took out of the closet was a Winston Fly Rod cap. Walking to Hawk, she put the cap on his head, stopping to give him a passionate kiss before pulling the bill down to his eyebrows.

"No cowboy hat! I don't want those beautiful Spanish women flirting with my handsome cowboy."

Within minutes, Hawk and Custer left, headed for the airport, with Sue Ann, Betsy, and Trapper waving from the porch.

Betsy felt guilty for the lie Hawk told her mom, but she soon found out she had nothing to worry about.

"So—what have Tobi and Angel gotten themselves into? I know Hawk and Custer are going to Central America and not Washington, D.C."

"Mom, how do you do that? I had to threaten with looking up the conference on my laptop to get Hawk to come clean, and you just let Custer go right on with the lie with no explanation. How did you figure it out?"

"Well, let's see. Custer being a representative for the Tribal Council to attend a conference in D.C. is about as believable as Custer attending the National Democratic Convention! The man hates politics. Besides, I saw on the computer where he had purchased two tickets to Costa Rica."

Betsy told her mother why they really went to Costa Rica, and they both became torn with worry.

"Let's go to the mountains, Betsy. We have some praying to do."

Chapter Three

Angel got off the airplane and wished immediately she had chosen Spanish as her second language in college rather than the French that could do her no good here in Costa Rica. Tobi, who had no foreign language to speak of, also wished his fiancée were fluent in Spanish. Going through customs was quicker than either of them had thought possible, but then the real problems began.

Going from the airport to downtown San Jose, the capital, was like stepping into a bustling, aromatic sauna. The tropical breezes so prevalent in literature such as Somerset Maugham's novels could not be felt with the mass density of tourists.

"Well, it seems a few other people like Costa Rica besides Dad." Angel looked around, wondering how they would ever find her father. "The needle is not the problem. Finding the haystack is the problem." Angel was talking to Tobi, but when she looked beside her, Tobi was not there but several paces ahead and moving fast.

"Tobi!" Angel ran in his direction, her backpack slowing her down.

Tobi, hearing his name, stopped and turned to Angel, who he'd thought was by his side. He hurried back to her, running into two different groups of tourists and having to apologize.

"Angel! I'm sorry, sweetheart! I thought you were with me. I was talking away to whoever it was beside me." Tobi took Angel's pack and carried it while they headed for a taxi just up ahead.

"So where is our hotel?" Angel asked as she crawled into the taxi ahead of Tobi. "We never even talked about where in Costa Rica we'd start the hunt. What did you find on the Internet?"

As soon as Tobi got in, he searched his wallet, found the note where he'd written down the name of the hotel, and handed it to the taxi driver. At the same time, his cell phone beeped, indicating a message.

"It's from Custer." Tobi answered.

"Find a hotel on the Pacific side. You are probably being followed, so be careful. Keep a low profile and wait for my call later tonight. Do not call your mom or Betsy." Tobi read his message to Angel but kept his voice low so the driver could not hear. "This is a strange message. What is Custer up to?" Tobi put the phone back in his pocket and turned to Angel. "We don't need a taxi. We need to rent a vehicle."

Tobi got the driver's attention and in mostly sign language managed to get him to take them to a car rental company rather than the hotel where Tobi had booked a reservation. After renting a Jeep, Tobi headed for the hotel he had located on the map given him by the car rental agency, a map in English. They would need to cancel their reservations, and perhaps the hotel could suggest somewhere to stay on the Pacific side. Tobi had no idea why Custer told him to do this, but he also knew Custer was seldom, if ever, wrong. He would have to wait for Custer's call.

Tobi had a hard time trying to explain to the hotel

clerk how they needed to cancel their room and wanted to know about a hotel on the Pacific side. Angel stepped in and with the few phrases of Spanish she remembered from the introductory course she'd had in college, she was at least able to cancel their reservation. As they walked away from the desk, a young man approached them.

"Hi, I couldn't help but overhear your dilemma. I think I can help you. My name is Marshall Chapman. I recently moved here to work in my father's business. I know the country well."

Tobi and Angel shook hands with Marshall.

"Weren't you on the same flight with us from Miami?" Angel asked.

"Yes, I was. I was home in Florida finishing up a graduate degree in banking and finance and just headed back here today. You said you want to stay on the Pacific side, right?"

"Yes, that would be great, if we can find a place. Do you know of a hotel?" Tobi looked hopeful.

"I can do better than that." Marshall took out his cell phone. "How many nights do you want to book?"

Tobi looked at Angel and held up his hands.

"Let's book for two nights for starters, and then we'll decide after we have a look around and see what all we want to do. Is that okay, Tobi?"

"Sounds like a plan." Tobi agreed as he watched Marshall pull out his cell phone and dial.

"Maria, this is Marshall. I have an American couple with me who need a room for two nights. Do we have a room available?" Marshall smiled at Angel and Tobi. "Great! Thanks. His name is…" Marshall looked at Tobi.

"Tobi Parish."

"Tobi Parish, Maria. Yes, they will see you in about two hours."

"Gosh! That was nice of you, Marshall. Thanks. So does your family own the hotel?"

"Yes, as a matter of fact, my parents own two hotels and the resort where you will be staying. It's called Villa Benito Bonito, named after a wealthy Portuguese pirate from the 1800s. And no, we won't rob you. It's very economical for a luxury resort. I guess you have a map, since you rented a Jeep."

Tobi looked surprised that Marshall would know about their vehicle.

"I saw you pull up in front while I was checking in. I'm not going over until tomorrow, but you won't have any trouble finding it. Just follow the map, and it will take you right to it."

"Thanks again, Marshall. Maybe we'll see you tomorrow."

"Seems like a nice guy." Angel made the remark as they got in the Jeep, but Tobi remained silent.

As soon as the Jeep pulled away, Marshall took out his cell phone.

"Yeah, they bought it. Villa Benito Bonito. How's that for doing business? So what time will your flight come in tonight?" Marshall's gaze found its favorite subject while talking—the attractive women coming and going through the lobby. "I'll pick you up at the airport. I hope you're not wearing that black shirt and shades again. Makes you look like a bad-ass...a government agent bad-ass!"

Marshall laughed as he hung up. As he dialed the next number, he walked to a corner of the lobby where a window looked out at the busy sidewalk. Hidden by massive palm plants, he started a new conversation, but this time his entire conversation was in Spanish. As soon as he hung up, he headed for the bar, smiling with self pride.

Chapter Four

Whiteman put Haji and Saka through hours of vigorous guerilla stealth training exercises, and by the end of the muggy day, he was sweating profusely and drained of energy. Rather than heading straight to the shower like he usually did every day, he stopped at the cooler, grabbed a cold beer, and literally fell into a lawn chair, turning the beer up and guzzling it.

"Why do you work yourself harder than those damn trainees, Whiteman? You know neither of them will live to see their twenty-fifth birthday. Seems like a waste of time, but then…I guess that's why you make the big bucks." Reaching required much effort for the man who had to extend his short arms over his big belly and rock his chair toward the cooler just to retrieve his third beer. He waited for Whiteman's smartass rebuttal with a "shit-eating grin" as Whiteman referred to it.

"Not your business, Ferguson. Maybe if you'd get off your fat ass you could make more than minimum wage." Whiteman drained the bottle, never looking toward the man he found so disgusting.

"Since when is two hundred an hour minimum wage? I know it's not the million you probably get for being 'Captain…' " Ferguson smirked as he made the sign of quotation marks with his fingers. "But I don't crawl through the jungle on my belly; nor do I stink at the end of the day. For what you make, you ought to have servants and do nothing but yell orders and kick ass. Oh, yeah! You do kick some serious ass!"

"Sitting is not my style, Ferguson. You just stick to your computer, and I'll stick to what I do best—teach men how to kill." Whiteman held his beer up as a sarcastic toast, drained the bottle before adding it to the heap of empties behind Ferguson, and left his chair. He was tired of Ferguson's obsession with lifestyle and money. Whiteman began stripping, heading for the shower outside his tent, and ignored Ferguson's yell.

"Heard your phone beep. Didn't know you had a close enough relationship with anyone to get a call." Ferguson laughed, knowing he was pissing Whiteman off. Truth was he wanted to know more about Whiteman, the elite commander of this secret military training center, but as hard as he tried to find out about him by using his expert computer skills, he was still unable to come up with one personal fact, or even his name, for that matter, and that had him intrigued.

****

Whiteman sat on his cot naked and looked at the caller ID on his phone.

"Montana!"

Whiteman turned the volume down as low as he could get it and still be able to hear the voicemail. With trepidation, he punched play.

"Angel is in Costa Rica looking for you and could be in danger. She knows you're alive, and so do others who want to collect on your hide. I'm going after her. Call me. Not negotiable!"

Whiteman listened to the message two more times, unable to believe what he was hearing.

Hurriedly, he dressed and then began packing up

his equipment, leaving the uniform. With his pack on his back and carrying a gun case in each hand, he walked out of the tent, loaded everything in the Jeep assigned to him, and sped away as Ferguson yelled after him, asking where he was going.

Whiteman knew he would never be back to West Africa, or any country that needed the type of military training services he offered. Angel knew he was alive, and he had to get to her fast.

He changed his contacts from green to dark brown before leaving the hotel in Kinshasa, Congo. His next stop was Ndjili International Airport, where his Lear Jet and co-pilot would be waiting for him.

Chapter Five

Angel could do nothing but gaze out the French doors at the Pacific Ocean's white sand beach and indigo blue waters surging in the moon's vibrant glow. Inside, she wished this were a real honeymoon for her and Tobi and not a dangerous game of hide-and-seek between her, her father, and whatever criminals might be trailing them.

Even though she was worried and knew Tobi was, too, they both began stripping as soon as Tobi bolted the door. When the last clothing was dropped on the floor, Tobi swooped Angel into his arms and headed for the shower.

"Just close your eyes, sweetheart, and pretend we're under the waterfall." Tobi took the body wash and began rubbing it all over Angel, slowing at his favorite spots. When he finished, he took Angel's hands and poured a generous amount of the tropical fragrance in her cupped palms and directed her hands to his most vulnerable spots. As they reenacted the wonderful wet foreplay made famous at the waterfall, the water washed away the soap. Tobi picked Angel up and maneuvered himself into her. Holding tight to her hips, he moved from the shower to the bed without withdrawing from her.

They lay wrapped in a tight hold, with Tobi on top, and Angel moaned, locking her legs around him, pushing his hips with her heels, demanding he drive harder.

"Now, Tobi!" Her breath caught in a gasp as she pleaded. "Now!"

He plunged into her, holding taut, bringing both to maximum fulfillment. She shivered under him as he felt himself quake during the longest climax he could ever remember. Liquid passion filled his fiancée, and it seemed there was no end. Panting, he felt his release finally begin. Turning onto his back, he pulled his pixie on top of him, where he caressed her back and hips while engulfing her mouth in his.

They lay still for a few minutes, both wishing their lovemaking did not have to end, but both feeling insecure.

"I've been thinking, Angel."

"What, my love?"

"Something just doesn't add up."

"You mean about Marshall and this room being available when the resort stays booked months in advance, according to what I found on my phone."

"Oh? You went farther in your investigation than I did. I just depended on gut, and my gut tells me we need to pack up and get out of here while it's still dark."

Angel sat up, straddling Tobi.

"As bad as I hate to leave this position, I know you are right."

****

In the early hours before daylight, the three men dressed in black, ski masks over their faces, charged into the romantic oceanfront cottage where Tobi and Angel had checked out, unofficially, two hours earlier.

"Damn!" Marshall jerked his mask off and threw it against the wall.

"Well, Mr. Hotshot, what's your next plan, since this one worked so well? Daddy will be so proud!" The tall guy retrieved the ski mask, smiling sarcastically. He knew he was getting the rich kid riled up, but he didn't care.

"It's okay, Mr. Marshall. Eventually we'll have her location when the signal from her phone tracker is picked up. Good thing we have our little CIA tricks, huh?" The shorter man knew how Marshall hated the CIA, especially since he was only a step away from being on their wanted list, something he and his partner reminded Marshall and his father of constantly in case they got any ideas of not helping them find Shockey.

The threesome began searching the room for any clue as to the whereabouts of the two Americans. Finding nothing, they put their ski masks away and headed to the bar to regroup with a few cold drinks.

Marshall chose not to socialize with the two he considered beneath him. He had to call his father and give him the news of the couple's escape, and he did not want the two so-called agents with him when he received a good ass-chewing from his domineering parent.

****

Tobi pulled the Jeep into a parking area on the beach, far away from Villa Bonito. Angel was afraid to check into another hotel, so they sat in the Jeep, watching the moon cast a spell on the water and wondering if they had misjudged Marshall. Both wished they were snuggled under the covers of the beautiful king-sized bed at the hotel they had left, but neither wanted to risk going back.

Tobi decided to call Custer and see if he could offer any advice and discovered he had no cell phone service. Angel checked her phone and "No Service" greeted her also.

"Okay. We need to go somewhere closer to a city where we have service, but not San Jose. As they drove, Angel held her phone out the door, checking for signal. Just as they got to the top of a hill, Angel's phone rang. She answered it quickly, thinking it had to be Custer. A synthesized voice surprised her, and she punched speaker so Tobi could hear.

"You were right to leave Villa Bonito. Chapman is not to be trusted. The best place to get lost is not the natural reserves. Try the big cities, San Jose being your best bet since it is the biggest."

"Who is this and how did you get my cell number?" Angel motioned to Tobi to pull the Jeep to the side of the road so she would not lose service.

"It doesn't matter who I am. What matters is that you listen to me. Get off the road you're on. It's the first road they'll travel looking for you. Check your map and find a back way to the next town. You may hit some rough roads, but you will be fine in the Jeep. When you get to the town, park behind the cheapest-looking hotel you can find, leave the Jeep, and catch a taxi to San Jose. Take refuge in any church you see, but pick a small one. Don't go back for the Jeep. You can report it stolen later." With this, the caller hung up.

Angel stared at the phone in her hand before speaking. "Who was that, Tobi? What is going on here? It's like a bunch of strangers know where we are, yet we don't know where we are or what we are doing.

First the Postman, now the Voice." Angel's head flew back against the seat when Tobi took off fast. "What are you doing, Tobi?"

"Call me crazy, but I'm taking the back road to this next little town. And when we get there, we are leaving the Jeep and taking a taxi to San Jose."

"Why San Jose? It is so big and crowded."

"Because that is where the Voice told us to go. At this point, he or she seems to be leading us away from trouble, and let's just pray *it* continues warning us."

****

Tobi grabbed the backpacks from the taxi and paid the driver, giving him a nice tip. Together, he and Angel started walking toward the quaint little church they had seen as they passed on one of the side streets in San Jose. Once inside, they each knelt and said a prayer of thanks as well as for their continued safety and the safety of their family so far away from them. Angel added a few special words asking for help in finding her dad. Moving to the rear, they found a back corner where they would not be seen and lay down behind the pews.

"I'm putting my phone on vibrate, just in case." Tobi held the phone so he could feel it if Custer or Hawk called, and then spooned tightly to Angel's back with his arm around her. Soon, they both fell into an exhausted sleep.

****

Custer tried to sleep on the two-hour last leg of the flight from Miami to San Jose, Costa Rica, but all he could think about was the synthesized voice who called to warn of danger for Angel. He also kept thinking about Shade and wondering if he'd gotten the message he left for him and, more important, if Shade would act on it. There was no way Custer could check his phone while in the air, but he hoped by the time they landed he would have a message. Still, the first thing he would do when he could access his phone was call Tobi to make sure they were okay and to give him the name of the wildlife refuge he thought Shade used as one of his safe havens. How they would get in would be another problem to solve.

Hawk was antsy going through customs, and Custer told him to get in control or the authorities would delay him, thinking he was a fugitive from American justice. Custer was glad Betsy had made Hawk change from the cowboy look to the fly fisher look, more appropriate and less attention-getting. Still Custer noticed how all the women drooled over his nephew, and he caught a few snapping pictures. He chuckled as Hawk looked embarrassed.

Then Hawk began to notice how all the older women were staring and smiling at his Uncle Custer with his long gray braids. One American lady, who looked to be in her late eighties, grabbed Custer's arm as he came out of customs and handed Hawk her digital camera to take her picture with Custer. It happened so fast, Custer didn't know what was happening. Hawk bent double laughing when he heard the lady telling her friends she just had her picture taken with Willy Nelson. She began pointing to Custer, who refused to make eye contact with her.

"You old fool!" One of the woman's friends prodded, "That is not that skinny old Willy Nelson. Didn't you look at his body? That's Sam Elliott with braids. I bet he's here to star in that western they're filming over on the ocean side." The three older ladies headed off, still arguing over the identity of the famous movie star.

Custer dialed Tobi's phone but got no answer. He had the same result with Angel's phone, and both he and Hawk grew uneasy. Every five minutes, Custer tried them again but to no avail.

As they rode in the cab, heading for downtown San Jose, where they would rent a car, Custer's phone rang. The caller identity was blocked, and Custer felt his heart skip a beat.

"Yes."

"So you made it to San Jose. Good job. Tobi and Angel will need your help. They have already run into problems and had to leave their hotel on the Pacific coast in the middle of the night. Tell the driver you want to go to St. Christopher's Chapel. You will find Angel and Tobi there." Click.

"It was that crazy voice again. It's so disguised, I still can't tell if it is male or female." Custer shook his head. "Who would have my number, and how did they get it?"

"And why are they so interested in Tobi and Angel, and you?" Hawk added as he hailed a taxi.

"St. Christopher's Chapel," Custer told the driver, and then when the driver stared at him without moving, Custer pulled out his English-to-Spanish dictionary. "Cristóbal Iglesias." Custer did not call Tobi's or Angel's number again, deciding to wait and see if they were in the chapel.

****

Hawk opened the chapel door and found it lit only by candles. No one was inside that he could see.

36

Keeping his backpack on his shoulder, Hawk began going up and down the aisles looking for Tobi and Angel. He hadn't gone far before he heard low snoring coming from the back corner behind the pews.

Custer motioned Hawk over and put his fingers to his lips. They lay down on the floor near the two, using their packs as head rests. In no time, they were snoring right along with Tobi.

****

Beams of sunlight shot through the stained-glass window, casting waves of rainbows over the entwined bodies of the young couple. Tobi jerked to a sitting position and looked around while feeling for his cell phone that had somehow escaped in the night. For a minute, he had lost all perception of where he was. Hearing something that was not Angel's breathing, he got on his knees and looked around.

"Custer? Hawk?" he whispered, trying not to wake Angel.

Custer sat up and saluted. Hawk was next, rubbing his eyes and stretching.

"What the hell are you two doing here?" Tobi asked, a faint smile forming at the corners of his mouth.

Chapter Six

"The first thing is we have to have a vehicle," Hawk said as they packed up to leave the church.

"I'd like a shower," Angel remarked, and they all agreed it would feel good but was not a top priority at the moment.

"We could go back and get the Jeep, but the bad guys may have it staked out by now." Tobi added, "You or Hawk need to rent this one, but not a Jeep. It's too open." He rose from the floor and held his hand out to Angel. They all put on their backpacks and headed out the door.

An hour later, the foursome was headed down the highway toward the Pacific side but more northward this time, in the direction of Monkey Paradise, the game preserve they believed stood as a front for Raven's private sanctuary. Custer had decided not to disclose Raven's suspected location until they were closer, not wanting Angel to get too excited and rush them without taking proper precautions.

"I can't believe Dad left the information on the back of the Northern Lights painting." Angel had been in deep thought ever since Custer told her of his discovery. "Do you think he wanted us to find him, Custer?"

"No. Your father would never put you in harm's way, but I do think he put it there for just such a circumstance as we have now—an emergency, in case he needed to be found, if any of you were in trouble and needed his help disappearing. Shade was a planner, but only for those he felt the need to protect. He had no thought of needing anyone for his own preservation. Shade was selfless and independent to a fault, and that is why he disappeared even though he was reported drowned in Alaska."

Custer still didn't know if Shade had received the message he'd sent him. He also wondered how they would get into the game preserve, since it seemed to have a huge gate with No Trespassing signs barring the entrance, according to the secret painting.

Before they made it to the main turnoff to the preserve, Custer's phone rang.

"Eagle, turn around. There's a roadblock up ahead, and the men in uniform are not who they appear to be. They are waiting for Angel and Tobi and know they want to be on the Pacific side of Costa Rica. Turn around now, before it is too late!" The caller hung up.

"It is pretty obvious we have tracking devices on us somewhere. I'd say we need to dump our phones, but whoever this voice is, he or she seems to be steering us away from danger. Maybe we'll keep him…at least for now." Custer put the phone back in the holder attached to his belt. I've gotten calls and you've gotten them on your phone, Angel, so our phones will be the first to be trashed when it's time."

"But how? My phone has never left me." Angel had been through this in her mind a hundred times since arriving in Costa Rica. When could someone have accessed her phone?

"Not exactly true, Angel. I got all your contact

numbers off your phone when you left it in your room." Custer looked at Angel but saw only surprise and no anger.

"Well, you don't carry yours half the time, Custer. I know because I checked your phone for calls and messages from my dad several times a day." Angel smiled, knowing Custer was watching her reflection in his side mirror. "I didn't find any, by the way."

"Turn down that path, Hawk. We need to regroup, and we don't need to go through a roadblock!" Custer pointed to a dirt road heading into the rainforest. "Hope this four-wheel drive works. It's pretty wet in here. Guess that's why they call it a rainforest."

As soon as Custer made the comment, the Land Rover hit bottom in a deep rut.

"That didn't sound good." Tobi remarked, but Hawk ignored him, gunning the vehicle and pulling out of the rut.

Hawk pulled into a side path that looked seldom traveled. After pulling behind a clump of dense low bushes, he stopped the car but did not turn off the ignition.

"Where's that map you picked up at the car rental place, Custer?" Custer reached into the side pocket of his pack sitting at his feet and unfolded a road map. Butting heads, he and Hawk traced the highway they had just left to see if it led to the monkey preserve.

"Would you two mind letting the rest of us in on where it is we're going?" Sarcasm edged Tobi's words.

Custer turned but cast his gaze at Angel. "We're going to find Raven."

Angel's gasp quickly turned to a smile. "But how…"

"The secret information left on the painting, but that is all I can explain until this pans out. Pray it will." Custer turned his eyes back to the map to avoid more questions.

****

As soon as the Lear Jet was airborne, Whiteman pulled out his cell phone and hit redial on one of the numbers he had called often. After five rings, a woman answered in Spanish.

"Speak English, Sophia. Get everyone together. Code 13. ETA 1400. Stand by."

The next call Whiteman made was to Alaska. The phone rang numerous times and when someone answered on the other end, all that was heard was a click.

"It's time!" After speaking only these two words, Whiteman shut his phone off and nodded for his copilot to take control. Whiteman put his head back, folded his arms across his chest, covered his face with his cap, and closed his eyes.

****

Hawk and Tobi stared at the map, trying to figure out the most secluded route to Mono Paraiso Preserve.

"Call it coincidence, but it looks like if we follow the rough road we're on, we'll come in on the back side of the preserve, away from civilization. Going by the legend, it's maybe twenty miles, winding around through the rainforest."

Tobi pointed to the legend. "Yes, but it says the road is mostly impassable. It has "arriesgado" which translates as "hazardous" in English, according to the footnote at the bottom of the map."

"Let me look." Angel leaned up to get a good look

at the map and followed the trail with her fingernail. "Okay. It looks passable up to this point, say halfway, which should mean we have about ten miles left to get to the preserve. I can hike ten miles."

Angel looked to Tobi and then to Hawk. Hawk dropped his eyes, and Angel knew he was worried about Custer making it ten miles.

"Remember the vision, Hawk. I'm trusting my ancestors on this one." Custer directed his argument to Hawk, knowing he would be the one to try to protect him. "If I can't make it, I'll stay with the vehicle until you come back for me. Now, let's get this chunk of horsepower moving."

Hawk hesitated, rubbing his hands around the steering wheel as if thinking.

"I don't know, Unk, but I can tell you I won't be leaving you in the middle of a jungle. Sue Ann would never forgive me if something happened to you."

"Drive, Hawk! Trust me. My heart is strong right now, and I'm trusting the vision Grandfather gave me." Custer looked straight ahead, refusing to give in to Hawk's worried glances, and Hawk put the Land Rover in motion.

The vehicle bumped and ground its way through the deepest potholes imaginable and through mud holes so deep they had to fight to get out of them. Twice, Tobi and Hawk had to strip to their boxers and wade in to push the vehicle out with Angel behind the wheel. Custer tried to get them to let him help, but Hawk and Tobi refused.

"We're saving you in case we need a sharpshooter, Custer." Tobi hoped he was joking when he made the remark.

"There is only one problem with that thinking, Tobi. I don't have a rifle."

Two hours into the trip, Tobi's GPS showed they had gained six miles.

"Well, we can't turn back now," Tobi announced. As soon as he got the words out of his mouth, he heard a sound that made his heart jump. ATVs with their motors wound out were approaching fast through the jungle to the west of them.

"Tobi, take Angel and head through the jungle to the east. If it's that Marshall guy and his men, they will be looking for you and Angel. Take your packs and get as deep in as you can. We'll meet up with you later. And silence your phones!" Hawk began pulling on his zipped-off fishing pants and his hiking boots while Tobi and Angel grabbed their packs and headed into the jungle. In no time, they were out of sight.

Custer left the vehicle and began tromping through the mud, not wanting to look different from his driver. He pulled a low bush up from its roots and covered Tobi's and Angel's tracks in the mud. Both men jumped back into the vehicle and began scrutinizing the map together just as three ATVs drove up beside them. Each ATV held two passengers—six men, all dressed in Park Ranger uniforms.

"You see couple…American? They steal Jeep from park." The one speaking pointed to his park ranger patch on his shirt.

"Jeep? No… We have not seen anyone." Hawk spoke slowly and louder than he needed to.

"Any good fishing?" Custer spoke softly and pointed ahead as he asked the rangers, not wanting to show any curiosity about the American couple who stole a Jeep.

"One river...small...catch small fish!" The man showed fish in the ten-inch range with his hands. "Better to fish ocean—big fish!" This time he showed the size of the fish by stretching his hands as far as they would go.

Custer was not impressed with the fishing knowledge of the park rangers, but it really didn't matter, since neither he nor Hawk had brought their fishing gear.

As soon as the men pulled away, Hawk started the engine, prepared for even worse trail conditions. As he drove, he kept his eyes peeled for Tobi and Angel. Not seeing them made him anxious.

"Where in the hell are they?" Hawk mumbled under his breath.

"Drive slower and gun the engine every once in a while so they can hear us."

After driving for fifteen more minutes, Hawk really became worried. Tobi and Angel still had not shown up back on the trail. Custer directed Hawk to pull over and park in the bushes. Hawk had no idea what his uncle was doing until he began taking off his hiking boots. When he opened up his backpack and pulled out his lace-up moccasins, Hawk's thoughts were confirmed, and he knew exactly what his uncle was doing.

"It's time to track. You can come with me, or you can stay with the vehicle, but either way, you have to stay behind me and stay quiet."

Before Custer headed into the jungle, he emptied his backpack of any extra clothing or toiletries, and motioned for Hawk to do the same. Hawk was surprised when his uncle strapped on a large sheath holding a hunting knife.

"How did you get on the plane with that, Custer?" Tobi asked.

"I didn't. I bought it off a street vendor when you were renting the vehicle."

"Damn! I wish I had known. I would have bought one, too."

Custer smiled as he dug into his pack and pulled out a second knife and sheath a little shorter than the first and handed it to Hawk, who gave a big smile of thanks.

With Hawk following, Custer headed into the jungle to try to pick up Tobi and Angel's trail. In no time, his mind took him back to the bad days, something he'd hoped never to think of again.

After an hour of walking softly, looking deep, and watching for any overturned leaf, twig, or stone, Custer found footprints.

"This has to be Angel's tiny boot print, and here's Tobi's beside hers." Custer set off in another direction a few feet away from Tobi and Angel's trail and left Hawk standing, looking confused until he figured he'd better stay with his uncle.

"This is not good." Custer stopped and put his fingers down into a track he had found in a soft spot of vegetation covered with mud. "Someone is following Tobi and Angel. It has to be Angel's phone being tracked. I should have made her leave it in the car. Those devices are so tiny and sophisticated nowadays, it's hard to figure out which part is foreign. We should have all gotten different phones once we landed."

Hawk said, "Not only is the device small, but really, no device is needed. If they have a phone number and the right high tech software, any phone can be tracked. I saw it on TV. Should be handy when Trapper gets to be a teenager. I'm kind of thinking about getting one surgically implanted when he has his thirteenth birthday."

Custer scoured the ground and soon came up with more tracks. "Now it's worse. Two men are tracking them and may have overcome them by now. We need to be extra quiet and stick close to the heaviest vegetation. They can't be that far away. Tobi's and Angel's tracks are heading straight in the direction of the preserve. Keep your ears open, Hawk."

Chapter Seven

Tobi followed a few steps behind Angel. He had lightened her pack, placing some of her heavier objects in his pack, but still she trudged on, her boots often weighed down with mud. A path, possibly a game path, had appeared out of nowhere, and after studying his compass and the aerial map he had pulled up and saved on his phone earlier, the two decided the narrow trail led to the preserve.

Angel was operating on pure adrenaline now as they got closer to the preserve. Tobi had said they should be within a mile of the outer perimeter, but what lay ahead of that he had no clue.

She was quiet, thinking. Would her dad welcome her with open arms, or would he be standoffish, not wanting to show affection for fear of his daughter wanting to stay with him? And then, what if she got to the preserve only to find her dad a decrepit old man, perhaps using a walker, or in a wheelchair? As her mind sped, so did her short legs until Tobi came beside her and took her arm.

"Pace yourself, sweetheart. I know you're anxious, but we need to give Custer and Hawk time to catch up with us. We don't know what waits for us ahead." He reached into the side pocket of her pack and pulled out her water bottle. "Here…drink. You've hardly had any water, and you're sweating pretty good. You don't want to get dehydrated."

As they stood side by side, a snap was heard back down the trail. They both turned their heads at the same time and then looked at each other.

Tobi motioned for Angel to keep going. He was going to circle around and come in behind whoever was behind them and hope like hell it was his two family members.

Angel shook her head vehemently and grabbed Tobi's arm, pulling him toward her. No way was she letting him out of arm's length, and after convincing him, the two continued following the trail at a faster pace.

****

The tall man, dressed in camouflage, stopped to look at his map and the device that showed the two he was tracking. Pulling out his phone, he typed in a quick message to his partner before putting his phone away and continuing.

Almost time, Jon Shockey. Almost time! And my birthright will be mine.

He rubbed his hands together in anticipation of the millions that awaited him in Switzerland once this job was finished. All he had to do was show a photo of Shockey's dead body with fingerprints on the page matching those left with the overseer of the money. Then the money would be transferred to his own bank accounts already set up and scattered all over the world. Only one problem lay in his path, and that was time.

Exactly six weeks from today, the money and the account would cease to exist, arranged for by ONE thirty years ago when he, the owner of Tiger's Eye, set it up in anticipation of a lifetime cat-and-mouse chase that would either end TWO's life or send him into hiding. ONE was in prison at that time, put there by Jon Shockey turning state's evidence against him to a CIA agent.

Once the deadline passed and the money was unclaimed, all twenty million, plus interest, was set to be dispersed to various illicit accounts, mostly to anti-U.S. organizations. The tracker had a problem with this and used it as rationale for the kill he was going to make. If he got the millions, terrorist groups who hated the U.S. would not get the money.

The would-be assassin mentally retraced the steps leading to his finding out about his father and the millions left in blood money. He was more than annoyed with his mother for not letting him know in time to do something to claim the money, but she, too, was dead now, leaving her son not much better off financially than she had been.

If only my mother had not waited until she was on her deathbed to tell me who my father was. She fought hard to keep me from being like him, mostly by not telling me who he was in reality, and she almost succeeded. But her lawyer, the greedy bastard, gave me all the pertinent information after she died, with the stipulation he would get his own cut out of the deal for disclosing how to access it once Shockey is dead—again. It didn't take much convincing for me to partner up with the lawyer, and what better position to be in for getting information than being in the CIA, my mother's dream fulfilled—and mine until I found out about the millions. Guess my bad genes finally pre-empted the hero worship I had for my mother's older brother who retired from the CIA.

And then there were those within the Agency who could add to the plot to find Shockey. Their help was crucial if the deadline was going to be met. Besides, the plot within the Agency was already in motion when I was asked to join the efforts to find and kill Shockey. But I can't believe the big boss made me prove myself by attacking Angela and stealing her briefcase, even if it turned out to be the wrong briefcase. It was a good thing he was waiting in the car and knew I didn't have time to break the lock and steal the document for myself. And he had the original document all the time— he was the one setting Angela up, knowing she'd lead us to her father. "Just testing you before I allow you to join us on cashing in on Jon Shockey's skin!" he told me. I was pissed and almost took a swing at him.

After taking a swig from his water bottle, he continued following the trail Angel and her fiancé were on, but from the jungle thickness. It would be easier following on the actual path, but the old man's reputation for tracking made it necessary to be extremely careful. In one spot, he had no choice and had to get on the trail because the vegetation was so thick he could not get through it without sounding like an African water buffalo on the attack.

It won't be long now, and I'll have the bait needed to draw Shockey out of his hiding place. Poor sweet Angela!

He wondered just how good Marshall and these local guys were. The boss had hired them, but why had they not known Shockey was hiding in their country? Then he remembered they did not have the resources he had with the CIA. The only bright one in the bunch of hired guns seemed to be the Chapman kid, and that was saying nothing. His balls would probably drop off when the gunfire started.

Hell, they don't even have a military in this country! Paramilitary border patrols are the closest thing they have to an established military, and they are certainly no threat to the likes of Jon Shockey—or me. And then there is the matter of gun control. Weapons registration is done online with proof of sound mental state, fingerprints on file, and a few other details, all easy to fake, a piss-poor effort to strengthen gun control. The Costa Rican government must be run by comedians, or maybe by the protected monkeys of Mono Paraiso.

He smiled at the thought and wondered what the locals would think when they heard gunfire in their jungle paradise. *Oh, let's check online and see who has guns registered in the area!* The man chuckled under his breath.

Shockey had planned well, choosing the preserve and the country as a safe haven, if in fact this was where he was hiding. He would have to trust Shockey's daughter on this one.

Following Angela is my best bet for finding Shockey. Mono Paraiso is totally off limits to the tourist industry, and with no decent trails in, the complex is the perfect location for hiding, so it has to be where they are going. I wonder how much Shockey pays the Costa Rican government for his little "research facility," as the border patrol employee called it, a border guard who gave me directions to the complex after a little gift was laid in his palm.

Closing off all thoughts, he continued trailing the two, keeping far enough back that they would not hear him as he pushed his way through the dense vegetation. He kept just enough distance from the trail to avoid being seen or tracked, he hoped.

****

Custer gingerly placed one moccasin in front of the other, looking right, left, and front for any signs of vegetation disturbed, of stones kicked up out of the earth, or branches bent from someone pushing through, and he found the trail.

"There…a stone kicked away from its original location, broken twigs, and a half boot print in a clear spot," he whispered to Hawk. "Angel and Tobi have company. The same man who left the other print is on their trail and closing in."

Hawk looked at the evidence and was in awe of his uncle.

"What do you want me to do, Unk?"

"Stay on the trail, but go slow, make no noise, and follow Tobi's and Angel's boot prints. I'm going to follow this one who is trailing in the jungle, off the path. Keep that knife where you can get to it, but hope we don't have to go that far."

Custer left Hawk and went farther away from the path Angel and Tobi were using. Not only did he want to see if his gut feeling was paying off, but he wanted to put a nitro tablet under his tongue without Tobi seeing. The heavy walking in the tropical heat was taking a toll on him, but he couldn't let Hawk know. He had a job to do—his last—and protecting Angel and Tobi, and even Raven, was top priority.

At one point, when he felt he couldn't go on, Custer sat on a tree felled a long time ago and stared into the rainforest full of tangled vines, low trees, and bushes with leaves big enough to use for nap pads or rain cover, and trees that seemed to end high above the clouds. For a moment, he had the sensation of being young again; it was the time he wanted to forget, the bad days, but his mind overtook him.

Crawling on his belly through stagnant jungle water, Custer hoped not to run into a punji trap or other booby traps set around the perimeters of the VC camp. His job was to get close enough to put the enemy officer in the crosshairs of his rifle, the officer's one-way ticket to hell. Other kills were not events to solicit pride like this one, and Custer tried to purge memories of those bad ones from his soul.

A vision he had seen before replaced the nightmare. The young brave, dressed only in loincloth and moccasins, rode bareback in the midst of a herd of ponies, their mane keeping time with the beat of hooves on ground hard like the plains of Montana. The cadence of loping horses formed background music for dancing manes and the rider's body moving in harmony with his horse. The scene reminded Custer of the last dance, Ashéeleetaalissua, The Dance Through Camp, a dance for a young eagle warrior like Custer envisioned himself, exhibiting power given him through a vision quest. But the dance also invoked future happiness and success embodied by the pipe carrier, an honor only to be held by one who had seen combat and returned to his people without any sign of injury. Custer had seen combat, but he carried with him mental injuries and self-loathing, secret wounds he would carry to his grave.

A fiery red sky highlighted the scene, filling it with energy needed for battle; the brave and his ponies paused, silhouetted in the crimson glow like ghostly shadows left over from the Little Bighorn battlefield. The distance closed between the two, and the young brave cast a glance Custer's way, nodded his head, and pointed in the direction Custer needed to go. In the whirlwind left behind by the Crow brave, Custer heard the voice of Grandfather speak in the language of his people the Apsáalooke, Children of the Large Beaked Bird:

"Be silent as a mountain breeze, fierce as a prairie fire, with the eye of an eagle and the cunning of a coyote!"

Custer left his resting spot and followed the direction pointed out by the brave his ancestors had sent to guide him. He had checked his phone twice while tracking, but he was not greeted with a message from his old friend and fellow mercenary Raven.

****

Thirty minutes had passed, and Hawk was getting worried. There was still no sign of Tobi and Angel, but their boot prints were still heading toward the preserve by way of the path. He had heard not so much as a twig break since leaving his uncle, and he hoped he would not have to explain to his mother-in-law how he had left Custer to his own devices in the middle of a tropical jungle. Just as he was about to go off trail in search of Custer, he heard a muffled sound, a moan, followed by a series of stifled, guttural yelps.

"What the hell?" Hawk took off in the direction of the sounds into the forest on the other side of the trail.

Chapter Eight

Whiteman's plane landed at a small private airport used by only a few pilots. As soon as he disembarked the plane, he boarded a chopper, its blades running, ready for liftoff. Whiteman did not take the controls as he usually did but directed the pilot to "hit it, and hit it fast!"

Within minutes, the chopper was being lowered to the helipad inside the tall fenced compound of Mono Paraiso. Ducking low, Whiteman ran from the helicopter and headed for the tallest of four towers, one in each corner of the compound. As he cleared the chopper, he was escorted by a woman, heavily armed, and two men, also armed.

"What's up, Whiteman?" Sophia asked, never breaking her stride beside Whiteman.

"No time for explanations. I need to get to the monitors and search the rainforests for a small group of probably two men and a petite woman. I want men at each tower, as well!"

****

Hawk hurried, making his way to where the muffled sounds were coming from and hoped he would find Tobi and Angel okay. He also needed to get to Custer. He did not have a good feeling about this escapade, regardless of what his uncle told him. *Custer looked pale, even though he would not admit to having*

55

any problems—the selfless old coot! In an effort to put worries of Custer out of his mind, Hawk turned his thoughts to Tobi and Angel and hastened his step.

****

Tobi had watched with alarm as the two men carried Angel away through the forest. Her hands were tied behind her and her mouth duct-taped, but he could hear her muffled scream through the gag. Hard as he tried to loosen his hands, he could not pull free. The attack had come quickly, catching him completely off guard, something he would never forgive in himself. He had fought them with everything he had, but in the end a blow to the head with the back of a pistol put him out. When he came to, he was tied to a tree, with duct tape over his mouth. A glimpse was all he had gotten of the two men, one carrying a bound, kicking and screaming Angel while the other spoke on a cell phone.

Time crept as Tobi continued to struggle with his bindings. His head hurt like a son-of-a-bitch, but it would not stop him from going after the bastards who had Angel. It seemed like an hour had gone by and still no Hawk or Custer. Tobi felt out of control and knew he was about to go unconscious again. Then he heard footsteps coming through the heavy vegetation and not on the trail.

****

Hawk broke through and ran when he saw Tobi tied to the tree. Taking his knife out of the sheath, he cut the ropes as Tobi jerked the tape from his mouth. Blood gushed from Tobi's head, running down his face and pooling around his left eye. Still, he tried to get to his feet, only to stagger back into the tree that had held him captive.

"You're hurt! I need to get you to a hospital!" Hawk held to his brother-in-law, holding him upright, but Tobi pushed him away.

"Two men...took her...got to go..." Tobi collapsed, but Hawk caught him and eased him to the ground. Moving to the stream, Hawk pulled a T-shirt from his pack, wet it, and ran back to Tobi, applying it to his injury and wiping the blood from his face and eye.

Tobi was unconscious, and Hawk knew he also needed to get Custer. This time he dialed his number rather than texting.

"Signal! Thank goodness! This place probably has its own cell tower."

****

Custer felt he was getting close to whoever was following Tobi and Angel and was angry when his cell phone vibrated.

"I told you I'm fine, Hawk. You shouldn't be calling me. I'm still trailing whoever is after Tobi and..." Custer was whispering but did not get to finish his conversation. Hawk cut him off and began talking fast, telling him what had happened and giving him directions, as best he could, to where he had found Tobi. He knew Custer would track him. By the time he hung up, Tobi was again trying to get to his feet.

"Go after her, Hawk! Please!"

"Custer is on his way, but I don't know how far he is. He was tracking another guy he thought was following you and Angel." Hawk combed his fingers through his hair. "Damn! If we were in Montana, our odds would be so much better, but I don't know anything about Costa Rica or jungle fighting. I was too young for Vietnam."

"Help me up, Hawk. I've got to do something… anything!"

"Which way did they take her, Tobi, and how long ago?"

Tobi pointed in the opposite direction from where they had come.

"This road is too rough to go very fast. I'm going to try to catch up with them. You are in no condition to go, so you wait here for Custer." Hawk hurried off through the rainforest, hoping and praying he could catch up with Angel's abductors.

****

Custer hurried to the location Hawk had given him. He was breathing hard, and his heart had begun to palpitate, probably out of fear for Angel. As he made it back to the trail Tobi and Angel had been on, he heard someone running through the forest back in the direction from which he had come.

No need for me to follow. I could never catch him. Besides, he's probably with the two who have Angel. I need to get to Tobi. Knowing Hawk, he's in hot pursuit of the two kidnappers.

****

Hawk made no pretense of trying to be quiet as he jumped bushes and vines, and broke mud holes wide open without trying to go around them. He could see the footprints of the two men and hoped Angel would kick and squirm enough to slow the men down and give him a chance to catch up. He did not take time to look at the map, but he thought he remembered a road to the east of where they had gotten on the trail, and his sense of direction told him this was where the kidnappers had probably parked their getaway vehicle.

As he neared the edge of the rainforest where he thought the other road was located, he heard a vehicle start up. Reaching inside for strength, Hawk tore out in that direction. He reached the road in time to see a yellow Jeep bumping its way down the road. Not letting up, Hawk ran after it, giving it everything he had…until the bullets started flying.

Hawk did not stop but began zigzagging his way after them, decreasing their chances of hitting him. He gained on them when they tried to dodge a huge mud hole and straddled an unforgiving thick bush. The shooter got out of the Jeep and began hurling bullets at Hawk, but Hawk ran in a different direction away from the scene. To his amazement, the Jeep drove off, leaving the shooter behind. Hawk decided that in order to lose the shooter he would have to do something unpredictable. Up ahead he could see a small clearing. His long stride took him to it in no time. His hope was to find more forest where he could hide and double back on the shooter, using his knife if necessary. But when Hawk reached the clearing, he found only small clumps of trees around the edge, and he thought he could feel and hear the ocean behind these. Only one tree stood in the clearing, the strangest-looking tree he had ever seen, but he had no choice but to take refuge in it.

The tree looked like a giant green mushroom, or perhaps a really fat, giant spear of broccoli, but regardless, the trunk was about seven feet deep, big enough to hide a big man's frame, and the cap of thick green canopy cupped, touching the ground in a huge circle. The tree was a cinch for Hawk to climb, and he lifted himself into the green covering. Once he was balanced in the tree limbs, he pulled his knife out and waited.

****

Custer hurried, not giving in to the palpitation of his heart, and soon reached Tobi, who was by that time talking out of his head, the victim of a bad concussion. Custer gave Tobi a drink from his water bottle but would not let him stand.

"Where's Angel, Custer?" Tobi asked as if they were back in Red Lodge and Custer might have given her a ride to Betsy's.

"Take it easy, son. She'll be back shortly." Before Custer got the last word out of his mouth, Tobi was unconscious again.

****

Hawk had one peek hole through the thick green canopy, but it was enough to see the shooter, now wearing a bandana over his mouth like he was in an old-time western movie. He was making his way across the clearing and looking toward the tree. Hawk thought about getting down and running back into the thick rainforest, but decided to wait. Besides, capturing the shooter might be their only way to find Angel. He had been in worse messes than this, and he had a knife, even though the quality was not wonderful and the blade was so dull it wouldn't have been able to slice Betsy's southern cornbread he loved.

Within seconds, the kidnapper was walking on the outskirts of the tree canopy with no thought of Hawk hiding in its high branches. When he got to the edge of the canopy's shade, Hawk knew this was his chance.

Gingerly, Hawk slipped down the tree, making his

way to the kidnapper while staying close to the edge of the canopy. As the shooter cleared the tree, Hawk took off. Running, hurling his body toward the man, Hawk knocked him to the ground. The man managed to get his handgun out of the holster, but it did him no good. With one good Montana Grizzly barroom brawl punch, he was out.

Hawk tore the man's shirt off, cut and ripped it into strips, and tied his hands behind his back. With another strip, he gagged him. As the man came to, Hawk jerked him to his feet and marched him back in the direction they had come. Angel was gone with the other kidnapper, but Hawk knew they could make this one talk, whatever it took.

When Hawk made it back to Tobi and Custer, Tobi was lucid. When he saw the man with his hands tied behind his back, he tried to get to his feet, ready to tear into him, but dizziness and a firm hand by Custer prevented it.

"So what do we do now, Hawk?" Tobi asked the question. "And don't tell me we're taking him to the police. He knows where Angel is, and the son-of-a-bitch will talk—or we'll let Custer scalp him like he did that guy on the reservation in Montana."

Custer was sharpening his knife on a smooth stone he had picked up in a stream and never cracked a smile when Tobi made the threat. Instead, he moved to the man, who pretended not to understand English, and pulled his hair back as if examining his hairline. Custer held the big knife in front of the man's eyes, which grew bigger the closer Custer held the knife to his face.

Hawk motioned for Custer to join him out of earshot of the captive.

"What now, Custer?" We can't just stay here, and we have no place to go. I say we head toward the preserve and see if Shade is really there. He's our only chance of finding Angel. Besides, we need a place, an isolated place, to force our man to talk, and Tobi needs medical attention."

"What about Tobi?" Custer asked. "I'm not sure he can walk. It's too far to go back for the Land Rover, and from the looks of the road, it would never make it to the preserve."

"I can walk, and I'm not deaf, Custer." Tobi stood, but he grabbed the tree when he felt himself falling and did not take a step.

Hawk put the gag back on the captive's mouth, motioned with the gun barrel for him to get moving, and then handed the gun to Custer, who looked at him in surprise.

Moving to Tobi, Hawk helped him up, knelt in front of him, and told Tobi to get on his back. When Tobi refused, Hawk lit into him.

"Ditch the pride, Tobi! Angel's life is in our hands. You are holding us up, so get your ass on my back so we can get to the preserve and see if we can save her. If you don't, I'll throw you over my shoulder, but I don't think the blood needs to rush to your head right now."

Tobi climbed on, wrapping his legs around Hawk's waist and holding around Hawk's neck to the front of his shirt. Knowing there was no way he could carry Tobi through the rainforest itself, Hawk hurried toward the trail.

Chapter Nine

Angel awoke to find herself in a cottage like the one where she and Tobi had stayed for a short while the night they arrived in Costa Rica. Her head hurt, and she was having a hard time keeping her eyelids open. Then she saw the small bruised area on her arm where someone had jabbed a needle, and she knew she had been drugged, but how long had she been lying in this room comatose?

Leaving the bed, she made her way to the French doors leading out onto the deck overlooking the ocean. Just as she thought, the doors had been secured from the outside and a guard was positioned a few feet away from the covered deck. Next she made her way to the front door, but it, too, would not budge.

"No escape!" she said under her breath. Looking around, she found her backpack and searched in it for her cell phone, but it had been removed, along with her jewelry. She was glad she had convinced Tobi to put the blue diamond ring in the safe deposit box before they left Montana. At least the thugs hadn't been able to steal it. She would never have gotten over that.

"This can't be happening!" She spoke aloud but was glad no one was there to hear her or to try to make her tell where her father was. Angel looked down and saw her legs were still covered in mud. She was glad to know no one had tried to undress her and put her in the shower. Risking her captives coming back any minute, she decided getting a shower was a must.

Later, wrapped in a towel, Angel dug through her pack one more time, hoping her cell phone would show up this time, but it was not there. As she stuck her hand to the bottom of the side pocket, she found her meds. Inside the small plastic container, her sleeping pills and her birth control pills stared at her, and she thought of Tobi.

"I hope I have a reason to keep taking these, Tobi, and I hope you're okay." She spoke aloud and remembered how Tobi had fought the two men, yelling for her to run, but it had done no good. As soon as she took off, one of the men had hit Tobi with the butt of his gun, knocking him to the ground. Unable to leave Tobi, she had run back to bend over him and then cradle his bleeding head in her lap. But the other man had given her no time with Tobi, instead tying her hands behind her back and duct-taping her mouth. Next he threw her over his shoulder and began moving through the forest as fast as he could while carrying her. The second man soon caught up to them, and she worried that he had done more harm to Tobi.

Angel knew the only way she could sleep would be if she took the sleeping pills that had become almost a necessity ever since she received the first document. But she didn't think she would be taking those pills while in captivity. She needed to stay alert and ready to grab any opportunity for escape.

Sleep can come later, when I'm safe in Tobi's arms.

Angel pulled out a pair of shorts and a shirt and quickly dressed. Then she rummaged through the cottage, looking for a knife or anything she could use for a weapon, but all she found was a set of plastic throwaway utensils. While she was searching, she noticed fresh fruit, cheese, and pita bread, plus bottled water in the fridge, and she helped herself, surprised at how famished she was until she remembered she had not eaten all day.

In the door to the fridge, individual bottles of liquor were lined up, two whiskeys and two bourbons, popular American brands. She was tempted to drown her sorrows, but today was not the day for that. She had to stay focused. Also in the fridge door was a small bottle of raw honey, something probably left over from the last customer, or possibly another abductee. She tried to screw the top off but found it had dried on like glue, indicating it had been there for a while. Rather than putting it back, she threw it in the trashcan and then wondered why she was bothering.

Angel jumped when she heard the door rattle and knocked her bottle of water off the table. As the water streamed across the floor, she ignored it and closed her eyes, willing herself to look fearless and in control.

It's my father they want, not me. They will keep me alive as bait to get to him and the blood money.

When the rattling stopped, the door opened and in walked Marshall Chapman, his handsome face covered in a huge grin.

"You!" Angel exclaimed giving the young college grad, if that was what he was, her best "go to hell" look.

"Have a seat, Miss Baird, or is it Miss Shockey? You have almost as many names as your father." He crossed to the refrigerator and took out a bottle of water and one of the small bottles of whiskey. After pouring the whiskey into one of the small plastic glasses on the counter, he topped it off with what looked like a tablespoon of water.

This guy is serious about his whiskey. Angel watched as he took a drink and then held up the glass to her.

"May I offer you a drink? It's Crown Royal, imported just for Americans like you and me. No Guara for me, thank you very much."

Angel shook her head and folded her arms.

"What do you propose to do now that you have me, Mr. Chapman?" Angel used a derogatory tone and said the guy's name as if she wanted to follow it with a gigantic wad of spit aimed at his pretty face.

"Well, let's see. I could take you to bed, but I have a woman, not that this would stop me. I could hold you for ransom, but your father chooses to remain aloof, or perhaps estranged, from his only child. Not much of a father, if you ask me." He smiled as if this statement should get a reaction from her.

"You don't know my father, and I don't know where he is. I thought he was in Costa Rica, but the informant who was going to meet us did not show. I think it was a hoax to get money from us." Angel had made up the story while in the shower. She would not tell about the possibility he was hiding in the Mono Paraiso.

"So you were out in the rainforest to meet an informant? That is preposterous, Angela." Marshall took his whiskey and sat on the sofa. Angel remained standing.

"Where would you think an informant would meet someone in this country? In the middle of the capital building in San Jose among a crowd of about ten thousand?" Angel did not correct his calling her Angela, but she found it suspicious. Only the people who had known her in D.C. called her Angela. After getting another water from the fridge, Angel took a seat in the easy chair opposite Marshall.

"So what's your plan? Do you really think my father will show himself after over twenty years and rush out to save me? I think not."

"Then why are you here, Angela? And don't tell me to have an early honeymoon with your fiancé…what's his name?"

"He does not concern you. I did want to get away with my fiancé, and I once overheard my father mention Costa Rica to the woman he was living with in Alaska, but that was when I was a teenager. I've always wanted to come here, just in case my father was alive." Angel dropped her eyes, pretending sadness had overtaken her. "You want to kill him, but you're too late. He isn't here. He died in Alaska, and my thinking he is alive is just the dreams of a girl who suddenly realized she is getting married and has no father to walk her down the aisle."

"That is so touching, Angela! However, I know different. I know Costa Rica provides one of many sanctuaries for Jon Shockey, and I know you recently found out your father is, indeed, alive. We are putting the word out on the street in all the places your father might frequent, or might keep informants. In due time, he will make contact to save you." Marshall rose from the sofa, guzzled the rest of the whiskey, and walked to the door.

"Oh, don't be alarmed when you hear workers

outside your windows. They will have all possibilities of escape boarded up within the next hour. Until then, guards are on duty."

Angel stood and glowered at Marshall with her arms crossed.

"Um…um…um! I love the way you look when you pout. Maybe I'll take you to bed after all." Marshall moved to Angel and put his hand under her chin and then moved it to her mouth, running his finger over her bottom lip. "Pretty little China doll. Oh, what I could do to you!" Marshall put his lips to Angel's and kissed her, pulling her bottom lip with his teeth.

Angel stood stoic and did not resist or kiss him back. Her mind began to plot her escape.

"I'll come by later this evening, and we will discuss your impending marriage—and see if we can get your mind off your predicament?"

Marshall ran his fingers down her neck and chest, letting his fingertips circle over her nipple. Angel stood rigid, refusing to show fear.

Yes, Marshall, please come by later. I'll have a nice surprise for you.

Chapter Ten

Custer prodded the captured gunman with the pistol to walk faster as the four made their way up the pig trail in the direction of Mono Paraiso. He had no idea if Raven would be here or not, but his gut told him he would.

As they walked, Custer sensed being watched. Hearing rustling on both sides of them, he stopped and fetched his water bottle from his pack, allowing Hawk time to move up beside him.

"We have visitors. Be ready." Custer whispered, but Hawk was carrying Tobi and knew he could do nothing to prepare.

Suddenly, they were surrounded by armed men, all dressed in camo that blended perfectly with the jungle surroundings. Custer took one look and knew this was not the ordinary camo from Cabela's but was custom designed by an artist, one who had the gift and the eye, not to mention experience in blending in with the scene, of matching surroundings perfectly where the person wearing the outdoor clothing became part of the picture. The only identifying mark on the clothing was a patch across their left shirt pocket labeled "Mono Paraiso Ranger."

Custer put the pistol in his waistband and held up his hands in surrender.

"Custer Larson?" A beautiful woman, also dressed

in camo and armed, stepped from behind the men, stopping a few feet in front of Custer.

"Yes," Custer answered, lowering his hands.

"Follow us." The woman started to leave but said something in Spanish. One of the men grabbed the kidnapper by the arm and ushered him ahead, and two others took Tobi from Hawk, carrying Tobi together.

****

Whiteman sat glued to the monitors and waited, watching from the edge of his seat for a glimpse of Custer and his daughter.

Dear God, what am I doing wanting my sweet Angel to show up on this monitor? If she's here, her life is in jeopardy. But if I can get to her before others... But then, there will always be others!

Whiteman had watched as the guards drew together and then separated, fanning out on each side of the trail leading to the compound. He rubbed his beard and his heartbeat grew faster as he watched the rangers circle a group on the trail.

Move, Sophia! Get around them and get them back here to the preserve!

As Sophia came into focus, Whiteman could hardly believe what he saw. A tall, Indian man with long gray braids walked behind her.

"Custer!" Whiteman said aloud and then moved closer to the monitor, hoping for a glimpse of his daughter. Next he saw a man with his hands bound behind him, a local of Spanish descent, and Whiteman's fears surfaced. Behind him were two of the rangers carrying a younger man with blond curly hair. The young man's head was slumped and blood had dried on his head and face.

"Come on, Tulen, my little Angel! Where are you?" Again he spoke aloud as if the monitor could answer. Standing in front of the monitor, he leaned in, putting pressure on his hands, now pushed down hard on the table, as he glared at the screen, waiting.

Behind the blond man was a tall, muscular guy with dark hair. The look on his face was all seriousness, and he looked Indian. Whiteman knew this had to be Betsy's husband Hawk.

He wished he had kept up with the books after Sue Ann married Custer, but all he wanted to do was forget. Even if he could go to Sue Ann now, she belonged with Custer. He knew Sue Ann and Betsy had written a book, Sue Ann's biography, but he could not bring himself to read it as he had all the fifty or so romances Sue Ann had written since they parted, and he had loved Betsy's book about meeting and marrying Hawk. Betsy was like a daughter, and in a few minutes he'd meet Hawk.

Tulen, whom he had protected since her birth, had been catapulted into his life when her adopted mother was murdered by ONE. Even with his fear for Angel's safety, he was anxious to see her, to hold her in his arms again. But this was a dream that could not be fulfilled. Angel would always be a target now that the word was out that he was alive.

Again Whiteman moved his eyes closer, within inches of the big monitor, and he scanned every inch.

"Where is she?" No longer able to control his emotions and fears, he left the monitor and headed for the outside.

****

As the group of armed rangers and captives

71

approached the compound, large wooden doors, like the ones in the scene Shade had painted on the cardboard, opened automatically. More armed men stood guard in the two corner towers looking down on the approaching group.

"I feel like I'm in a scene from *Jurassic Park!*" Hawk said as he followed the guards inside the compound, where a massive setup of modern buildings lay spread out in front of them.

The rangers had dispersed, except for the few who were helping with Tobi and detaining the kidnapper. Custer stopped at a covered patio area and dropped into a chair.

"Are you okay, Uncle Custer?" Hawk's use of the respectful name and title showed his concern.

"Could we have some water, please?" Hawk directed his request to the woman who had introduced herself as Sophia.

Sophia used her radio and spoke Spanish to the person on the other end, and in what seemed like seconds, a server brought a tray of cold drinks, water, fruit, and sandwiches piled high with meat and cheese, which they placed in the center of the patio table.

Custer had his head back with a second nitro tablet already dissolving under his tongue. When the water was brought, he took a glass and drank in slow sips.

"I think I might live." Custer looked up toward the fan and closed his eyes.

But a few minutes later, Custer watched the long stride of the man approaching from one of the buildings, and his heart began the irregular beat he had not experienced since his visit to the Sacred Hoop. He could do nothing but stare as Shade Dubois, Raven, approached, his eyes already zeroed in on his old friend.

Shade's "raven wings" as Sue Ann had called his hair, were no longer the shiny black of the bird that was Shade's animal spirit. Though the thickness remained, his hair, like his beard and mustache, were silver. His physique was as ever—fit, strong, commanding, even though he was the same age as Custer.

Custer remained seated until Shade stood over him.

"Eagle!" Raven held out his hand to his old friend.

"Raven. We must talk. We have a problem." Custer rose to his feet as Raven scanned the tired, muddy group.

Raven's eyes fell on Tobi, who had been placed on a lounge chair with his feet on the stool. His head was back and covered with a towel that had been dipped in cold water and wrapped around ice. He remained quiet, lapsing in and out of consciousness.

"That is Tobi Parish, Betsy's twin brother, but the story will have to wait. He is Angel's fiancé."

Raven turned to Sophia and spoke in Spanish. Within minutes, a man dressed in scrubs and carrying a medical bag strode toward the patio, putting his stethoscope around his neck in preparation.

"I'm Hawk, Betsy's husband." Hawk held his hand out to Raven, who shook it firmly, putting his other hand on top of Hawk's in a gesture of affection Hawk admired, affection he knew was for Betsy.

"Where is my daughter, Custer? I'm guessing the local with his hands tied has something to do with her absence. I won't ask you to tell me she's safe. It is obvious she is not, but we need to debrief as quickly as possible. Now that I know she's in Costa Rica, I have to have her with me." With Custer moving slowly beside him, Raven headed toward the building he had come from, calling back, "Hawk, join us. When Doc is finished with Tobi, they will bring him to us on a stretcher. I'm sure he wants to be involved, since he is to be my son-in-law."

Thirty minutes later, Raven knew the whole story. He had remained calm, but Custer could see his mind working.

"I knew this could happen as the deadline grew closer. I'm almost glad Angel came to Costa Rica where the climate is healthier, and I am not referring to the amount of rainfall or the temperature, but I will withhold that judgment until she is safe with us here at the preserve. Costa Rica is considered one of the safest countries in the world. That's the reason it draws so many retirees and expats like myself, although retirement is not my reason for being here."

Hawk and Custer relayed everything they knew about Angel's abduction, including the part Marshall Chapman had played when they first arrived. Raven shook his head in recognition of Chapman's name.

Tobi had been brought to the building and was helped into an easy chair shortly after they began their tale, and Raven moved to sit beside him. Tobi said he felt much better and wanted to be part of the discussion and the plans for rescuing Angel.

"Tobi, tell me everything you remember about Marshall Chapman. I know him, or at least his father, and he should be easy to find with my connections with the local officials. By the way, my name here is Dr. Thomas Whiteman." He turned to face Custer. "Just what I needed, huh, Custer, another alias." Again, he faced the group. "I fund the research facility here as a private, not-for-profit organization that contributes generously to the Costa Rican economy, and the government. They never deny my requests, and they do not bother me in the way I run Mono Paraiso."

"You do research on monkeys?" Hawk asked.

Raven smiled at Hawk's question. "My scientists do all kinds of research to protect the animal species of Costa Rica, and a new lab is being built for medical research for humans. We hope to find a species of vegetation in the rainforests that can be used for cures for catastrophic diseases." Raven cast his eyes at Custer. "Such as cancer...breast cancer in particular."

Custer knew Raven had gotten his message, but he also knew his friend would not discuss the message with him.

"Now...let's get my daughter back. My people are already gathering every resource available and getting them on this. Hopefully, Angel will be here before the day is over. With the reward I'm offering, I do not think she will be harmed, but I want her found quickly before her abductors try to move her out of Costa Rica. What name does Angel go by now?"

"Angela Shockey." Custer watched as Raven's eyes showed both pride and fear.

****

Raven left the room after telling Sophia to take the men to quarters so they could shower and change. He had her get their sizes and provide more clothing as needed for each, since their backpacks had been left in the rainforest. Raven offered for Tobi to rest in the infirmary so the doctor could watch him, but he refused. He wanted to be where any information on

Angel was received.

Retreating to his personal quarters, Raven got on the phone, making calls to high officials in the Costa Rican government. They all assured him his daughter would be found and found quickly.

He knew Marshall Chapman's father, but it was not a good relationship. Known to Chapman as Dr. Whiteman, he had hired Marshall Chapman's father to take care of some of his accounts for the preserve, until discovering funds missing. Raven had promised not to turn him in but told him he would hold all evidence of his illicit use of the preserve's funds in case he ever needed it. Since he was not sure if Morris Chapman had anything to do with Angel's abduction, Raven would not make a call to him, but he would have stakeouts surrounding every hotel, resort, and business owned by the elder Chapman, including residences. Raven had heard Chapman's son was a no-good, and he could easily be in on Angel's abduction.

That night, Raven met with Custer alone for the talk he had needed to have for the last three years. They would go for a ride over the preserve, he said. Custer was surprised when Raven picked him up in an Argo UTV.

"Going off road, are we? Could have used this today." Custer climbed in and Raven gunned the machine, heading out through a gate on the back side of the preserve.

After plowing through deep mud holes and motoring down shallow rivers, Raven pulled to a high point overlooking the Pacific Ocean. Raven cut the motor and told Custer to get out.

The two walked only a short distance, to a rustic

bench made from a tree trunk.

As Raven remained quiet, Custer wondered what this was all about. But it was not his style to rush anyone with a heavy heart. After long minutes of silence while watching the moon over the blue waters of the Pacific Ocean, Raven spoke. Custer listened intently.

"So you think you are dying, Custer? Pardon me if I don't quite believe you, after seeing you still very much in action today." Raven paused as if giving himself time to organize his thoughts into words. "You told me Sue Ann will need me when you're gone and that she has never stopped loving me." A long pause followed, long enough that Custer felt obligated to speak.

"Yes. I said all those things, and yes, I am dying. Doc says I need a heart transplant, but that is not my way. I have a reprieve right now, granted by the Creator. I suspect when Angel is with you, and all is well so that you can go to the woman we both love, my time will be up."

"You know I never stopped loving Sue Ann, but I cannot go to her and jeopardize her life and the lives of the others. You should not have come here, and you should have stopped Angel from coming." Raven rose from the bench, put his hands in his pockets, and stared at the ocean. With his back turned, he began to speak. "How did Angel find out I was alive and in Costa Rica?"

Custer relayed all that he knew and told Raven he felt her informant was someone with the CIA, a bad agent who wanted to collect on the millions still riding on proof of Raven's death, and he was using Angel as bait once again. "As for stopping Angel from coming here—she is your daughter in every sense." Custer then asked the question he had wanted answered since earlier that afternoon.

"What did you mean by, 'I knew this would happen as the deadline drew closer?'"

"I should not have said that, but you have a right to know." Raven turned to face Custer. "When ONE established the account with the unidentified corporation in control of verification of my death, he put a thirty-year deadline on anyone claiming it. The deadline is in just under six weeks. I've put it out of my mind, feeling someone might extend it, but as far as I know, the deadline will hold."

"I knew about the blood money, but I did not know about the deadline." Custer paused. "So after four weeks, you will be free again and can take care of Sue Ann should I leave this realm." Custer waited for Raven's answer.

"I don't know, Custer. I'm not sure I can ever put the fear I have for her out of my mind, even when the deadline comes. At one time, I trusted Marshall Chapman's father explicitly as my personal financial consultant and investor. I paid him hundreds of thousands of dollars for his services, only to have him mishandle funds for the preserve, which ended in his termination. He was angry…still is, and that could be where part of the problem lies. I had him look into ONE's Swiss bank account and the organization overseeing it, telling him the target of the money, Jon Shockey, was an old friend and had died in Alaska. I told him the money had never been collected. Chapman is the one who found out about the deadline. I believe he was telling me the truth. He went bad when he got involved with a drug cartel, and although that association has been broken, his son Marshall stays in trouble repeatedly. I will never trust Chapman again."

"When a man hurts Raven, the man is a dead man." Custer repeated what he had heard Raven say many times when they were young and invincible. "Is that still your motto?"

"No. I've mellowed with old age, but I do teach other men to kill, the underdogs in countries or areas without the means of fighting strong rebel armies. Besides, jungle warfare keeps me fit, in both mind and body." Shade sat beside Custer and folded his arms.

"What is it you want to tell me, Raven? You didn't get me away from Hawk and Tobi just to tell me about the deadline and about Chapman."

"You were always very perceptive, Custer, whether tracking, killing, or just reading minds." Raven leaned forward, resting his elbows on his knees.

"Does this have anything to do with the beautiful Sophia?" Custer asked.

"Partly," Raven answered. "I never looked for anyone until you and Sue Ann married, but then I let myself feel something for Sophia, something I acted upon—and still do." He looked down for a few seconds before raising his eyes, making his next comment. "I remain very much a man, Eagle, even though seventy is just around the corner." He gave Custer time for his admission to sink in.

"Sophia needed a place to hide. We are much alike, although she is much younger, closer to the age of my daughter. She was instrumental in bringing down one of the leaders in the Mexican drug cartel, but the Mexican government forced her to leave the country, knowing they could no longer protect her."

"Do you love her?" Custer asked, not making eye contact with his friend.

"I care about her." Raven answered in a low voice. "Could I ever love her, or any woman, as much as, or more than Sue Ann? You and I both know that is not possible, but it has been a long time, Custer. What if Sue Ann's love for me has died after all these years— after being your wife? You gave her something I could never give her—stability without fear."

"This is a decision you alone can make, Raven, but now Angel is in the picture. She wants to marry Tobi and become Sue Ann's daughter-in-law. Angel will not let you leave her again…no matter what. Are you going to swear her to secrecy and remain dead?"

"These are things I will have to contemplate, but I wanted you to know what's in my life and in my head." Raven returned to the Argo, and Custer followed. "Now, we have to find my daughter."

They rode in silence back to the preserve. When they got back, Hawk and a much improved Tobi were waiting on them. Tobi was angry.

"Why are you not out searching for Angel, Shade? You say you have resources; well, use them, for God's sake! I want her back now!" Tobi tried to stand, but Hawk pushed him back down.

"Good! Now I know you love my daughter. I have people everywhere, but mostly I have Marshall Chapman and anyone associated with him under surveillance. The man you captured today is known to do dirty work for Marshall, but he's not talking. As soon as I get word Angel has been spotted, or that

Marshall Chapman has been spotted, I will head to that location. If it takes too long, then I'll use other means to make our captive talk."

"I'm coming with you if you go after Angel!" Tobi announced.

"We'll see if you're able when the time comes." Raven turned and headed for his office to monitor calls. Hawk followed him.

"What can I do, Shade? I can't just sit here, and you know Tobi is in no condition to go with you, and neither is Custer. Regardless of what he says, his heart won't last much longer."

"Yes, he told me. He tries to be discreet about putting the nitro under his tongue, but during our little ride he reached in his pocket three times. He needs to go home to Sue Ann."

"And what about you, Shade? Do you want us to tell Sue Ann you are alive?" Hawk knew a world of hurt was in store for his mother-in-law, hurt when Custer did pass on to the next realm, as he called it, and hurt to know Shade was alive all these years when she could not get over him.

"We will decide when the time comes, Hawk." Raven walked away and then turned back. "If I get a call that Angel has been found, I would like for you to go with me but not Custer. He needs to rest."

"What about Tobi?" Hawk asked.

"Doc will give him something to make him sleep. I'll tell him to add it to his antibiotic so he won't have to tell him. He needs to stay healthy for my daughter."

Chapter Eleven

True to Marshall's warning, the French doors and every window had been boarded up so that the only light in the cottage came from the lamps, but Angel did not mind the dim light. It would make it easier for her late visit with her captor. During the long afternoon, Angel had formed a plan of escape.

Angel smiled as she removed her medicine container from her pack and moved to the kitchen area. After taking the little whiskey bottle, Marshall's favorite, out of the fridge door, she unscrewed the bottle cap and poured out a tiny bit of the liquid. Opening her medicine box, she took out four of the high-powered prescription capsules for insomnia. After breaking them open with the serrated edge of the plastic knife, she carefully poured the powder from each capsule into the whiskey bottle and rotated the bottle in her hands until the medicine was completely mixed.

As she reached for the cap to the whiskey bottle, she realized she had a problem.

Damn! It will be too easy to unscrew and he'll suspect something!

Angel tried to think what she could do to make the cap appear as if it had never been opened and her eyes fell on the trash can. Reaching in, she took out the old bottle of honey and tried to unscrew it, but the cap was stuck tight.

Perfect!

Angel turned the hot water on in the sink and let it run until it was too hot to touch. Placing the honey under the stream, she let it run over it just enough to loosen the honey under the cap. Once she was able to screw the cap off, she reached for a toothpick she had seen in a drawer and went to work on the whiskey bottle cap. After coating the inside of the small cap with honey, she took it into the bathroom and turned the hairdryer on low to help harden it just enough before screwing it tightly on the bottle.

After a few minutes in the fridge, Angel tested the cap, and it had dried too tight for her to remove it.

Bingo! Now to make sure he chooses the whiskey and not the bourbon.

Angel screwed off the cap of one of the bourbons and poured it down the sink, leaving the empty bottle on the table. Then she removed the other bottle of bourbon and mixed it with a plastic cup half full of water. After pouring most of it down the sink, she placed the cup on the table on top of a napkin. She hated bourbon, but later when she would hear Marshall rattling the key in the door, she would take a quick sip to get it on her breath, and then act like she'd been enjoying her drink.

She also hated the part of her plan in which she would be dressed only in the short terry robe left for guests. It would not take much to seduce Marshall after his earlier scene, but for him to drink the laced whiskey was imperative if the plan was to work.

Her next move was to find something heavy to use as a weapon on the guard at the front door. In the bathroom, Angel got down on her hands and knees and looked under the sink for a chrome pipe she could take off. Using all her strength, she tried to loosen the main pipe, but it wouldn't budge.

Now what?

Angel looked inside the closet but saw nothing—until her eyes stopped on the steel rod. Getting a chair from the kitchen table, she stood on it to see if she could remove the rod. Two screws held the bracket in place. Retrieving one of the plastic knives from the kitchen, she used it to loosen the screws. It worked. She only had to remove the bracket on one side in order to take down the rod.

Now all I have to do is wait for you, you egotistical bastard!

Angel tapped the rod on her other hand in anticipation of using it like a baseball bat—or better, a club.

I may be petite, but I can swing a billy club with the muscles I built up working out. Look out, Marshall! This China doll is going to do some serious damage to you and your guard!

Chapter Twelve

Angel sat at the table dressed only in the short terry robe from the bathroom. She had even put on makeup to make herself more irresistible. The bedcovers were pulled back and the pillows fluffed like she was eager for company. With her drink in front of her, Angel drummed her fingers on the table. Her thoughts had been on Tobi all day, and in her mind she could still see him lying there with blood covering his face. With her eyes closed, she prayed he was okay. She also prayed her plan would work on Marshall.

By now, maybe Tobi, Hawk, and Custer were inside Mono Paraiso getting to know her dad. Just as her thoughts began to overtake her, she heard Marshall talking to the guard at the door in Spanish and then the key rattling in the door. Nervously, she took a big sip of the bourbon, forgetting how bad it tasted when not mixed with her usual Coke. Collecting herself, she pulled one bare knee up in the chair and slinked back, pulling her robe open at the top and putting on her most alluring, sultry, intoxicated look.

Marshall pushed the door open and was surprised to see Angel sitting at the table with a drink in her hand. His view of her bare knee and the way her robe dangled open, exposing a little of her small breasts, made him smile. He closed the door and secured the deadbolt, adding one final order for the guard. "*No molestar!*"

Marshall said to him with a huge smile.

"*Si, si, señor!*" The guard replied with a hearty laugh.

Marshall pulled off his coat and tie, following them with his shirt as he made his way to Angel. She smiled as she took a sip of her drink and tried not to cringe when Marshall dropped to the floor in front of her, running his hand up her leg and under the robe. As he caressed the top of her thigh, she closed her eyes and moaned like it was the most wonderful feeling in the world. Then she decided to play hard to get and put her knees together, squeezing her thighs against his hand while laughing hysterically.

"Ah…my little China doll wants to play!" Marshall pulled off his pants and shoes and stood in front of her in his boxers. Taking her hand, he placed it down in his boxers and wrapped her fingers around his engorged penis.

"Just le' me finish my drink firs'." Angel pulled back her hand and wrapped her fingers around her glass, slurring her words as her head rolled back on her shoulders.

Marshall took the glass from her and smelled of it before putting it back in front of her.

"Bourbon? Good! You left the whiskey for me. A girl after my own heart…and everything that goes with it." Marshall chuckled as he reached for the whiskey bottle in the fridge. "You drank both the bourbons? You are a little fish, aren't you? No wonder you're so relaxed." Marshall pulled off his boxers and posed for Angel.

Angel smiled as if approving the object of his pride, but what she wanted to do was saw it off with the dull, serrated plastic knife, the one she had used as a screwdriver. The thought made her smile bigger, and Marshall moved his hips suggestively, thinking he was really turning her on.

He took the whiskey bottle and began trying to turn the cap, but it was stuck too tightly, thanks to the very old honey now in the trash can.

"Damn! I can't screw it off! I'll tell the guard to get me a bottle out of my car." Marshall started toward the door, but Angel stopped him.

"Here!" Angel stood but remembered to feign wobbliness. "Le' me show you how it's done, Mis'er!" Angel took the bottle and staggered to the sink, where she turned on the hot water and let it run over the cap. In no time, she had the cap unscrewed and handed it to Marshall, who smiled with approval.

"No screw too hard for me." Giving her best drunken laugh, Angel sat on the edge of the table and picked up her drink while Marshall poured his whiskey into the same plastic glass he had used earlier.

"I think I'll drink it straight so I can catch up with you, little darling, but in bed. Don't want you to pass out on me before I get my fill." Marshall took a big swallow from the glass, and Angel held her breath, hoping it would not taste different to him.

Marshall licked his lips and took another big gulp. "American! Has a bite to it." Taking her hand, he led Angel to the bed, but stopped her beside it and snatched her robe off. After taking another big drink of whiskey, he began the foreplay he thought she wanted. Angel lay on her back with one hand over her head and her eyes closed, pretending this was not happening.

Maybe this wasn't such a good idea after all.

She heard him fumbling with the whiskey glass as he took one more gulp and finished off the whiskey.

"Now…le' see wh' I ca' do!" Marshall's speech was already slurred as he climbed on top of her, trying to insert what was obviously his pride and joy, considering the way he flaunted it, but it seemed he was having trouble with his aim. Angel lay still, praying the capsules would work exceptionally fast, and was rewarded with his dead weight dropping on top of her, followed by one gigantic snore. Rolling him off her was no easy chore, so she inched her way over and pulled herself out from under him. Quickly, she dressed in her panties and bra and threw on the short robe. She would have to call the guard in and knew it would look suspicious if Marshall was naked and she was fully dressed. Hurrying to the kitchen sink, she mixed dishwashing detergent in hot water, making a thick foamy solution.

Angel tugged at Marshall until she finally got him on his side. Again, she was tempted to use the plastic knife on him but decided there just wasn't enough time. Instead, she smeared the foam all over his mouth and let it drizzle down onto the bed. Pulling the rod from under the bed, she propped it behind the door and then began calling for the guard and beating on the door.

"*Señor Chapman! Ayuda! Ayuda!*" Angel hoped she remembered the Spanish word for "help" correctly and continued to call and pound on the door. The guard began knocking and saying something in Spanish she didn't understand, and then she remembered the door was locked from the inside.

Unlocking the deadbolt, she jerked the door open as the guard rushed in. Angel pointed to Marshall's naked body lying on the bed with the foam still seeming to pour from his mouth. As the guard began shaking Marshall and feeling for a pulse, Angel grabbed the rod and tiptoed up behind him.

With one hard swing, she knocked the guard away from the bed. He lay rolling on the floor, holding his head and moaning. Angel held the rod over her head and brought it down on him again as hard as she could, and then one more time for good measure. Blood spurted from the man's head, and he lay still.

"Sorry!" Angel whispered as she hurriedly dressed and put on her socks and boots. Once outside, she took no time to look for other guards but headed for the Jeep driven by the guard.

"Please, God, let the key be in it!" Angel climbed in and was rewarded for her prayer. After starting the Jeep, she slammed it into reverse and slid sideways out of the parking area. She had no idea where she was going, but she intended on getting there fast. When she hit the main highway, she headed north, the direction she and Tobi had gone when they left Villa Bonito the first time.

"Should I hide in the rainforest or head to the nearest town? Tobi, where are you when I need you?" Angel was talking aloud, hoping it would help her make a decision. Remembering the bumpy trail and the sounds of animals, and not wanting to repeat that in the dark, she decided to head for the nearest town, twenty miles ahead.

*** *

Hawk woke with a start. Raven was leaning over him, shaking him.

"Let's go!" Raven was glad to see Hawk had slept

in his clothes, ready to go on a moment's notice.

"Someone spotted her?" Hawk asked as he crawled into the big SUV.

"Yes. She's in a borrowed Jeep, if you know what I mean, and is heading east toward San Pablo. If we hurry, we can cut her off. Fasten your seatbelt. This will be a rough ride."

Raven headed out a different gate from the one the rangers had brought them through, and Hawk hoped the road would not be as rough.

Driving on the other one was a son-of-a-bitch! Hawk held tight to the roll bar, just in case.

For ten minutes, they bounced and careened all over the dirt road, but it was better than the road from the previous day.

Up ahead, Hawk could see the main road. Raven hit it without looking to see if any traffic was coming, and they lucked out. Skidding sideways and squealing tires, Raven floored it. Within ten miles, they could see blue lights up ahead, and Hawk hoped this was a roadblock of Raven's doing and not a wreck with Angel in the middle of it.

Raven slammed on his brakes at the group of police cars that had the road blocked, jumped from the SUV leaving the door open, and ran in the direction of voices and people.

As the lights circled, Raven saw her, sitting on the ground beside one of the police cars. A white Jeep sat with two wheels in a ditch to the right, teetering on the passenger side. The police officer had squatted down beside her and was writing information on a pad, information he could not understand since his English was not very good.

"Angel!" Raven yelled. The girl stood, cupping her hand over her eyes so she could see through the blue strobe, looking around to find the voice she thought she heard calling her name. Two men were jogging toward her, and for a second she was afraid it was Marshall back from his dead sleep, but the way one of the men moved seemed familiar. The lights hit him, and she saw his hair was silver and he had a beard.

"Angel!" Raven called again, but when she didn't respond, he yelled, "Tulen!"

Leaving the policeman with his notepad, she ran toward the man who was no stranger to her even though he looked totally different from the man she remembered.

"Angel!" Raven called once more as the girl neared him. Tulen, his little pixie Angel, leapt into her father's arms.

Chapter Thirteen

When Tobi woke in the night to a throbbing head, he reached for the pill the doctor had left for him. But as he pulled his arm from under the cover to reach, he felt a warm body next to him. Slowly, he turned over, and there she was, Angel, sound asleep, with her hands under her cheek.

Tobi brushed his fingers over her other cheek and smiled through his tears. She was safe. Shade had said she would be found and home before the day ended—but why had he not come for him? The pounding in his head reminded him of why he couldn't go, and he lay back and said a prayer of thanks for Angel's safe return. Wanting to be pain-free when he awoke in the morning, he reached for the pill again. With his arm around his fiancée, Tobi drifted into a peaceful sleep.

The next morning was a celebration and a renewal. Angel had found her dad and openly announced she would not lose him again. Raven smiled but kept quiet, and Custer knew he was worried about how this could all come to fruition.

Tobi was much better, or so he said, and he pulled Angel onto his lap every chance he got. Several times, he caught Shade smiling as he watched the two of them, and Tobi wondered if Shade would be the one to walk Angel down the aisle. He didn't know what Custer and Shade had discussed when they left the preserve, but

Custer seemed worried.

Hawk watched his uncle like the hawk he was named for, worried that this was all too much for Custer's heart. He knew Sue Ann, at home in Montana, was wringing her hands in worry for Custer as well as for Tobi and Angel and him.

After breakfast, Custer asked to speak to Raven in private, and the two men went into the office.

"It's time for me to get back to Sue Ann, Raven. What time I have left, I want to spend with her. Angel will not leave you, and that was to be expected. I don't imagine Tobi will leave Angel, so that means Hawk and I will be heading to the airport without them."

"Custer, I don't know what to say. I can only thank you for risking your life to protect my daughter and for taking care of Sue Ann and Betsy all these years. I hope you are wrong about your heart, but please enjoy what time you have left without worrying about Sue Ann. She's a strong lady. She proved that when she took Betsy to Alaska all those years ago, and when she fought and won her battle with breast cancer. How wonderful that Tobi found his way back to her, and now she has grandchildren."

Custer made no reply to Raven's remarks, knowing he was trying to justify not coming back to Sue Ann.

"Can you get us a ride to the airport?"

"Of course. I'll get one of the rangers to drive you." He pulled out his cell phone and dialed. "Sophia, have one of the men pull the SUV around. Custer and Hawk need a ride to the airport."

The two men shook hands before Custer turned to leave the office. As he reached the door, he spoke to his old friend with the Crow wisdom he was famous for, but he kept his back to Raven.

"It is better for a man to act on what is in his heart rather than on what is in his head." Custer walked through the door without looking back.

****

Angel hugged Custer and Hawk as they left for the airport and thanked them for coming to the rescue for her and Tobi. She did not say when, or if, she would return to Montana but asked them to give her love to Sue Ann, Betsy, and Trapper. Hawk decided it was best not to tell Sue Ann the truth about what had transpired in Costa Rica, and they agreed just to tell her Angel had unfinished business she needed to take care of before she and Tobi married.

Tobi was in no condition to travel and wanted to stay with Angel until he had to return for his visit with his daughter in two weeks. Before Hawk and Custer left, Tobi confided in them that he was afraid Angel would not leave her father. With handshakes and hopes for happiness, Custer and Hawk got into the SUV that was waiting for them.

To Custer's surprise, Sophia drove them to San Jose.

It was a quiet ride, with only small talk when there was talk. Sophia's first language was Spanish, but Custer knew that was not why she was quiet. When they reached the airport, Hawk got out and opened the tailgate, retrieving what little was left of what they had brought with them to Costa Rica.

Hawk, sensing Sophia had something to say to Custer, walked inside the terminal to wait on his uncle.

"This Sue Ann...she loves Whiteman very much?" Sophia spoke in English.

94

"More than life itself," Custer answered and turned away from her.

"I love him, too." Sophia called to Custer before getting back in the car.

Custer made no reply other than to thank her for the ride and kept walking toward the terminal door held open for him by Hawk.

****

He watched as the two men headed for their gate to board their flight back to Montana. Angela was nowhere in the terminal.

Damn that Marshall! I should have known he and his two-bit cronies would botch everything. I should have listened when the boss told me the Chapman kid was all dick and no brains. And who wouldn't risk it all for bedtime with Angela? I should know. If she's with her father in that compound, I'll never get to her. Besides, that ex-detective from the Denver Police Department is with her. I'll have to find different bait— maybe in Montana. The CIA report from Alaska said Shockey was shacked up with the school principal, Dr. Sue Ann Parish. He went by the name Shade Dubois back then. Dr. Parish lives in the mountains out from Red Lodge, now. If I had known how difficult Costa Rica would be, I'd have watched Sue Ann Parish's place instead of watching Tobi with Angela. Now that was a hard scene to watch without rushing down and shooting the bastard, but I'll be more careful when I take Dr. Parish. She's in her sixties, so she should be an easy capture.

The man left his hiding place and headed back to San Jose. He had one more chance at Angela, and he wouldn't leave Costa Rica without trying. Besides, he wanted some time alone with her himself, and he knew she would not be leaving Costa Rica any time soon, at least not until after the deadline, and by then, she'd be an adult orphan again.

Chapter Fourteen

Sue Ann and Custer sat on the porch looking at the Beartooths in silence until Sue Ann reached over and placed her hand on top of her husband's.

"You were so restless in your sleep last night. Are you feeling all right, dear? You probably need to get checked by Doc after the trip to Costa Rica. I still can't believe you wouldn't tell me the truth about where you and Hawk were going."

It was the first time she had spoken of the trip in the week since Custer and Hawk had been back. She seemed to accept the explanation of Angel staying to complete her assignment for the CIA, and that he and Hawk had found out Angel was being followed and so headed to Costa Rica to protect her and Tobi. Sue Ann missed her son and her future daughter-in-law.

"I'll be fine. No need to worry Doc to death about something he cannot fix." Custer entwined his fingers with hers.

"I'm glad Tobi will be home tonight, and in another week, Carrie will be here for her summer visit." she added, changing the subject from Custer's weak heart, which gave them both undue grief.

"Yes. It will be good to see Carrie again." He reached into his pocket for a nitro tablet as he felt his heart's erratic beat.

"I think I'll get a cup of coffee. Do you want a cup,

Custer, and maybe a piece of strawberry rhubarb pie? I saved the last piece for you since it's your favorite."

"Yes, that would be nice. Thank you, Sue Ann." He held to her hand, preventing her departure, and pulled her down for a kiss. "I love you, my wife. You are the essence of all that has been happiest in my life. I hope you know that."

Sue Ann placed her hand on her husband's face, kissed him, and smiled into his eyes before going inside.

Custer closed his eyes and leaned his head back, trying to lessen the hard pain he felt in his chest. As the gentle touch of a mountain breeze brushed across his face, the pain left him, and he knew.

Opening his eyes, he saw the brave descending the mountain trail, leading a second pony, the great appaloosa stallion from Custer's own youth. This time the brave stopped and beckoned to Custer to come. Stepping off the porch, Custer found renewed strength and a strong heart, and when he looked down, he was wearing moose-hide pants and moccasins but no shirt. His chest felt tight, robust, strengthened by muscle sinew perfectly placed by the Creator of All Things, and he puffed it out in pride. Custer was a young warrior again, with black braids hanging to his waist and the headband wrapped around his forehead holding a single white feather, the tail feather of his animal spirit.

The brave handed Custer the reins of the appaloosa, and with one fast swing of his body, Custer mounted it, ready to ride bareback. Trusting the brave to lead, Custer rode beside him, but soon the mountains ceased being the Beartooths. The Pryor Mountains formed shadows around them, reminding Custer of his birthplace on the reservation. He was home.

The Crow Fair, a highlight for his people, was coming to an end as "Ashéeleetaalissua," The Last Dance, began. Custer, honored by his people, was handed the pipe by his grandmother, a carrier for the Tobacco Society. Custer no longer felt unworthy and took the pipe, leading the four eagle dancers around the parade grounds. Custer had seen combat and returned to his people without injuries. He was forgiven for his bad days.

Looking into the glowing crimson of this, his last sunset, he lifted his hands and gave thanks to the Creator for bestowing such an honor on him in the last moments of his earthly existence, and he thanked Him for Sue Ann.

With the Pryors in the distance, the young braves, now silhouettes against the crimson backdrop, kicked their steeds into full gallop, giving a final war whoop that rolled across the sky like crackling thunder; red cinders shot from their horses' hooves, fire to be added to sunsets that others, like Sue Ann, would see, and they would remember. Horses and young braves faded like ghostly shadows, heaven bound, as Custer's feather released from his headband and gracefully floated back to earth. His final feather had fallen.

Chapter Fifteen

Angel ran, following the trail the compound map had shown. She knew her father would have objected to her running without a guard, but she needed to be alone. She missed Tobi and was wishing she had gone back to Montana with him. She loved being with her father, but he was suffocating her. He had told Sophia to know where she was at all times, and this had really ticked Angel off. She did not like the beautiful Sophia, and she knew Sophia and her dad were sleeping together. She had forgotten to knock when she walked into her father's quarters one morning early. Her dad was gone, but when she walked into the bedroom, she found Sophia naked in his bed. Sophia had sat up when she walked in, not bothering to cover herself and just smiled at her as if to say, "He's mine!"

She wanted to talk to her dad about Sophia, but she could not get up the nerve. Maybe she'd talk to him tomorrow.

****

He had his binoculars focused on Angela as she rounded the corner of the compound. He had been told the northwest tower was rarely guarded since it overlooked the Pacific Ocean, and this proved to be true. Digging a hole under the fence, he had been able to infiltrate the compound with little effort. As he hid in the shadows, a good spot near the trail where Angela liked to run, he opened the bottle of chloroform and poured some on the bandana.

Once she's out, she will be no problem to carry through the trees to the boat tied below on the beach. I'll have my bait; I'll have Angela. My man just better be ready and have the boat running.

****

A few more feet and Angel would make the turn that would take her back to the front of the compound. It was an easy run, and mixed with the wonderful gym equipment her father had, she could stay fit and gain in strength. Her father had promised to teach her Tai Kwon Do, something that might save her from another scenario like the nightmare she had gone through earlier in Costa Rica, as well as the incident when her briefcase was stolen.

Just before reaching the turn, Angel's cell phone rang. Looking at the screen, she saw it was Tobi. She stopped in the shade, smiling to herself.

"Hi, babe! I miss you." As Angel listened, her smile faded.

"Oh, no! Poor Sue Ann!" Angel wiped at the tears running down her cheeks. "I wish I was there with you, but there's no way Dad will let me come back until he's sure it's safe. I'll call Sue Ann and Betsy later. Will you tell them I'm thinking of them and I love them?" She started jogging back the way she had come. "I love you, too." She sped up to a run, and before her stalker could get near her, she was out of sight.

"Damn!" he said under his breath as he made his way back to the trailhead.

****

Angel glared at Sophia as she walked up to the

patio where the woman sat beside her father.

"Dad, I need to speak to you—in private." Angel kept her eyes on her father, refusing to look toward Sophia.

"Sure, sweetheart. Let's go up to my quarters." Shade put his arm around Angel. "Where did you run? Did you stay on the main trail like I told you?"

Angel ignored her father's question, knowing he would be mad if he knew she had been on the ocean side, but she loved to look out over the deep blue water. Rather than answering, she dove right into the news from Tobi.

"Dad, Custer died this morning. A heart attack."

Shade stopped at the door to his quarters.

"What?" He looked at his daughter, hoping he had not heard her correctly.

"Custer is dead." Tears ran down Angel's cheeks, and her dad pulled her to him, hugging her and kissing the top of her head.

"I am so sorry, sweetheart." Shade led her to the sofa, where he sat by her and held her hand. "This has to be devastating to Sue Ann and Betsy, and of course Hawk, Trapper, and Tobi. Eagle was a good man. No— he was so much more than that. He was a great warrior."

"Dad, we need to go to her...to Sue Ann. She needs us. She needs you."

"Angel, you don't know what you're saying. I can't go back to Sue Ann. I don't want her to know I'm alive—for her sake and for Betsy's."

"You mean for Sophia's sake!" Angel folded her arms and waited to see if her dad would defend his woman.

"Don't take this out on Sophia. She has enough problems of her own, Angel."

"She didn't seem to have any problems when I saw her two days ago—in your bed."

"What are you talking about?" Shade stood waiting for his daughter's explanation.

"I forgot to knock. It was early, and I thought you and I could eat breakfast on the patio. I opened the door and she was...she was naked...in your bed."

Shade combed his hands through his hair. "I'm sorry you saw that, Angel. You should have knocked. I was going to tell you, but..."

"I don't want to know anything about Sophia. You can't possibly love her like you loved Sue Ann. Admit it!"

"Angel, please...this is not up for discussion. I'm sorry for Sue Ann's loss, but it's been too many years...too much has happened, and I could still put her at risk."

"I want to go back to Montana. Sue Ann, Betsy, Hawk, and Trapper are my family. They are Tobi's family, and I need to be there for them."

"I'm sorry, Angel. It's too dangerous. You can't go right now, but as soon as it's clear, I promise I'll take you myself if I have to."

"And risk seeing Sue Ann?" Angel was crying again.

"No. I can't see Sue Ann, Angel. It could never work."

Angel ran from her father's quarters, almost bumping into Sophia, who stood on the stairs and trailed her with her stare.

Shade gave Sophia the order for Angel to be

watched closely the next few days, afraid she would try to leave and go back to Montana. He did not leave his quarters the rest of the day or that night and didn't answer the door when Sophia knocked.

Moving into the one room where no one but he was allowed, he took a bottle of whiskey and sat in the easy chair with the big ottoman, the same chair where he had held Sue Ann after she wrecked on the Alaskan mountain pass; the chair he had directed his old friend Jake to rescue before burning down the cabin. He turned the lights off so the room was pitch dark and hit the remote.

The wall rumbled softly as the huge painting appeared from nowhere; strobe lights danced across the canvas, illuminating the masterpiece that reached from the floor to the ceiling, giving it the illusion of moving like real skies. Classical music softly surrounded him with memories, flashbacks of loving beyond the boundaries of forever. The handsome couple stood spellbound, looking up into nature's incredible display, and Madame Aurora danced. Golden tresses of hair spilled from under the woman's green velvet hood as eyes already dazzling green changed in hue with each twirl of Madame Aurora's silk skirt. Sue Ann's emerald eyes gazed up through a white wolf ruff into her lover's face. Tightly, he embraced her, as he beheld her, his only love, through eyes so blue they cut ice daggers through the effervescent glow from the goddess's heavenly stage. He smiled through raven wings, the smile of total, unequaled contentment only love brings, love that could never be matched or duplicated in this world.

Custer's words invaded Shade's nostalgia.

"It is better for a man to act on what is in his heart than on what is in his head."

****

For over a week, he waited on the ocean trail inside the compound, but Angela never showed. With time getting too close to the deadline that would either make him a multi-millionaire or doom him to poverty like his mother, he packed up and headed for Montana to capture new bait for Jon Shockey.

Dr. Sue Ann Parish will not get away like Angela.

Chapter Sixteen

Sue Ann sat on the porch alone, trying not to think. It had been days since Custer's death, but she could not let him go.

I never realized how precious he was until it was too late. All I could do was compare him to Shade, and in so doing, I missed out on so many wonderful years we could have had together.

Rising, she went inside the cabin to shower and dress. She was meeting Betsy in town for lunch at the Pollard. Perhaps they would go on a little shopping spree, even though Sue Ann's heart was not in it. She knew Betsy was grieving for Custer as well, but she had to restrain her show of emotions to try to help Hawk come to terms with his own grief.

Carrie was at the end of her summer visit with her dad, but almost as soon as she got to Montana, her dad had taken her to Costa Rica to get to know Angel, since Angel didn't think she would be back before Carrie's visit ended, especially since that was sooner than originally planned.

As Sue Ann entered the great room of the cabin, she stopped and once again let her eyes move to the portrait over the fireplace. With only one quick glance, she turned away and ascended the stairs, ready to remove herself from all heartache for at least the afternoon.

****

Betsy and Sue Ann both ordered soup and salad, something light and with very little sustenance. They were not good for each other in their dissimilar states of grief, but each played at cheerfulness for the other's sake.

"I'm thinking of going to Mississippi, Betsy. Elizabeth is begging me to come, and I need to get away for a while. I've not seen her in so long. Will you be all right while I'm away?" Sue Ann put her hand on top of Betsy's.

"Of course, Mom. I have Hawk and Trapper to help keep my mind off..." Betsy did not finish what she was saying. At the moment, she felt she would burst into tears all over again if she said Custer's name. "Let's go to Billings before you leave and do some heavy-duty shopping and maybe take in a movie. Hawk will keep Trapper. Neither of us have been to town in a long time, and I know you need a new wardrobe to take to Mississippi. Elizabeth will not like you looking drab, especially since you've lost more weight."

"Good idea, Betsy. And while we are in Billings, I'll get my hair trimmed on the ends." Sue Ann reached for her braid and pulled it to the front so she could examine the ends. "Maybe I should think about getting my hair colored so I don't look so old and tired."

"Mom, you are beautiful as you are. Yes, you need some color in your cheeks, but Mississippi sunshine will fix that."

Just as Betsy and Sue Ann were about to leave, a man dressed for business approached their table.

"Mrs. Sue Ann Larson?" he asked as Sue Ann pushed her chair out from the table.

"Actually, I'm Dr. Sue Ann Parish, but I was married to Custer Larson. I'm an author, so I kept my maiden name. How do you know me or my husband?"

"Is there a place we could speak in private?" The man was not from Red Lodge, as evidenced by his expensive suit and non-cowboy/all-business demeanor. Sue Ann and Betsy looked at each other, both questioning why someone like this had business with her.

Moving to a corner of the hotel lobby, Sue Ann and Betsy sat on one of the sofas and waited while the man rummaged through his briefcase.

"Here we go." The man took a seat across from them and opened the manila envelope he was holding. "Oh, I am so sorry. I forgot to introduce myself. I am Ben Abernathy, an attorney with Dunlap & King in Billings. This is concerning the estate left to you by your late husband, Custer Larson."

"Estate? I have no idea what you are talking about. I am on the deed for Custer's land and cabin already, and I get his retirement from the Forestry Service, not that I need the small check. Custer never mentioned anything about an estate."

"I think you will definitely want to hear what I am about to tell you. There is a substantial amount of money in an account in Billings…"

"An account in Billings?" Betsy turned to her mother. "Mom, you didn't know anything about this?"

"Excuse me, but there is more." He cleared his throat before beginning again. "And there are substantial amounts in accounts in New York City and Memphis, Tennessee, just to name the domestic accounts."

"The domestic accounts?" Sue Ann asked. "How many accounts did my husband have, Mr. Abernathy?"

"Please call me Ben." Again he cleared his throat before answering. "Three in the U.S., one in the Cayman Islands, and one in Switzerland."

"This is preposterous!" Sue Ann stood and walked to the window, Betsy on her heels.

"Mom, what is going on?" Betsy whispered. "I'm calling Hawk and telling him to get over here." Betsy reached for her cell phone, but her mother stopped her.

"No, Betsy. Not until we hear Ben out. Whatever is going on, or went on, could be just as big a shock to Hawk as it is to me, or it could be nothing." Sue Ann returned to Ben, looking as if this whole scenario was unbelievable.

"Let's start again…Ben." She took a deep breath before asking the next question. "How much are we talking about in these mysterious bank accounts?" Sue Ann reached for Betsy's hand as if knowing this would be a bombshell.

"Let's see." Ben turned pages, adding numbers on his phone's calculator. Taking his glasses off, he looked up to see two pairs of eyes staring at him.

"I can't give you an exact figure because some of the money is invested, but it is in the neighborhood of ten million dollars for your part, plus there will be interest to add."

"What do you mean 'for my part'?" Sue Ann eyed the man.

"A portion of the estate was left to Mr. Larson's nephew, a…" He looked back to another manila envelope. "A Hawk Thomas Larson, but I'll have to speak to him about that, since it is confidential."

"Mr. Abernathy, I'm Hawk's wife, Betsy."

"Please. Call me Ben. I'm sure we will know each other well by the time this estate is settled. You will be happy to know our firm is well educated and experienced in matters of international banking and in dealing with the proration of large estates. Mr. Larson, Mr. Custer Larson, has been with us for twenty-five years, in fact."

Sue Ann turned to Betsy. "I think it's time for you to call Hawk, but let's move this conversation to your house, Betsy. Too many people come in and out of the Pollard."

By late that afternoon, Sue Ann, Betsy, and Hawk all sat in shock, not understanding where all this money had come from in joint bank accounts in their names as well as Custer's.

Hawk sat especially quiet. Sue Ann suspected he knew more than he was telling, while Betsy stared at him. Finally, Hawk jumped to his feet and stood by the window. His thighs were getting the same treatment they always did when he was nervous, and would be raw by the end of this conversation.

"Okay! Here's as much as I can tell you." He turned to face Betsy and Sue Ann. "Uncle Custer had a past, one he regretted, and one I only recently found out about. I knew he had made money, but I figured he had given it all away to charities. I had no idea…"

"Past? What kind of past? Open up, Hawk. As his wife, I deserved to know, but he never even gave a hint. What kind of past is so lucrative a man has to hide his millions in…" Sue Ann counted on her fingers and held up one hand fingers spread apart. "Five banks, including the two international?"

"I can't tell you any more, Sue Ann." With this, Hawk grabbed his hat and headed for the barn with Trapper on his heels. Soon Betsy and Sue Ann watched as Hawk and Trapper headed off across the pasture on their horses.

****

A week later, Sue Ann and Betsy did indeed go on a shopping spree, but it was not for what Betsy thought it would be. She and her mom hit every fly shop in Billings, updated their fly fishing equipment to the best Winston had to offer, bought new waders, and everything they could think of for life in the Montana outdoors. Then they stopped by Red Lodge and purchased exotic cowgirl boots, jeans, and everything western they could find and desired, making the sisters at Whispering Pines very happy, as well as Heidi in Paris Montana. Sue Ann also purchased a wonderful primitive pie safe that Lynette in Twice Touched told her had originated in Mississippi prior to the War Between the States. This would be delivered when Sue Ann got back from her trip, but the back of Betsy's Suburban was loaded with all the other treasures. Betsy could tell her mother had something on her mind, and it was confession time.

"Mom, I know you love to fly fish and you haven't been able to do any in several years, but how and where exactly are you going to do all this fishing?" As Betsy hit the bumpy road to her mother's cabin, she glanced over at her and noticed her mother smiling as if she had a secret she was bursting to tell.

"Let's unload all my new gear, get a glass of good old southern sweet tea, sit on the porch, and I'll tell you what's on my mind, daughter." Sue Ann literally jumped from the vehicle and began loading her arms and carrying everything inside.

It took several trips, but before long her haul was unloaded and filled the dining portion of the great room. After pouring the tea over ice, Sue Ann handed Betsy her sweet tea, and they headed for the front porch, to the rockers that held many secrets, much misery and sadness, and more than a fair share of happiness and contentment, not to mention having been the inspiration for several contemporary western romances over the years.

"Okay, Betsy. Here's the new Dr. Sue Ann Parish—the customized Dr. Sue Ann Parish." Sue Ann took a sip of tea before starting.

"For years, I've been the queen of doom and gloom, first over losing Tate and then Tobi and having to raise a daughter alone—one I adore, by the way, but one I allowed to consume every bit of me just to make sure she was happy. I was eaten up with guilt, better known as Unwed Mother Syndrome." Betsy started to protest, but Sue Ann threw up her hand to stop her. "Just hear me out, Betsy."

Betsy sat back and took a sip of tea, giving her mother her full, silent attention.

"Then, just when I had resigned myself to being alone…in bed…for the rest of my life…Bam! Shade Dubois! Need I say more about that?" Sue Ann rolled her hand toward Betsy to let her know she could speak.

"Movie-star good-looking! I'm following you so far." Betsy began to rock as she waited for the rest of her mother's story.

"After Shade, I spent years writing romance rather than looking for and experiencing romance; living vicariously from hero to hero—all fictitious hunks with extraordinary endowments, if you get my jist, bigger than the Big Sky Country—and getting my real-life battery recharged about three times a year with visits to Montana..." Sue Ann cut her eyes and leaned toward Betsy. "And Custer."

Betsy almost choked on tea with this disclosure but managed to regain her composure.

"Don't mind me! Continue, Mom. I think we have a tell-all exposé in the works for our next book." Betsy and Sue Ann laughed, and Sue Ann began again with proclamations performed like a Broadway actor, with many side conversations and directions—a soliloquy with her audience of one.

"After years of denial and the resurfacing of ghost Tate, I bit the bullet, chose to marry Custer—something I regret not doing years before—only to lose him after three years of heavenly married bliss." Sue Ann spoke softly and sighed as if worn out with the drama of her life.

"My life has been wonderful—to an extent. Tragic—way more than necessary. One full of regret." Sue Ann looked down, shaking her head in supposed sadness. Looking up at Betsy, her sadness was replaced with a wide grin as she became louder and more animated. "NOT...FOR...ONE...DAMN...MINUTE!"

At this, Betsy applauded, then twisted her fist in the air and hooted.

"Shout it out, Mom! You've needed this outburst for years. Don't stop now. You're on a roll!"

"But..." Sue Ann stuck her finger up to make her next point to her daughter and to the mountains if they were listening. "I'll not replay even one second of it, no matter what. I'm getting my unfit skinny ass off this porch. I'm not sitting here talking to the mountains that talked back only to my darling Crow husband Custer. I'm buying myself a nice new rig that will get me wherever in the hell I want to go, in comfort and at great expense at the gas pump. And I'll go anywhere in the world I choose to go! All of this paid for with the millions my dear sweet husband made selling himself to the devil, or in some other dastardly way I prefer to remain, in an author term, *unbeknownst*. Do I make myself clear, daughter?"

"Yes, ma'am. Clear as the Montana sky over the Beartooths!" Betsy was smiling from ear to ear as she stood and held up the wine of the South.

"A toast to my mother, always my inspiration, and a person I hope to envy in her new adventure."

Sue Ann stood and clicked her tea glass with her daughter's.

A new book—a book of life renewed—was about to be written.

Chapter Seventeen

Dr. Sue Ann Parish packed up her laptop and two suitcases of new outfits and left the next day for a health spa in Arizona. She tried to get Betsy to go with her, but Betsy just could not leave Hawk and Trapper. To Sue Ann's surprise, Elizabeth joined her at the spa two days later.

After her friend had gotten over the initial shock of Sue Ann's decision to "customize her life" as she called it, and her disclosure about Custer's secret life that included millions left in an estate, the fun set in.

"Okay, now, Sue Ann, why exactly am I here? Yes, I need to lose ten or twenty pounds, but look at you. You look wonderful—well, maybe a little too thin. So here's the deal. Anything I want to eat, I'll hand over to you."

"Yes, but I want to look wonderful-er! I guess that would be more wonderful, but I'm having so much fun not being me, it's hard to stop myself!" Sue Ann grabbed Elizabeth's arm, and they headed to the suite they would be sharing for the next week.

"Are you pretending, Sue Ann? I know when I talked to you two weeks ago, you were terribly depressed over losing Custer. That can't have changed."

Sue Ann's smile left her face for a few seconds.

"Of course, I miss Custer, and yes, I'd go back to

the old me in a second if I knew it would bring him back to me, but I can't hole up there in the mountains anymore. I've done nothing but brood for years, decades actually, and I don't want to spend the time I have left on this earth grieving over things I can't change. I'm cancer-free, but I don't know I'll stay that way, so I just have to pull myself up by the bra straps and take drastic measures. Oh, wait…I don't have any boobs, so I don't have a bra by which to pull myself up. Will I go back to Montana and the cabin in the Beartooths? Absolutely! It will always be home, and once I get myself fit and on track the way I used to be, I'll enjoy it even more. I'll hike, ride horses, and fly fish with Betsy, Hawk, and Trapper, and hopefully Tobi and Angel will be back at home by the time I get back. And I've got my friends Wanda and Devery looking for a vintage camper for me, so I can travel with Sisters on the Fly, something I've wanted to do for a long time."

"All right. Where do we start?" Elizabeth held Sue Ann out away from her and gave her a good up-and-down look.

"Well, I already walk three miles every day, and each day I get a little faster. I'm taking online classes to teach me how to eat healthy, and I peruse every magazine I can find to see what women in their sixties look like who are considered chic."

"Uh-uh…no, ma'am, I will not let you cut your hair to where you can't have braids when you go back to Montana. That would be a big mistake, Sue Ann."

"No, I won't cut my hair, but the gray is about to go. And you and I both know I won't spend the time to straighten my hair every day, so I'm going *au natural*…curly." Sue Ann picked up a magazine and showed Elizabeth a picture of a woman a little younger than she, with long, naturally curly hair. "This will be me—blonde and curly, sassy…even for an old fart."

By the end of the week, Sue Ann was the target of many flirtatious instructors, ages forty and up, but Sue Ann was not ready for romance. Regardless of the façade she wore, her heart still ached for Custer.

Sue Ann and Elizabeth hugged as they went to their separate gates at the airport. Selfies galore were messaged off to Betsy and Tobi, whose mouths gaped in disbelief on the other end in Montana and Costa Rica. Betsy had told her mother she looked very young with her blonde curls and her daughter would have to think about covering the few gray strands cropping up in her own hair or risk looking older than her mother.

In Costa Rica, Tobi wanted to show Shade a picture his mom had sent, but he decided against it. Shade hadn't discussed her with him, and Angel thought Shade was still in a relationship with Sophia, the manager of the preserve. Angel had seen Sophia coming out of his quarters early in the morning on several occasions since Tobi had returned to Costa Rica.

Tobi tried to talk to Shade about the deadline on the blood money in the Swiss bank account to see if he trusted it enough to let Angel go home after it ended. Angel was getting cabin—or preserve—fever and often felt she was being held captive by her father, but Shade was just not sure the information he had gotten was trustworthy.

Chapter Eighteen

Shade stayed close to the monitors, not because he thought there would be a threat to his daughter's safety, but because he did not feel like conversing with anyone. The man who had saved his life all those years ago was dead, leaving Sue Ann, the woman he and Custer both loved, unprotected. He thought about talking to Tobi, convincing him to go back and stay with Sue Ann, just in case. Angel had told him what was in the document left for her by an informant.

Some son-of-a-bitch out there knows everyone who has ever been important to me, and I'm not there to protect them.

He was interrupted by a knock at the door, a soft undemanding knock. Sophia.

She entered the office and took a seat at one of the monitors beside him.

"I am sorry to have to report this to you, but there has been a breach in the outer perimeter." She knew this would alarm him, and she was not wrong.

"What?" Shade jumped up from the desk. "Where?" He headed for the door, and she followed him.

"Pacific side, northwest corner. Someone dig under wall. Footsteps on beach below, boat is come and away, and footsteps go up to ridge."

"Get Tobi and Angel."

In minutes, Shade, Tobi, Angel, and Sophia were tearing through the compound on the Argo. All were armed, and two other guards followed in a second Argo.

When they reached the tower, Shade disembarked first, seeing the breach.

"Damn! How did this happen? Sophia, I told you I wanted all guards in towers at all four corners while Angel is here. ¿Comprendes?" He was so angry with Sophia that even Angel felt sorry for her.

"I am sorry. I thought it better to have guards closer to your daughter." Sophia moved to one side with her phone and called for guards to report to the back towers immediately.

Shade began following the trail to see if he could find footprints, but all he found was an old, dried set of very small tennis shoe tracks. Sitting on his heels, he measured the tracks with his hand, which more than covered it. Without saying anything, he raised his eyes and looked straight at Angel.

Angel folded her arms and looked away.

"Do I need to say anything, Angel?"

"But that was two weeks ago—during the dry season."

"I fix problem. No need for...how you say... preacher?"

"Preaching." Angel corrected and smiled at Sophia as a way of saying thanks for taking up for her.

"Call in every person on payroll. I want this compound secure."

Shade got back in the Argo, and everyone followed except Sophia, who had her ear to her cell phone.

That evening, Shade called Angel, Tobi, and

Sophia into his office, directing them all to take seats.

"Sophia, I will be leaving—indefinitely. I am leaving you in complete charge of the preserve. As soon as I can find someone knowledgeable about what we are doing here to help the people of Costa Rica as well as to keep the medical research going, I will let you know, but consider this your home for as long as you want it. Our connections in the government will assist you as they have assisted me."

Sophia looked at Shade as if begging to go with him, but he offered no sign of wanting her along. Knowing he had made a decision that did not include her, she left the room, closing the door on her way out.

"Angel, Tobi, get packed. We leave at midnight."

"Where are we going, Dad?"

"Montana." With that, he began shutting down the monitors.

Tobi could tell Shade wanted to be alone, so he took Angel's hand and led her back to their quarters.

After the two left, Shade returned to the secret room, his room where only memories of one woman were allowed. Reaching into the side pocket of the chair where he had spent years reminiscing, he pulled out a small velvet drawstring bag. Reaching inside, he pulled out a gold nugget ring with a huge emerald in the center and placed it on his ring finger, left hand.

He remembered the night Sue Ann had given him her father Zeke's wedding ring, telling him her mother had the band set with a big emerald the color of her eyes because Zeke always loved looking into those eyes. When the CIA agent, his friend, told him he needed to send something to Sue Ann to make his death believable, Shade had looked down at Zeke's wedding ring but he simply could not part with it. Instead, he had the agent get an exact copy of the ring made, a copy that could be taken to Sue Ann.

As he fixed his eyes on the ring, he remembered the words Sue Ann had said to him when she placed the ring on his finger: *You are the man I have loved more than any, the man with whom I want to spend the rest of my life, and now is the time for me to take my vows just as you did when you gave me my ring. I promise to cherish you, to honor you, and to protect all that we have together for as long as I live. I love you unconditionally, Shade Dubois. I will love you forever—and then some.*

Shade remembered sleeping with the curtains open that night in Moose Springs, Alaska, with their bodies and hearts enraptured as the Sky Dwellers watched over them. Neither suspected it would be their last time to make love under Northern Lights.

And now, here he was about to see her again. She had been through so much heartache, and through physical suffering with the breast cancer. He knew already how he felt about Sue Ann. His heart was no different now than it had been all those years ago when he first met her. What he didn't know was if she could ever forgive him for deceiving her, even though it was done to protect her, Betsy, and Angel. And he still had to be sure the blood money was no longer available. The deadline was only days away, and if it meant his really dying to save the ones he loved, then so be it.

For now, he had to keep Tobi and Angel with him, and the best place to do that and protect all those he loved was Montana.

Chapter Nineteen

Shade landed his Lear Jet in Missoula rather than Billings, figuring anyone with knowledge would think he would pick Billings since it was the closest major airport. Once they left the jet, he decided it was time to explain the rest of his plan.

"I have a ranch cabin rented in Nye, about fifty-six miles from Red Lodge. It's a remote area in the middle of the mountains, so cell phones won't work there. Here." Shade handed each of them a satellite phone, knowing the younger generation would think it was too big and gaudy, but it would connect them with any phone they needed, regardless of how isolated they were. He was surprised when neither of them complained.

"It's okay to get new cell phones to replace the ones you had, but don't let them out of your sight. No more risk of tracking devices."

Shade had backpacks filled with anything and everything they would need for survival and had each of them put them on to see if they were too heavy.

"So are we renting a vehicle?" Tobi asked and was surprised when Shade gave a little chuckle.

"I have something better and faster in mind." Shade took off walking fast toward another private hangar, with Tobi and Angel in tow. After unlocking the door, Shade pushed the button to automatically roll up the door and disclose a small helicopter inside.

"So you can fly this, too?" Tobi asked, but he already knew the answer.

"We do have vehicles waiting for us at the ranch house I rented, so you won't be going to the grocery store in this—" Seeing the smile on Angel's face, he corrected his statement. "Not that you will be going to the grocery store or anywhere. The cabin is well stocked."

After buckling in, they all put on headsets so they could speak to each other without screaming or going deaf from the noise.

When they began their descent into the valley in the middle of the Beartooths, Angel gasped, in awe of the scenery. But when they flew over the next rise, and Shade began to land, Angel's mouth flew open and remained that way. The rental cabin was a huge log mansion, surrounded by mountains with a new sprinkling of snow on their peaks. Off to the left, a herd of mule deer grazed, totally oblivious of the helicopter and human visitors.

"Funny how they seem to know it's not hunting season," Tobi remarked, smiling. "As much as I love this location, I wish I was home in my own little log cabin." He reached for Angel's hand.

They landed, and as they climbed out of the copter, Angel asked Shade, "So when do we gather together all of the family and surround them with armed guards?" It was a question Tobi was thinking also.

"Hawk already knows the plan. He and Betsy are expecting Sue Ann home from a trip to Florida and Mississippi tomorrow. For now, I am staying out of the picture, but I won't be far away. That's why you have the satellite phones. I'll be a sniper's distance away at all times unless something changes for the worse. There are more satellite phones inside the cabin."

Shade had no more than gotten these words out of his mouth when his satellite phone rang. He moved several yards away to take the call but only talked for a few minutes. When he came back, he had a scowl over his eyes.

"Everything all right?" Tobi asked.

"No. It's just as I expected. Two Americans, one CIA and one unknown, just landed in Billings, and they flew from Costa Rica by way of Miami. Neither one is to be trusted, whether they are working together or independently. I suspect one of them, probably the CIA agent, has been tracking Angel, the reason he knew you were in the rainforest that day."

"Do you think the synthesized voice is one of these bad guys? It's hard to believe, since he, or rather it, told us to leave the Villa Bonita and then told us to ditch the Jeep and take refuge in the church. He even knew Hawk and Custer were coming in and gave them directions where to find us." Angel squeezed Tobi's hand, remembering the ordeal they had survived.

"What about Marshall? Is he still a threat?" Tobi took Angel's hand.

"No. I had a nice little chat with his daddy, and Marshall is grounded, so to speak—in a secure rehabilitation institution for drug and alcohol abuse. Besides, you embarrassed him pretty good that night, Angel. I don't think he wants to tangle with the pint-sized Ninja warrior." Shade gave Angel a hug, showing how proud he was of her gutsy plan. "As for the Voice, I'm not sure who that is, but my gut tells me your informant—the Postman as you called him—was with the CIA, a bad cop, so to speak, who wants to claim the millions ONE left for killing me."

"It would be hard to believe the Voice was out to hurt us. Everything it told us seemed to be for our protection. Only good came from those calls." Angel looked to her father for an answer.

"We may never know, sweetheart, but for now, let's get the chopper inside that huge barn, and we'll go inside and see if your accommodations suit you. I need to go before Hawk and Betsy get here."

"Does Betsy know you're alive, Dad?"

"No. I asked Hawk not to tell Betsy or Sue Ann. If the deadline does not go through, I will need to disappear again, and it's better I only die once, especially for Sue Ann. She's been through too much pain already." Shade saw the look on Angel's face, and he went to her and took her in his arms. "Don't worry about it until it happens, Angel. I wouldn't trade the time we've had together these few weeks for anything, but I want you safe."

****

The two men who got off the same flight in Billings pretended not to know each other. The first man, a tall guy with chiseled good looks, rented an SUV, a luxurious black one, and filled the back with backpacks and outdoor gear, but cases that looked suspiciously like they could hold rifles and ammunition took up most of the space.

The second man was shorter and huskier, with a bald head that he covered with a baseball cap. His dress was casual bordering on sloppy. He, too, got a rental vehicle, a cheaper SUV, tan in color. Both headed out of Billings on I-90, and both were on their cell phones constantly.

****

Sue Ann arrived at Billings on a late flight. Her new adventure had started in the Arizona spa with Elizabeth, and from there she had gone to Florida and done a book signing in a local book store, something she had missed during her years of recuperation from breast cancer. Then it was back to Mississippi to relax for a few days at Parrish Oaks and spend more time with Elizabeth, Annie, and the grandchildren. But try as she might, Sue Ann could not shake her longing for her Beartooth Mountains. She headed for the airport in Memphis on the spur of the moment, not even calling Betsy to tell her of her change in plans. She would surprise them tomorrow and could hardly wait to hug Trapper.

As she glanced in her rearview mirror and saw her reflection, she could not help but smile. One thing she did like was her new look. She looked so much younger than she had with her gray braids. Her hair was still long, but her natural curls reminded her of the way she had looked in Moose Springs.

"Good memories," she whispered to herself as she turned onto I-90 and headed for Red Lodge. "And some nightmares, too."

As she drove along the interstate, her thoughts went first to Custer. She wondered what he would think of the younger look, but deep down she knew it wouldn't matter if she was bent over with a walking cane or the perfect image of Christy Brinkley, he would love her just the same. Then her mind regressed to Alaska, and she remembered the first time she and

126

Shade made love. He had loved her long blonde curls, really more of a fascination than love, and he wanted to know how she got the tangles out. She had bent her head over, run her fingers through the mass of thick curls, and when she slung her head back, her curls were all back in place.

Sue Ann wondered if her little log cabin in Moose Springs was empty. Perhaps she would buy it back and return to the little village that had been home to her and Betsy. After Betsy started college, Sue Ann had alternated between Alaska and Red Lodge, never quite able to decide which one suited her best. But falling in love with her grandson Trapper had brought her to her cabin in the Beartooths more often and then permanently.

What a biography the other half of her life would be! She thought that might be what she'd write next, since *The Gully Path* ended with Tate's abandonment of her when she was pregnant. The book ended when she and Betsy moved to Alaska on a whim, and then there was Shade. She still had to write *Under Northern Lights*, Shade's story, but she was not looking forward to that. It brought back not only sadness but trauma.

"Well, enough thinking." Sue Ann realized she was talking to herself but decided she was old enough for that, so she continued the conversation. "I'm ready to get home and do that thing I thought was too boring and lacked excitement. I'm going to sit on my porch, drink coffee, and speak to the mountains. Maybe now that Custer is up there, the mountain breezes will talk to me."

It was after midnight when she pulled onto the forestry road leading to the cabin. She hoped she had not overdone it, buying this big expensive SUV. Maybe she'd get another Jeep, just for fun, a second vehicle. She could certainly afford it.

She grabbed one of her suitcases, leaving the other one until tomorrow, and made her way into her cabin. Stopping on the porch, she breathed in the antiseptic smell of pines, aspens, wildflowers, and the smell of rich pioneer history that emanated from her historic log cabin. Soon it would be cold enough to build a fire in the big old stone fireplace, another mountain smell she loved. A streak of sadness swept through her when she remembered she had no one to share all of this with now that Custer was gone. Unlocking the door, she stepped inside—to home, memories, peace, and loneliness.

Chapter Twenty

When Angel and Tobi got up the next morning, Hawk, Betsy, and Trapper were already settling in, and coffee was made. Trapper was eating chocolate chip pancakes, but he gladly left his breakfast long enough to give his uncle and future aunt a hug.

Angel looked around for her dad, but he was gone. Hawk looked at her and reminded her, with his eyes, not to mention anything about Shade.

Conversation did not come easy, and Betsy had many questions she wanted answered, but no one was willing to answer them.

"So we told Darlene to hold our mail because we were going out of town. We also said we'd be picking Mom up at the airport to take her with us, even though we know she had her own vehicle waiting for her. None of this makes sense. Angel, if you resigned from the CIA, why is someone still after you, and why do we have to hide with you? I want…no…I *deserve* answers."

"I'm so sorry to bring you three in on this, but my boss thought it was worth staying low, all of us, until these guys are under arrest. They are not your average criminals. As soon as he calls, things can go back to normal." Angel put her arm around Tobi's waist, needing his reassurance, and he put her in a tight embrace and kissed her. "Besides, we have a wedding

129

to plan."

This brought a smile to Betsy's face.

"Do I have to be the ringbearer again, Mom? I'm in second grade, you know. I'm too old. I want to be best man." Trapper protested through a mouthful of pancakes.

"We'll see, little man, or I should say Big Man. You are getting awfully tall, like your daddy." Angel reached down and kissed him on the cheek and got a taste of pancake syrup. "Um…that's good!" She licked her lips. "Got anymore?" Angel looked at Betsy and grinned.

****

Betsy used one of the satellite phones to call her mother's cell phone.

"I cannot wait to see Mom! I haven't been away from her this long since Hawk and I married. And then there's her new look I haven't seen except in pictures." After several rings, Betsy hung up. "Are you sure these walkie-talkie-looking things work? Mom doesn't answer."

Betsy tried several times but got no answer.

"Here, Sis. Let me try. Maybe you're hitting the wrong keys. It's kind of awkward for your little hands." Tobi let the phone ring even longer, but he got no answer either. Seeing her worried look, he said, "I'm sure she's okay, Betsy. Maybe her flight was late. Let's call the airline and see."

Tobi got the airline agent on the phone and began to pace while she checked Sue Ann's flight status. "Are you sure? She was supposed to be on a flight this morning." Tobi cast a look of alarm toward Hawk, and Betsy noticed.

130

"What's wrong?" Betsy went to her brother as he hung up the satellite phone.

"She said Mom came in on a late flight last night. She arrived at eleven p.m."

"Hawk, we've got to go check on Mom. Something is wrong. She would have called by now to let us know." Betsy's face was covered in terror.

"Calm down, sweetheart. I bet she was tired and just overslept. You and Angel stay here with Trapper. Keep the doors locked and the curtains closed. And keep the satellite phone handy. Tobi and I will go check on Sue Ann and call you."

Tobi kissed Angel and whispered for her to keep the gun handy.

****

Shade watched through binoculars as Tobi and Hawk took off in one of the SUVs.

"Where in the hell are they going?" Pulling out his satellite phone, he rang Hawk's phone and repeated the question he had just asked himself.

"I hope it's nothing, Shade, but Sue Ann evidently came in a day early from Mississippi, got to Billings about eleven p.m., but she isn't answering our calls. Betsy is terrified, and to be quite honest, I am, too. This isn't like Sue Ann. She would have called first thing this morning to let us know she was home."

"Call me as soon as you get there. I don't like this. Maybe I'll just head that way over the mountains. I know there's a trail that goes from here to Keyser Brown. Custer took me fishing that way many decades ago. There's a side trail that should take me to Sue Ann's cabin. Still, call me when you get there. I'm heading out, and I'm bringing what I need."

****

Sue Ann talked to herself as she trudged along the wilderness trail.

I will not be afraid and will never exude anything but confidence and positive thinking. This is not the worst scenario I've been in, but thank you, God, for letting me see I needed to make myself fit, even though I never dreamed it would be for the purpose of being prodded along by a very large, muscle-bound man with a gun. Hawk and Tobi will find me.

Her mind returned to the night before, when she was awakened by a stranger, the abductor, standing over her in her bedroom. Her first reaction had been sheer, unadulterated terror, but then she got control of herself. He grabbed her cell phone, stuck it in his pocket, and told her to get dressed. "And don't think about going for the rifle in your closet. I've removed it." Before heading out her bedroom door, he added, "Dress for wilderness hiking, and dress in layers—for the high country. We're going into the Beartooth Wilderness, so prepare to be gone indefinitely."

Sue Ann wondered if Tobi and Hawk would find the clue she left behind. She had been pushed for time and had to think fast. As she pulled her hiking boots from the closet, she saw Custer's lace-up moccasins and his pack in the back corner, resting against the wall as if he expected to return any minute, pick up his gear, and head to the high country to fish, to give the woman he loved time to make life-changing decisions, or to build a sweat lodge and prepare himself for any visions the Creator might bestow upon him. Searching the side pockets of the pack, she found a forestry map of the high country and laid it, unfolded, on top of the pack.

Now, something for writing a message!

Leaving the closet, she quickly returned to her dresser. No pen was lying around, but her tube of bright red lipstick was there, one of the lipsticks she had bought but did not like. She had not included it in her packing for her new adventure to disguise herself as the blonde bombshell she was thirty years ago—in other words, as someone else. Hearing her abductor on the stairs, she quickly removed the top and circled the words "Beartooth Wilderness" on the forestry map.

Her abductor had refused to answer any questions. Her first thought was of Angel and Tobi and the dangerous case left over from her CIA job.

"Is Angel all right...and my son Tobi?"

"Not your biggest concern, Dr. Parish." This was the only answer the man had given, letting her know this was going to be a frightening chapter in her book.

Hearing how he addressed her, including her title, made her wonder about this guy's background. He did not have the demeanor of an everyday thug, but she was not sure if this was a good thing or a bad thing. One thing she was sure of—he would not be sharing his resumé with her.

What bothered her the most was the fact that he had not camouflaged his appearance. He had no facial hair, no ski mask, no tacky fake wig. His hair was neatly trimmed and covered only by a baseball cap with no discerning logo. In another scenario, her abductor could have been a handsome hero from any one of her romances, but she was too old and too smart to play Stockholm Syndrome.

As they left the cabin, he picked up a small pack from the porch and handed it to her.

"Here. Put this on." He did not offer to help her. The last thing he did was remove an envelope from his pocket and place it on her desk beside a copy of *The Gully Path*.

****

Hawk sped along the forestry road to Sue Ann's cabin, oblivious of the ruts. He and Tobi had ridden in silence, each trying to control their thoughts and fears.

When they reached the cabin, they noticed Sue Ann's new SUV parked in front. As Tobi walked by, he opened the front door and looked inside. A suitcase sat on the back seat, but he had no time or need to open it. He had to hurry to catch up. Hawk was opening the front door and calling for his mother-in-law.

Frantic, he took the stairs two at a time, still calling but receiving no answer. Her bedroom door was open, her bed unmade, looking as if it had been slept in the night before. Another suitcase sat on the floor, unopened.

Hawk noticed the closet door was open and stepped into it, letting his eyes absorb every minute detail of the room as he went. Pulled to the front of the closet was Custer's big pack, his lace-up moccasins beside it. But it was what was opened on top of the pack that got Hawk's attention. He grabbed up the map and took it to the window for more light as he heard Tobi calling from downstairs.

"Hawk! Come quick!"

Tobi's voice was panic-filled, and Hawk headed down the stairs, carrying the map still unfolded.

Tobi sat at Sue Ann's desk, his head in his hands, reading the message he had found. When Hawk walked up, Tobi handed the piece of paper to him, being careful

134

to hold it by one corner in case any fingerprints were left, although he doubted this would be the case.

"It has Shade's name on the outside, but I had to open it."

Hawk took the paper and read aloud. *I have Dr. Parish. If you want to see her alive, follow the instructions. As you know, time is of the essence, so hurry. You know what meets you at the end. Who do you choose to die...really die? You or Sue Ann?*

Instruction: Go to Keyser Brown, far end from trailhead, where stream from First Rock enters. Find large flat rock with small X in orange on top. 2nd set of instructions are there. Too bad Angela isn't with you. She would remember making love to Tobi in the meadow grass beside this rock. A very inspiring scene!

The trails are being watched. If anyone is with you, you will never see Sue Ann again...at least not in one piece. That's a promise.

"Whoever this is, he's been following Angel ever since she came here. He was watching us the day I taught Angel to fly fish, the first time we made love. If I could get my hands on this bastard..." Tobi's voice was filled with rage, not only because the abductor had watched as he and Angel made love but because the criminal now held his mother's life in his hands. "Call Shade. He needs to know every word of this note, and we need to go after Mom. We can be at Keyser Brown in a couple of hours if we hurry."

****

Shade hastened his movement rather than stopping to listen as Hawk read the note aloud over the satellite phone. He had Hawk read it three more times until every word and phrase was embedded in his mind.

"What now, Shade? Tobi is pacing, ready to go after the bastard. I know every trail and route possible in the high country, but we can't head out without proper provisions...and weapons." As Hawk folded the message, he remembered Sue Ann's clue. "Oh, Sue Ann left a clue in her closet...a forestry map opened and left on top of Custer's pack. She circled Beartooth Wilderness in red lipstick."

If Shade had not been so worried for Sue Ann's life, he would have chuckled at the symbolism of the red lipstick. Hopefully, some day, they might be able to share this anecdote.

"I have to do this alone, Hawk. You have to convince Tobi to stay at the ranch house. I need you both protecting the family. Do you know anyone who can fly a helicopter—someone who can be discreet and keep all this to himself?"

"Yes. Betsy and I have a good friend named BJ who works for the forestry service as a helicopter pilot. He knows the Beartooths well, especially from an aerial perspective."

"Perfect! Ordinarily, I would want as few as possible involved, but this is Sue Ann, and this guy is serious and deadly. If he can bring a forestry chopper, that would be even better, but if not, mine is in the barn, ready for use. I just don't want to draw suspicion. A forestry chopper would be a good front."

****

So many scenes from the past invaded Hawk's mind, and he hoped this would be the last time any of his family's lives would be put in jeopardy. He thought back to Custer's sharpshooting skills that had stopped a killer and saved Betsy and him at Devil's Canyon. Then he thought of Tobi saving Trapper from a killer's vengeful rage.

"Hawk!" Shade had called Hawk's name three times but he did not answer.

"Sorry, Shade. This whole thing is like déjà vu— I've seen my family in dangerous situations like this too many times for one man. I'm having a hard time taking directions."

"Trust me, Hawk. This man's motive of multiple millions of dollars puts it at the top of bad experiences, and I need you and Tobi to follow my orders this time. Sue Ann's life depends on it. Now, I'm heading to Keyser Brown and as high as I have to go to find Sue Ann and save her, but have BJ ready with that chopper, fully armed. From this point, I need to turn off the phone. Distractions are not part of a sniper's prowess."

Thirty minutes after they'd called BJ, he landed the forestry helicopter on the ranch. Hawk told him as little as possible other than that Sue Ann had been kidnapped and they had to sit tight until going in for the rescue when directed.

"I'm glad you called me, Hawk. Sue Ann is a special lady, and I want to help. As luck would have it, I'm on patrol today, looking for poachers, so the forestry service won't miss me."

Betsy had taken the news better than expected, at least on the outside, but Tobi was overly anxious. Hawk knew it would be all he could do to keep him from going to the high country.

Angel was exceptionally quiet, and Tobi knew she blamed herself for all of this. Finding her sitting on a rock looking at the mountains, he joined her, taking her in his arms.

"It will be all right, sweetheart. Your dad has more ability in tracking, locating, and solving these kinds of situations than any man alive—prowess, he calls it. And it is obvious he is still in love with my mom."

"I know. That prowess is what keeps him and us in danger. Where will this all end, Tobi? Will I ever get to have a normal father and family situation?" Angel put her head on Tobi's chest.

"Yes. It's in the cards. You need to think only positive thoughts, Angel."

They sat quiet, both in contemplation of the situation.

Angel broke the silence. "Tobi, I've been trying to go over everything since the informant left me the classified file from the CIA telling me my father is alive, through everything that has transpired. We must be missing so many clues that could help."

"I've been thinking along those same lines. You have gotten in the way of my logical thinking, which was my strongest point as a detective before coming here. Logic does not disappear completely, but it does need a revival every once in a while." Tobi got up, taking Angel by the hand and pulling her beside him. "It's time for me to be a detective again. Let's get Hawk and go to the office in the barn."

Hawk hated to leave BJ out, but he could not bring him completely in...not yet. When he got to the barn, Tobi had moved a dry eraser board full of ranch schedules and deliveries to where the three could gather around it and brainstorm. After erasing the obsolete information regarding the ranch, Tobi drew a timeline, with the first entry three months earlier, the approximate time of Angel receiving the first CIA document. Next was the second drop, the more detailed document giving all the information surrounding Shade's near death in the Tekooni River and Custer's saving him.

"And the only reason you thought about Costa Rica as a place of hiding for Shade was because you remembered hearing him tell Sue Ann about it right before his so-called death?" He directed the comment to Angel, who confirmed it with a nod of her head.

"Describe again for me the night you were attacked in the garage at your condo and your old briefcase was snatched. Don't leave out any detail, regardless of how minute. I am especially interested in a physical description of the assailant."

"Tall, about like Hawk, and maybe a little more muscular in his upper body, but a bit of a stomach. He had on a ski mask, so I couldn't see his face."

"What about his voice? Did it sound familiar at all?"

"No, not really, but I suspect he was making it gravelly intentionally. I really didn't get much of a look at him. It happened so fast."

"Okay. You think he was disguising his voice?" Tobi looked at Hawk, who was taking notes.

"Actually, that didn't occur to me, but yes, I do, now that I think about it." Angel frowned, showing she was in deep thought. "I could hardly understand what he said, and I think his heaviness in the middle could have been part of his disguise. When he had me on the floor with his knee in my stomach, I tried to push him off, but I could only reach his midsection. It was soft…too soft, like he had some kind of padding on to make him appear bigger."

"Good! Now we're getting somewhere. Could you see his hands?" Tobi watched Angel.

"No. He wore gloves."

"Did you see the car he left in?"

"No. He was on foot, and I was in a hurry to grab the correct briefcase and get myself locked in my condo."

"Okay. Now let's talk about people you know in the CIA who could have access to information about Shade. And let's not forget about your old boyfriend Randal." Tobi smirked when he said Randal's name.

"Oh, surely not Randal!" Angel frowned at Tobi. "He was introduced to me by my best friend in the agency, Herb Fellers. Herb is a good man and always had my back, or at least, I always thought he was a good man. Do you think he's involved in this and wants to kill my dad?"

"I don't know, Angel, but we cannot trust anyone. You said Herb is about ready to retire. Maybe his pension is not enough." Tobi looked toward Hawk. "Feel free to jump in, Hawk, if something grabs you."

"Well, I do have a question. It seems someone, probably several people, are tracking Angel, first to Montana and then to Costa Rica. It had to be by way of her cell phone for at least part of the time, since she got messages warning her of impending danger while in Costa Rica. But the messages stopped after Marshall took her cell phone. She's had none on the new one, so let's figure out exactly when someone could have placed a tracking device in the second phone, the one she got after losing the first one in the wreck."

"My Mercedes may have had a device on it, even though Randal said he tracked me through credit cards and through use of CIA resources. Problem with that is I only used a credit card in the eastern and central states. When I reached South Dakota, I began using only cash, just for the reason of not wanting anyone to know where I was going."

"So Randal lied?"

"Did you use a credit card to pay the wrecker?" Tobi asked.

"No, I didn't. But Randal knew my Mercedes had been wrecked. Remember? He asked about it the day he came to your cabin, Tobi."

"Okay. Think of that day, actually two days, since you put off explaining about the briefcase until you, Custer, and I had time to talk about what you should tell him."

Angel became quiet, thinking. All of a sudden, she jumped up with an excited look on her face.

"I know when he put the tracking device in the phone I bought after my wreck! Well, really, it doesn't have to be a physical device. He just needs information off my phone and he can use his own tracking software. Simple and deadly! Remember when Herb called during Randal's second visit? Herb called on my phone because Randal did not have his with him. What CIA agent leaves his car to interview someone about a case without his cell phone?"

"That's right! He walked out on the deck to talk to Herb in private—on your phone—and he even took it to his car! Good detective work, former CIA..." Tobi hesitated.

"Intelligence analyst." Angel finished his sentence. "And Randal did not have my new cell phone number, and I made sure not to give any information that could be used to track me when I got the new cell phone. But I did even worse by letting him use it."

"Okay. So what I'm hearing is you are both leaning toward Randal as the main suspect, but why? How did he find out about Shade being alive? Obviously, anyone after Shade is after the millions." Hawk added this.

"I don't know," Angel answered. "But I'm not letting Herb Feller off the hook until I know for a fact he is clear. They could be in this together, since Herb would have more access to classified documents, and he did introduce me to Randal, just before I got the first classified document."

"And there's darling little Marshall Chapman, whose daddy knows all about the blood money and the Swiss corporation in charge of determining who gets it. Let's not discount him." Tobi's face shot red just thinking about Marshall's kidnapping and harassment of Angel, not to mention that he'd put his hands on her.

"Marshall might have been a hired accomplice, but he really did not strike me as smart enough for anything else," Angel said, wanting to close the subject before Tobi got really angry.

"Well, all we can do now is wait to hear from Shade and hope we can get BJ up in the helicopter in time, armed and ready for action that will result in getting Mom back."

Chapter Twenty-One

Shade took out his forestry map of the Beartooths. It was over thirty years old, a map given to him by Custer a long time ago. He knew some of the trails might have changed, but high mountain lakes never change. Besides, he would be sticking to off-trail hiking except for picking up instructions.

As he reached the back of Keyser Brown Lake, he dropped to the ground, preferring to crawl to the spot where he could look over the whole area without being seen. He figured he knew this part of the mountains better than the man, or men, who had Sue Ann. He had to figure on at least two men, one watching to see if he picked up the instructions at the designated spot and one holding Sue Ann. The one holding Sue Ann captive would be the mastermind, the one with his eyes set on claiming the money.

Below, Keyser Brown Lake spread out in magnificence against a backdrop of steep, rugged mountains with only small pockets of snow left in the crevices. On one of the grassy knolls the same elevation as he was, he spotted a mountain goat grazing. He thought about Betsy telling Hawk in her first novel about having a staring contest with a goat at Keyser Brown.

Betsy! What a scrapper that carbon copy of Sue Ann has turned out to be! I owe it to her, Hawk, and their little Trapper to bring Sue Ann back to them unharmed!

Shade noticed something shining on the trail directly across from him and turned his binoculars in that direction.

A man was hunkered down behind a large boulder, his rifle resting on the rock. His stainless steel coffee cup reflected the low sun, and Shade marveled at the man's stupidity.

"Too easy!" Shade chuckled and began searching the mountains to the sides and behind the trail he recognized as the one going to September Morn, a place where he and Custer had caught several species of indigenous trout decades ago when Shade needed to disappear, a time before going to Alaska.

After leaving his high perch, Shade stopped and pulled out one of his camo suits to make him blend in perfectly with the greens, browns, and grays, with a touch of white—the colors of the Beartooths. The suit was made from a layer of breathable material with padding where it counted for belly crawling and for protection of elbows and knees. Once dressed, Shade put together his high-powered rifle, ready for taking out, or taking in, the man hiding across from him, a man who knew enough to hasten Shade's rescue of Sue Ann.

****

Sue Ann had no problem hiking on the trail, even after eight hours with only a few rest stops, but when they reached the boulders of First Rock, she looked up and wondered if she would be able to make it. Her abductor prodded her in the back with the pistol butt, reminding her she would make it or else.

As she climbed the first part of the boulder field, she remembered her younger days with Betsy, racing to see who would wet a fly rod first. Sue Ann now realized just how many years ago that had been, after she slipped into the first major crevice because of her short stride. Her abductor told her to stop.

"Take off your pack," he ordered, and Sue Ann did not hesitate. It was far too heavy for where she was having to go.

"Go through it and be quick about it, and take out at least half of what's in there. Leave the water bottles here except for two. Water is the heaviest thing you're carrying. I have a pump and filter and can fill from the streams. Socks should stay, along with your bedroll. Everything else can go. Keep the backpacker food. It doesn't weigh much."

When she finished, she left everything in plain view but figured he would make her hide it so anyone tracking could not find their trail.

"Where are you taking me?" she asked again as she fastened the straps on her much lighter pack.

"I told you, not for you to know. Get your pack on and move. I want to be there before dark. If you break a leg in the dark, I'll bind you and leave you for the bears."

"Pleasant thought!" Sue Ann mumbled as she slung the pack over her shoulders and tightened the chest and shoulder straps. She picked up the items left out of her pack and wadded them into a ball, prepared to stuff them in the crevice.

"Leave them out. In fact, spread them around so they are in clear view. The sooner he catches up, the better."

"He who? Who are you trying to trap using me as bait?" Sue Ann put her hands on her hips and stared at the man.

The man chuckled deep in his throat. "Wouldn't you like to know? But you wouldn't believe me if I told you. We'll just let it be a surprise."

****

Shade knew he couldn't be too far from the accomplice, so he stopped and put camo paint on his face and hands. Next, he reached into the other breast pocket and took out greenish-colored leaves. Coca was something he chewed often during a mission. The plant, also used in Coca-Cola and cocaine in its processed forms, was being grown in the Mono Paraiso, not for sale but for Shade's own personal use and for medical research. Not only was coca a natural stimulant, but it suppressed hunger, thirst, fatigue, and pain, all of which could be the real enemies on guerilla missions.

Shade crawled on his belly, elbows, and knees for twenty minutes without overturning a leaf or dislodging a stone in his path. When he reached the knoll that overlooked where he thought the man was, his stealth and adrenaline flow reached maximum proportions. He was Raven, and he was ready. This would be the second most important mission of his life, the first being the rescue of Angel and Betsy as teenagers.

Shade got his first peek at the shooter from a distance of less than fifty feet.

Perfect!

The man crouched over the small boulder, looking at Keyser Brown and the area surrounding it through high-powered binoculars. Laying his rifle on the ground as quietly as possible, Raven pulled his knife from the

146

sheath attached to the inside of his lower leg and then crept a few feet closer to the edge, rising on his knees and elbows while keeping out of sight behind a boulder. Reaching into his breast pocket, he removed a small flat rock he'd found on the trail and clutched it in his left hand.

The shooter stood, keeping himself hidden behind a second boulder beside him, and pulled a water bottle from his pack. Taking advantage of the man's attention focused on drinking and not on anything above him, Raven threw the rock down the trail, skidding it to cause more of a distraction as it kicked up dust.

The shooter grabbed his rifle, stepped into the trail, and looked toward the noise and dust.

Shade stood, poised for action, and stole along the edge, following above the shooter. With one giant leap, he knocked the man to the ground, punching hard with his right fist. With only a few punches, the man released his rifle and lay still. Raven tied and gagged him and pulled him off the trail behind a big crop of boulders with spindly evergreens growing from the crevices. One crevice was particularly deep, with no trees growing from it—a perfect punji pit.

When the man came to, his eyes got big as he saw Raven whittling on a long stick and making the end as sharp as any spear he had ever seen. Raven carried his spear, as well as a sadistic grin, toward the man and jerked the gag from his mouth. The man was bound completely around his arms, legs, and torso, with sticks underneath to act as splints that kept his body rigid and unmovable.

"Before I ask you this question, I want to give you a lesson in how to make a punji pit. First you use your very sharp knife, like this one." Raven held the knife so close to the man's eyes he was afraid to blink for fear his eyelashes or eyelids would be severed.

"After you get, oh, about a dozen of these sharpened to a really good point, you stick them firmly in the ground at the bottom of a pit so they stand tall…and deadly. Or, if there's no time for whittling, you can make do with one exceptionally sharp point aimed where it will penetrate a man's gut when he falls a few feet down on it. This point is mighty sharp. I'd say it could go right through that gut of yours, no problem."

"What do you want from me?" The man spoke in a deep, raspy voice, laced with fear.

"You know what I want. Start talking."

The man shook his head in refusal.

"Well, now. That's too bad, Mr. Vinson."

The man stared at Raven with a surprised look, obviously wondering how he knew his name.

"Fingerprints don't lie, Vinson." Raven held up a small flat device. "And this little piece of technology gets me ID quicker than your soul will join the devil in hell…if you don't talk. Now, where did he take her?"

Again the man refused to talk, but this time he answered only with silence.

Reaching to a rope dangling from a tree limb directly overhead, Raven gave it a good tug, and Vinson felt himself being dragged across the rocky terrain. When he gave a muted yelp, Raven pulled his gag back over his mouth and then continued to pull him higher on the branch. Wrapping the rope around another small tree, Raven began talking to the man who was now hanging perpendicular to a crevice about thirty inches wide by two feet deep directly below him. The man cast his eyes below him and saw another punji stick, even sharper than the one Raven held, aimed directly at him.

"What I neglected to tell you is that a punji stick through the scalp goes even deeper, even faster, and the pit takes a lot less time to dig—if you have to dig, that is. This natural crevice is perfect. I'll give you two minutes to think this through. After that, I'll let the rope down about a foot. Your maximum time allotted for talking is limited to two minutes total." Raven looked at his watch, remaining silent until he hit the one-minute mark. "One minute...thirty seconds...twenty...ten..." Raven unwrapped the rope and let him move a foot closer to the pit.

By the time two minutes was up, Vinson's head was down into the pit, inches above the spear. He began to mumble and tried his best to get the rope to move.

After pulling him up just to where his mouth was out of the hole, Raven pulled the gag down.

"There's a spider web in that hole! It's on my head! Don't do this! Please!"

"Arachnophobia? For real? You're more afraid of a spider than of the sharp spears aimed at your skull?" Shade walked over and peered down into the natural cavity. "Well, I'll be darned. You're right! There's a big brown, furry spider down there looking up with two big old eyes. I think he's waiting for you." Shade pulled the man up over the pit again.

"Second Rock...north side...at edge of boulder field in trees...temporary shelter left by outfitters. The woman will be inside."

"What's his name?" Raven demanded.

Silence followed. Raven let the man down to within an inch of the spear…and the spider.

"Okay! Pull me up!"

"Randal. Randal Davison. He's CIA."

"Who's the big boss in this job?" Raven demanded.

"Nobody. Just him, with me to help. He promised me a million when we kill you. Said time is running out. In a few days, it will be too late."

"Good deal!" Raven jerked the spear out of the pit, pulled the gag back up and checked to make sure it was tight. Then he loosened the rope and let the man back down into the pit with his head only inches away from the spider at the bottom. The man's muffled begging could not be heard unless a person was right up on him.

Quickly gathering his gear, Raven threw on his backpack and headed for a trail where he couldn't be seen going around Keyser Brown. He did not stop to look under the flat rock. After years of torturing the enemy into talking, he knew Vinson had spilled his guts.

Pulling out the satellite phone, he dialed Hawk's number.

****

Angel, Tobi, and Hawk were still at the dry erase board when the satellite phone rang. Wasting no time, Hawk answered.

"No time to talk, Hawk. Get your pilot friend ready and have him on alert. I need you and Tobi to hike into Keyser Brown ASAP, or go horseback if you have any available, to make it quicker. Go up the trail to September Morn. About halfway up, you'll see three rocks stacked on top of each other. Go fifty yards more and turn down hill. A man named Vinson, CIA, is waiting for you. He's a little anxious, since he's hanging precariously over a punji pit, or rather a spider pit, so don't dally around."

"What about Sue Ann? Who has her and where is she?"

"Another CIA named Randal Davison. I'm not telling you where he is supposed to have Sue Ann until I have her in my sights. Hurry." Raven hung up, and Hawk and Tobi sprang to action.

The rented ranch came with many horses, some of which were pack horses, since the owner was an outfitter. In no time, Hawk and Tobi were heading through the Beartooths to Keyser Brown. BJ asked no questions but got the chopper ready, complete with emergency medical supplies and weapons.

Angel explained what was happening and told Betsy the culprit was Randal Davison, an agent with the CIA who had pretended to be interested in her. She hated keeping Shade a secret from Betsy and decided she would tell her before the day was up, maybe after Trapper went to bed for the night. Angel also wondered if Herb Feller was involved, since he had introduced her to Randal.

One thing she did know. No one in the CIA was to be trusted now.

****

Hawk and Tobi ran the horses as hard as they dared and reached Keyser Brown in an hour. After stopping to water the horses in the lake, they remounted and headed up. They found Vinson still dangling over the pit. He was seriously happy when Hawk and Tobi took him down and allowed him to sit upright for a few minutes before badgering him with questions.

Having already told Raven everything, he freely repeated what he knew, including admitting his part in it. With his hands bound tightly, he was put on the pack horse, and they all made their way back to the ranch headquarters, arriving well after dark.

Betsy and Angel were sitting on the porch waiting for their men. When the horses reached the edge of the yard, both women took out running. Hawk dismounted first, met Betsy halfway, and swung her around in a hug.

"I was so worried, Hawk."

"Mind holding these horses so I can hug my girl?" Tobi sat on the horse looking forgotten.

"Tobi, what you don't know about ranching will never do. Just drop the reins and ground tie him."

Tobi looked skeptical but dismounted, did as he was told, and then grabbed Angel for a kiss.

"So who do we have here?" Angel looked up at the man still mounted, who tried his best not to look her in the eyes. Tobi led him to the house, and when the porch light shone across him, Angel stood staring.

"Vinson, what in the hell are you doing mixed up in kidnapping and murder?"

"I can't say any more, Angela. I have to wait for my attorney."

"My name is Angel, not Angela, moron!"

Hawk and Tobi tied Vinson up, gagged him, and locked him in a back room that had no exits or windows. Betsy did not want Trapper anywhere near this criminal.

As the foursome plus BJ sat drinking coffee, Angel asked to speak to Hawk and Tobi in private.

"I'm going to tell Betsy about Shade. It's not right

152

to keep this from her. She is worried to death about her mother, and maybe it will make her feel better to know Shade is going to rescue her."

Hawk looked down, contemplating the what-ifs, but when he did speak, he agreed with Angel. "What about BJ?" Hawk asked.

"If we trust him enough to bring in a forestry chopper without permission and risk losing his job, then I think we can trust him with the truth," Tobi offered. "He doesn't know Shade, but he's heard about him from Custer…at least the part about Sue Ann's undying love for him. Those forestry guys stick together, retired or active, and all the foresters respected and admired Custer."

****

The explanation of what was happening to Sue Ann left Betsy almost hysterical and in severe denial and anger.

"Shade is alive, and he never let us know? How could he do this to Mom, to all of us?"

Hawk put his arm around Betsy and let her cry a while.

"I know, Betsy. I had the same reaction until Uncle Custer reminded me that Shade did it to save Sue Ann, and you and Angel. He chose to die for you once when he took ONE into the Tekooni River. He will willingly die for you again, but we hope that won't be necessary. If this deadline is for real, maybe Shade can have a life with Sue Ann yet. It is obvious he still loves her. Even Custer knew that. That's why he called him on the day he and Sue Ann married…to let him know he would love her and protect her for as long as he lived. Then he found the clues Shade left on the back of the Northern

Lights painting, showing the four sanctuaries where he could be found, along with a phone number that was almost unobservable. It was a long shot anyone would find the information, but Custer did, probably a gift from the Creator." Hawk put his arm around Betsy who wiped her eyes and looked up at him.

"You're right. I can't blame Shade. Am I mad at Custer just a little bit for not sharing his secret? Damn right! I wish the old coot were here right now so I could reprimand him—and then give him the biggest hug possible."

"BJ, you've been awfully quiet through all this. Do you wish I hadn't called you?" Hawk asked, smiling at their friend.

"No. I'm glad you called me. Now ask me if I wish you hadn't stolen my girl out from under me." BJ reached over and took Betsy's hand and smiled.

"I think we have been through this before. See, if you came around more often, we could have introduced you to Angel before Tobi got his hooks in her."

Tobi frowned at Hawk. "Wait a minute, Hawk! I may not be as big as you are, but I believe I can take you."

The ringing of the satellite phone caused them all to jump. Hawk answered, knowing it was Shade.

"I'm within an hour of where Davison is supposed to have Sue Ann. I'm turning off the phone. At first daylight, be ready. Remember to get here fast. I will do what I have to do, but I don't want Sue Ann to see me if I can help it." The phone went dead.

Chapter Twenty-Two

Hawk, Tobi, and BJ sat up most of the night, thinking, plotting, worrying, until one by one they dozed off. Betsy was asleep with Trapper, and Angel was asleep on the sofa with her head in Tobi's lap.

All were awakened when Angel's satellite phone vibrated. Angel looked at Tobi, not knowing whether to answer or not. Finally, it stopped.

"How could anyone know this number? Dad said it was a secure number."

Before anyone could offer an explanation, the phone began ringing again, and this time it did not stop. Betsy walked into the great room, awakened by the ringing, just as Angel picked up the phone.

"Take the forestry helicopter to Keyser Brown. Approach from the south. Wait there for further instructions." The synthesized voice had begun talking before Angel could get up the nerve to say "hello." Angel held the phone out, staring at it as if it were some type of technological monster about to attack.

"Who was it?" Tobi asked.

Angel glanced from Hawk to Tobi, her face etched with disbelief and fear. She hesitated before answering.

"The Voice!"

****

BJ and Tobi sat at the controls in the forestry chopper, waiting, not knowing if they had done the right thing by leaving the others at the ranch.

"What if the Voice is with Randal Davison? What if he wanted us to leave so he could take the others hostage?" All Tobi could think of was Angel's abduction in Costa Rica, one of the safest countries in the world, or so Shade had said.

"We did right convincing Hawk to stay behind." BJ sat back, and Tobi knew it was story time. "Hawk's ruthless when it comes to protecting his loved ones. I saw him beat the hell out of one of the Doobie brothers one night at the Grizzly when all the drunk bastard did was dirty dance behind Betsy. And that was before he and Betsy were 'in a relationship' as they say on Facebook."

"Facebook? We have got to find you a woman, BJ!" Tobi looked at his watch again. "The sun will be coming over that mountain any minute now. Damn, I wish I knew what was happening!"

****

Raven was in full stealth mode at his position above Second Rock. His rifle was ready, and he had crawled within sniper range of the temporary shelter where Vinson had said Randal was holding Sue Ann.

Okay, Raven! Don't let this be the first time you've missed, when you see the son-of-a-bitch.

As he waited, he heard a female voice yelling from inside the shelter.

Sue Ann! he whispered to himself.

"I don't care what the hell you're plotting! I have to pee. Shoot me if you have to, but a girl's gotta do what a girl's gotta do!"

The canvas flap opened, and Sue Ann stepped out, holding herself low to the ground as if she expected a shot to ring out at any moment. After looking around, she walked behind the shelter. In a minute, she returned and stood at the entrance, again looking around as if wondering if her abductor was still around.

As she stood there, the first rays of the morning sun cast its glow across her, and Shade could only stare. Her hair radiated, the golden color he remembered from so long ago. As her long curls bounced, sunlight clung to them and she looked celestial, surrounded by heavenly light. She had aged some but not like he expected after her battle with breast cancer. She remained beautiful, alluring, and he wanted to drop the rifle and run to her.

A shot rang out, bringing Shade out of his reverie and back to reality. Then another shot hit in front of the shelter where Sue Ann had been standing only seconds before, and Shade saw Sue Ann sprinting toward the forest.

The bastard is shooting at her!

Pivoting his rifle, Shade moved his sites in the direction the shot came from, but he could see no one. When he glanced back to the shelter, Sue Ann was gone. He didn't have time to think about what to do. Grabbing his pack and his rifle, he backed toward the forest. He'd go around and see if he could see the shooter from another angle, an angle closer to where Sue Ann had run.

When out of sight, Shade sprinted through the thick trees, not being as careful as usual. His only thought was to get to Sue Ann before the shooter did.

As he made it to the other side, he stayed high, hoping to get his sites on the shooter.

There!

Shade caught a glimpse of him several hundred yards east of where he had been, but he couldn't get a shot. Just as he began going higher, he saw Sue Ann below, hiding behind a boulder.

Damn! If I can see her, he can see her! I've got to do something!

Shade intentionally moved to get the shooter's attention, but it wasn't soon enough. A shot rang out, and Sue Ann fell to the ground.

Running down the steep hill, zigzagging when possible, Shade put all thoughts of himself or the shooter behind him. He had to get to Sue Ann. He wished he had made the call to Tobi and Hawk, but he could not risk turning his phone on and having some unauthorized ring or sound give away his position.

Shade kept his rifle in front of him as he made his way to her. Staying in trees as much as possible, he hoped to God he could reach her in time. Finally, he was within fifty yards when two quick shots rang out, hitting the ground in front of him.

Shade dropped his rifle and raised his hands.

"Okay, Davison. You've got me! Come out and claim your millions, but let her go!"

Randal Davison kept his rifle pointed at Shade as he approached, stopping within thirty feet of him.

"Move away from your rifle and away from her. I don't trust you anymore than my father and his brother trusted you, or so I hear, but I hardly remember either of them."

"You're ONE's son." Shade realized too late who the shooter was. It was obvious when he came out in the open. He was the spitting image of ONE's cowardly brother.

"Bingo! They say I look like my uncle, the one you murdered. What was his number? Seven?"

Shade ignored Randal and looked toward Sue Ann. "She's bleeding badly. Let me help her, Randal. She's not in this."

"No. I have to finish her off anyway, or she'll identify me. You know how it works, Raven. Or do you prefer Jon Shockey...or maybe Shade Dubois? Damn, man! I bet you can't even keep up with who you are."

"Kill me, take your picture, and go claim your...what is it, twenty or thirty million by now? But don't kill Sue Ann. She's been through enough. By the time she could identify you, you'll be on a beach somewhere, drinking expensive champagne, surrounded by babes in bikinis."

"Twenty-eight million, but who's counting? How does a man spend that much money in one lifetime? Funny! I hated my father all my life for making my mother and me live in poverty. I never knew who or what he was until I started working for the CIA. Herb Feller knew who he was and started talking to me about him and you."

"Herb Feller? CIA, huh? That's a step up." Shade continued to talk, hoping Davison would change his mind or would be caught off guard long enough for him to rush him. "He tried to hire on with Tiger's Eye, but he was a worthless piece of shit even back then. Your dad wouldn't have anything to do with him."

"My old man was wrong. Herb is smart. He told me you had this bounty on your head, and that you were alive. Knew about the deadline, too. He introduced me to Angela, and it didn't take much romancing to make her fall for me. Herb told me someone was feeding

Angela classified documents that would help me find you. He said she got a drop that night, so I followed her back to her condo and snatched the briefcase—the wrong briefcase, as my sorry-ass luck would have it. Then Herb admitted he had set me up to see what I was made of…to see if I'd really go dirty. He was the one sending the classified documents all along."

Sue Ann moaned, and Shade took a step toward her.

"Stop! No closer, or I'll go ahead and put a bullet in both of you. Besides, I want you to know how close your little girl came to being snatched and taken where you would never find her body. Problem was, she had no idea where you were. Herb helped me set up the show in Costa Rica after Angela led us there. She figured out who Custer was before Herb did. Smart girl."

"What about Marshall Chapman?" The prick's name put a taste in Shade's mouth equal to pure venom. "I guess he got the information about the deadline from his father's international banking business. Was he hired by Feller?"

"That idiot? Surely you jest. That information required payoffs to the organization that manages the account in Switzerland, big payoffs. That was Marshall's contribution. He helped himself to some of the accounts his dad managed, and before you know it, a couple of the little guys in Switzerland became millionaires overnight. Of course, Daddy was not too happy. Marshall was good at skimming off his daddy's clients. You thought it was his old man stealing from your precious preserve's account, and you fired him. Guess you're not quite as smart as you think."

"So you'll meet the deadline?" Shade asked, not really giving a damn, but Davison wanted to talk, and the longer he talked, the longer Sue Ann could live.

"With a few days to spare. As soon as I pour bullets into your naked body and take your last profile picture, plus get your fingerprints as added evidence, I'll be on a plane for Switzerland to claim the money my father should have used to give my mother and me the life we deserved. It's too late for my mother, but it's not too late for me. Now, get undressed. I'll make this as quick as possible for you and her."

"One more question...who kept calling Angel, warning her of danger in Costa Rica and here?"

Randal arched his eyebrows and gave Shade a puzzled look. "Now you're talking crazy. Nobody warned Angela of anything, and it surely wasn't Herb Feller. Herb planted the drops of the classified documents, but that's all, other than reprimanding her about the lost briefcase and the documents he claimed were in it. That was just to stir her up and get her searching for Daddy. We were only two steps behind her the whole time. By the way, Herb will be meeting me in Switzerland to claim his share."

Shade ignored Randal's threat, walked toward Sue Ann, and sat down beside her.

"Do what you must, but if you want me undressed, you'll have to do it. If I'm dying with Sue Ann, I'll be by her side when we take our last breath together, where I should have been all these years."

"Suit yourself, TWO. That's real damn touching!"

Randal raised his rifle and pointed it at Shade, who covered Sue Ann with his body. Putting his arms around her, he pulled her to him, kissed her, and whispered in her ear, "I've loved you forever…and then some."

Two shots in rapid succession rang out, echoing through the canyon. Randal Davison lay on the ground, the back of his head shattered and the back of his shirt covered in blood. Shade jumped to his feet and grabbed his rifle, looking through his scope in the direction the shot came from. He saw movement in the trees above but knew he could not get off a shot. Besides, the shooter had saved his life and Sue Ann's.

Grabbing his satellite phone, Shade called Tobi.

"Second Rock! Hurry! Sue Ann has been shot!"

Chapter Twenty-Three

Herb Feller sat in the great room of the ranch house. He apologized for not keeping Angel safe and for not telling her he knew about her father.

Angel had been shocked when she opened the door and there stood Herb.

"How did you find me?" Angel asked but knew what Herb would say.

His standard reply to questions like this was, "I'm CIA...remember?"

Angel's next question was, "Why are you here?"

"I felt you were in danger, and I felt I owed it to you. I've not been very nice to you since you left the agency. You should have come to me and told me someone was feeding you classified information. Things like that can get you killed, you know."

"The helicopter is back!"

Angel heard the chopper coming and wondered why her father had not called. She and Betsy both headed for the yard, ready to see their men and hopefully Sue Ann. They both knew Shade was probably not on the chopper since he did not want Sue Ann to see him. They were dreading telling Sue Ann lies after what she had been through.

The chopper did not land but continued over the house, proceeding north, so Angel was not surprised when the satellite phone rang.

She answered it with a question. "Tobi, why didn't you land?"

"We're on our way to Billings to the hospital. Mom has been shot, and we're heading straight to the emergency room. Don't worry. She'll be all right. She was hit in the side, but the bullet went straight through without doing excessive damage. Get Hawk to bring you and Betsy and Trapper to the hospital."

Angel could hardly hear what Tobi was saying over the noise of the chopper blades, but she did hear that Sue Ann was shot and they were on their way to the hospital.

"Who's in the black SUV I saw parked in front of the house?"

"Herb Feller is here." Angel found herself yelling.

"What?" Tobi yelled back.

"Herb Feller is here." Silence followed for at least a minute.

"Tobi, did you hear me?"

Again, Tobi did not answer.

"Put Hawk on, Angel. Tell him to go on the porch."

Hawk took the phone and headed outside.

"Is Sue Ann going to be all right, and what about Shade?"

"No time for questions, Hawk. Get the gun. Herb Feller and Randal are in it together. Don't let him out of your sight." Tobi yelled before hanging up.

Hawk had started to answer when he felt a gun barrel in his back.

"So now you know. Too bad you won't get a chance to use your information. Now, this is a predicament. Sue Ann Parish is alive. What about

Randal? Is Jon Shockey dead?"

"Tobi didn't say. He just said Sue Ann was shot and they're taking her to the hospital."

"Get back on. Ask about Shade, but say Angel wants to know. I'll know from that if everything went according to plans. By the time Sue Ann is ready to talk, Randal and I will be far away."

Hawk dialed Tobi, and he answered on the third ring.

"Angel wants to know if her dad is okay."

After several seconds of silence, Tobi came back on.

"This phone is not working right. I can't understand you. I'll call from the hospital." With that, Tobi hung up.

"Something is not right!" Herb said, pushing the gun tighter into Hawk's back.

"Look, Feller. There's no need to hurt the others," Hawk pleaded. "They don't know what I know. Just take me if you have to have a hostage, and leave my family out of this."

"How brave and selfless, Hawk! Just like Jon Shockey, or Shade as you call him, but that won't be the case. Now, let's go back inside until I figure out how to clean up this mess, and then I'll be on my way. I'll give Randal a little more time to call me. He's a sharpshooter, the best, just like his father was. There's no way he screwed this up. Now, take me to Vinson. At least I'll have a little help."

* * * *

Shade had BJ land the chopper as close to the ranch as he could get and not be heard. Once on the ground, he armed himself and headed for Herb Feller.

165

BJ then took off for Billings with Tobi protesting that he needed to stay at the ranch, but Shade did not give him a chance to get out. BJ was not on the ground but a second when Shade was out the door and running, heading over the ridges, making his way toward the cabin.

As Shade ran he tried to figure out who the sniper was who shot Randal, but he had no idea. He would be eternally grateful, though, not for himself but for Sue Ann.

Maybe there are a few good CIA agents after all...Maybe it's the Voice again.

Shade dismissed this thought as fast as it entered his head as he followed the trail he had traveled the day before, going the other way after Randal Davison and Sue Ann. When he approached the ranch house, he noticed how eerily quiet it was, and he hoped and prayed he would find everyone safe.

Shade stayed low as he approached from behind the barn. The black SUV still sat in the driveway, along with Hawk's Suburban and the vehicles that belonged to the ranch. Taking to the woods again, Shade made his way to the back of the huge house. Hearing voices, he tiptoed to the window, where he ducked down and listened.

"I guarantee you Shockey killed Randal. You're no match for Shockey, and I'm sure as hell not willing to go after him again." Shade knew Vinson was thinking "spider pit" and had no desire to encounter Jon Shockey ever again. "I say let's set fire to this place now that everybody is locked in that back room. By the time anybody finds them, they'll be unidentifiable."

"You may be right, Vinson. I'm going to try

Randal's phone one more time. He should be in signal range by now. But if he doesn't answer, we're leaving, right after we do what you suggest."

Shade smiled and moved far enough away from the ranch house that neither he nor the phone's ring would be heard, pulling out of his pocket the cell phone he'd taken off Randal Davison's body. At such close range, it worked without problem, and he let the phone ring four times, then answered through his hand so that his voice would be muffled.

"Randal here. I'm on my way to the ranch. Give me an hour to get there, but be ready to leave." Shade hung up the phone.

His next call, on his satellite phone, was to the CIA agent who had helped him disappear years ago from his protected custody medical facility, the same one who had hired him for the training jobs connected with Forgotten Children. The agent felt he owed him a favor since his son was one of the GIs Shade had carried out of a prisoner of war camp in the middle of VC territory, but he also needed Shade in his humanitarian efforts.

The agent answered on the second ring and told Shade he'd caught him just two days before retirement. He also told him Kamanda was dead, shot by Haji. Shade changed the subject and quickly told him what had transpired. The agent assured Shade help would be on its way by air with one phone call from him.

****

Shade entered through the back door and could hear Herb Feller talking.

"Something smells fishy. If he's done the job, he should have been here by now. And why didn't he make sure the Parish woman was dead before he left the

167

scene? All I know is he better have pictures and fingerprints proving Shockey is dead."

Shade walked into the front room, taking Feller and Vinson by surprise.

"I don't think that's going to happen, Feller." Shade pointed his gun at Feller, who dropped his head on the table in disbelief.

After Shade unlocked the door and let Hawk and the others out, Hawk helped him tie the two criminals in chairs inside the same room where Hawk and the others had been held. Once they were secured, Shade headed back up front to join the others in the great room. He stopped at the door, stood back, and smiled at Betsy when she looked toward him.

"Come on, Trapper. Let's go check on the horses." Hawk headed out with his son in his shadow. Trapper looked at the stranger and gave him a smile that was quickly returned.

Betsy ran to Shade, and he enveloped her in his arms, kissing the top of her head.

"I'm so sorry, Betsy, so very sorry. You will never know how much I wanted to be with you, and Angel, and your mom."

Betsy was crying so hard she could hardly speak. Angel joined in the hug, and Shade felt like the luckiest man in the world.

"Don't worry about your mother, Betsy. She will be all right. She was so brave."

"Did she see you, Shade? Does she know you saved her?" Betsy asked, still holding on to Shade.

"No, sweetheart. She was in the back of the chopper with Tobi and kept dropping off to sleep after Tobi gave her the pain medication BJ had in his emergency kit. It has to stay that way, Betsy, at least until I know I can keep all of you safe. My old friend in the CIA is going to check everything out and make sure this deadline is for real. Once the money is dispersed and the bank account closed…well, we'll see. Please don't tell Sue Ann about me. I don't want her getting her hopes up. She doesn't need another hurt. I've got to go, girls. Take care of your mother, Betsy." Shade turned to Angel. "Do not try to find me. If everything is clear and safe, I'll find you. I'll always find you." Shade kissed them each and headed out the door.

Hawk and Trapper were inside the barn when Shade entered. Shade shook Hawk's hand and thanked him for being a hero to Betsy and Sue Ann.

Trapper looked up from under his cowboy hat, into Shade's face.

"Daddy is my hero, too. He and Uncle Tobi saved me one time from a very bad man—when I was little." Trapper held out his hand to the stranger. "I'm Trapper."

"Yes, he is your hero, Trapper. I heard about that." Shade took the boy's hand and was surprised at the firmness of the little boy's handshake. "You're a fine young man. I'm pleased to meet you, son. Take care of Sudi, okay?"

"I will." Trapper stared at Shade. "Who are you?" he asked, and Shade was glad Trapper had not heard his name mentioned.

"I'm an old friend of Custer's, Trapper."

"I miss Grampa Custer," Trapper said. "He died and went to heaven, but I still see him sometimes."

"Well, when you see him again, tell him…tell him an old friend said hello." Shade and Hawk rolled the small helicopter out, and Shade got into the pilot's seat. Giving one last wave to Hawk and Trapper, he started the engine.

As the helicopter flew out of sight, Trapper walked to the gate where the horses were and rubbed the mane of the old appaloosa whose back was swaying some from too many trips through the mountains.

Hawk watched as Trapper crawled over the gate and ran over to the base of the mountain, where he began talking to himself. "Come on, son. Let's go check on Mom and Angel, and then we'll go see Sudi."

Trapper picked up something and stuck it in his back pocket before he ran back and crawled over the gate.

"What did you find, Trapper?"

"Just something for Sudi…to make her feel better."

"Can you show me?" Hawk asked, but Trapper shook his head no.

Shade flew the helicopter over Sue Ann's cabin for one last look before making the call to Alaska.

"Light the fire in the stove and leave a lamp burning. I'm coming home, Jake."

An hour later, federal agents swarmed the ranch. Two choppers landed at the ranch, and two more flew over on their way to Second Rock to retrieve the body of Randal Davison. When Hawk offered to answer questions for the agent in charge, he just shook his head and told Hawk that would not be necessary.

****

With the feds and their prisoners gone, Hawk drove his family and Angel out the gate of the ranch, ready to make the trip to the hospital and Sue Ann. He stopped to close the gate, since they had no need to stay there any longer. As he pushed the gate shut, he noticed a sign attached to the back. He hadn't seen the sign previously because the gate had been open when they drove in. Holding his arms out in excitement, he called for Betsy and Trapper to get out and look. Before Betsy could open the door, Trapper was out and standing beside his dad. Betsy and Angel moved beside Hawk to see what all the excitement was about.

"This ranch is for sale, Betsy! Can you believe it? It has a huge barn and bunkhouses—all set up for outfitting! Put this information in your phone!"

Betsy pulled her phone out of her pocket.

"Okay, Hawk. I'm ready. Read it out just like it is on the sign."

"Cynthia Colbert Realty, PO Box 176, Fishtail, MT 59028, phone number 406-328-4000. Got it?"

"I've got it, Hawk." Betsy entered the information in her phone and smiled as she watched her husband, his arms draped over the top rail of the big gate, and his sidekick Trapper, with his arms draped over the second from the bottom rail. In synchrony, each one pushed his cowboy hat back, propped his right boot on a lower rail, and exclaimed "Wow!" as they looked across the valley at the expanse of the magnificent mountain setup.

"Hawk, you do know this ranch will be at least a million dollars—probably more?"

Betsy made the remark as she and Angel began snapping shots with their phones of the father and son cowboys propped on the fence, both drooling at the Beartooth Mountain Ranch spread out before them like a scene from a western movie—a scene only possible in the Big Sky Country.

"Just a million? What's your point, Betsy?"

Hawk continued to gaze at the property until he felt Betsy's eyes on him. Without looking at her, he stepped back and put his arm around his wife. Together, they stood, eyes locked on the ranch they both knew could be—would be—theirs. After all, they were multi-millionaires, thanks to Hawk's wayward Uncle Custer.

****

Sue Ann was awake when Hawk, Betsy, Angel, and Trapper got to the hospital that night. Tobi was drinking coffee and telling his mom what all had transpired on the mountain that morning, leaving out the main character, and Angel immediately hugged Sue Ann, being careful of her wounded side. Sue Ann was in a little pain, but putting on a good front for her family, she welcomed hugs from Betsy and Hawk, too. Her prognosis was excellent, with no surgery needed.

Angel cried, telling Sue Ann how sorry she was this had happened, but Sue Ann shushed her, wiping the tears from Angel's eyes.

"Think of the story this will make in a future book!" Sue Ann told her.

Trapper, ready for his hug, crawled up beside his Sudi, on her good side, so she could put her arm around him and hold him. He would never be too big for his grandmother's hugs.

"Got you a surprise, Sudi!" Trapper took his cowboy hat off and hung it over the toe of one of his cowboy boots, which he did not take off. "Yep. It's a goodun!"

"Well, are you going to keep me in suspense, grandson?" Sue Ann's voice was weak, but she loved having Trapper beside her, even if it was in a hospital bed.

Trapper reached in his back pocket and pulled out a beautiful white feather and handed it to his grandmother. Her eyes lit up seeing it, as moisture formed in the corners.

"Oh, Trapper, it's an eagle feather, one of his tail feathers! How beautiful! Thank you, sweetheart. This is a treasure."

"I got a message for you, Sudi, from Grampa Custer."

All eyes moved to Trapper.

"From Grampa Custer? Are you sure, Little Man?" Sue Ann wanted to hear the message but was hesitant to encourage Trapper's imagination to run wild.

"Grampa said, 'Tell Sudi when the sunset is red, happiness will find her.' He told me to give you this feather so you would know it was a promise."

Hawk looked at Betsy and whispered, "Where did that come from?"

Betsy shrugged her shoulders.

"Oh, one more thing he said tell you, but it's kind of long. I had to practice with him so I'd get it right."

Now Betsy and Hawk were really baffled but could hardly wait to see what their son would come up with next.

"Okay, Trapper. I'm ready. Tell me." Sudi stroked his cheek with the eagle feather.

"Grampa said, 'The Crow people think the raven is a trickster, but I think he got a bad rap 'cause he's real smart.' " Trapper was dramatic, drawling the words as if he needed time to get it right. He paused, putting his finger to his head as if trying to remember his lines. "Oh, yeah! Now I remember. 'Raven mates for life and only has one love. He loves her forever—and then some.' " Trapper smiled and then cut his eyes up at his grandmother. "What does 'mate' mean, Sudi?"

Sue Ann stopped tickling Trapper's cheek with the feather and asked him what Grampa Custer looked like, mostly to change the subject.

"He was young. His braids were black, and he wore Indian pants but no shirt, but I knew it was him, Sudi." Trapper sat up excited about the next part. "He rode a wild mustang, an appaloosa, but it didn't have no saddle! He could ride bareback real fast and didn't even fall off—just like he used to do when he raced with me before he got too old, but he rode in a saddle then."

****

When the family left, Sue Ann tried to remember all that Trapper had told her. One line stuck in her head. "He'll love her forever and then some."

She would almost swear she had heard Shade whisper that in her ear when she lay on the ground at Second Rock, but she knew she was unconscious at the time.

Well, I guess if Custer can come back and drop me an eagle feather, Shade can come back and whisper in my ear.

With words spoken by her two greatest loves stuck in her head, Sue Ann closed her eyes and dropped off to sleep.

Chapter Twenty-Four

Weeks passed, and Sue Ann had fully recuperated. She and Betsy walked every day, and even though Sue Ann did not wear lipstick, or any makeup for that matter, she liked her blonde hair and decided to keep it, at least for a while. She was healthy, and time was beginning to heal her heart once again.

The white feather stood proudly in the pencil holder on her writing desk, where she had started the second part of her biography. But sometimes she took her laptop and moved to the sofa, where she could stare at the wedding picture of her and Custer, which now sat on the mantel under Shade's portrait of her and Betsy. She didn't know why she had never put the picture there before Custer died.

It was fall, her favorite time of the year, when the air took on a crispness only possible in the mountains. Some nights she built a fire in the old stone fireplace, but it wasn't the same, sitting alone in front of a romantic crackling fire.

Tobi and Angel were married, and Carrie was talking of living with them when she graduated from high school. Hawk, Betsy, and Trapper had purchased the dream ranch and had named it Eagle's Feather in honor of Trapper's find, and of course for Custer, who had paid for the ranch. They begged Sue Ann to move in with them, since the ranch house was huge, but she had declined for now, telling them she would reconsider when she was old.

"No, I'll never leave my cabin in the mountains." She was talking to herself again, and she wondered if she should just let her hair go gray again and admit she was aging fast, but each time she looked in the mirror, she'd decide to stay blonde a little longer.

It was almost sunset, her favorite time for porch sitting. Grabbing the quilt from the back of the sofa, she headed for the door. For some reason, she went back and picked up the white eagle feather Trapper still swore was a gift from Grampa Custer.

As she rocked, she looked to her mountains and felt sadness creep over her again.

Alone again! Alone again! Maybe that should be the title of Part II of my biography. It certainly sums up the biggest portion of my life—at least where love is concerned.

As the sun began to hide behind the Beartooths, she noticed it had changed into the most brilliant red sunset she had ever seen, reminding her of the harvest moon she and her daddy Zeke always loved to look at for hours when she was a child in Mississippi. The vibrant red dwarfed the dying sun, something she didn't remember ever seeing before.

Running the feather gently across her face, Sue Ann pretended it was her own Eagle brushing his fingers and caressing her cheek like he had done so many times. It was then she remembered Trapper's message from Custer: "Tell Sudi, 'When the sunset is red, happiness will find her.' He told me to give you this feather so you would know it's a promise."

Okay, Custer. I've got the feather, and the sunset is

red, so keep your promise.

As she looked toward the mountain, a breeze came from nowhere, blowing her curls across her face. Then she saw him—a man on the trail leading from Betsy's Six Rocks and Keyser Brown. She started to go inside, remembering the terror of weeks ago, but there was something familiar about this man's gait. His steps were deliberate—a man confident. He was tall, strong, and commanding as his frame moved in silhouette against the backdrop of intense scarlet. His shoulder-length hair bounced, keeping rhythm with his steps, which seemed more energized the closer he got to her.

"Raven wings!" Sue Ann whispered as she stood, letting the quilt drop into the rocker behind her. She watched, spellbound, wanting it to be but knowing it wasn't possible. He left the trail and entered the yard, his eyes fixed on her. When he reached the porch, he stopped on the bottom step in front of her. Ice blue eyes, Raven's eyes, smiled at her, beckoning, "Believe!"

She stepped closer and put her hand on his face, smooth and clean-shaven just as she remembered. Running her fingers through his raven wings now silver, she kissed him with tenderness but not passion, testing for reality and for a sign she wasn't hallucinating.

"Did I die right here on this porch and not know it? Am I in heaven?"

Sue Ann glanced around to see if her body lay slumped in the rocker, but all she saw was the quilt she had dropped when she saw him on the trail.

Raven stepped on up to the porch and took her in his arms, lifting her chin with his hand. His lips sought hers, not testing but rekindling the passion that had never waned, for the only woman he had ever loved. As he pulled his lips away, he spoke, and she shivered under his glacial gaze even while it warmed her heart and body simultaneously.

"You're not in heaven, Sue Ann—but I am. I'm here, darling, and I'm never leaving."

As the two kissed, the mountain breeze blew across the porch, picking up the eagle feather that lay on top of the quilt. Dipping, sailing like wings on mountain breezes, the feather gained momentum as it swirled and danced, rising higher and higher until it found its way home. The young brave sat on the mountain and reached out to catch the feather, returning it to his headband, a symbol of his people, the Crow. With a hint of a smile, he turned and loped the appaloosa stallion into the red sunset, remembering the words he had once written:

You are free, Sue Ann, as free as you have always been, whether in Alaska or Montana; as free as you have always been when in my arms. Free is the only way I can think of you, and I love you more for it.

For you to have the love you deserve, I will no longer be a part of your life. Go with my love, my blessing, and always my heart.

Epilogue

Sophia stood at the window, staring into the jungle paradise she managed, at least for now. Whiteman, or Shade as he was now called, had not returned to Costa Rica after going back to Montana. The scene, the last time she had seen him, haunted her, playing over and over in her mind and refusing to leave.

He was by a high mountain lake in the Beartooth Mountains of Montana, lying with his body over the woman's, trying to shield her. As he lay there with his arm around her, he whispered in her ear. A gunman stood not far away with his rifle aimed at them.

Sophia had always known Whiteman did not love her. Their relationship had been physical, a training exercise for him, to keep him fit and virile, but not for her. Sophia had been okay with this until that day when she saw him with Sue Ann for the first and only time.

As Sophia put the crosshairs of her rifle on the assassin, she thought of redirecting them to the woman, but she couldn't do it, not to the man she worshiped. With her rifle sight set on the assassin, she squeezed the trigger twice and watched him fall. Wanting to see no more, and with her mission accomplished, Sophia fled.

When she realized Whiteman would never return to Costa Rica, she decided it was time to break into the off-limits room of the quarters at Mono Paraiso where she now resided alone. She never understood why

Whiteman would stay in the forbidden room for days at a time. Now she owed it to herself to see what secrets the room held.

The room was dark when she entered, and she kept it that way. In the light that crept in through the open door, she spotted a remote by an oversized chair, the only furniture in the spacious room. Sitting in the chair, she put her feet on the ottoman and snuggled in, imagining herself in Whiteman's arms. She pushed the button on the remote, and the wall began opening. As music surrounded her, she saw the reality of this man she had never really known until three years ago when she received the call from the American CIA agent, a "friend of Whiteman's" he had said. He knew of her abilities as a sniper and asked for her assistance in protecting Whiteman, promising her continued asylum in the country of her choosing.

Using sophisticated equipment secretly given to her by the CIA, Sophia had tracked Angel for months in the U.S. and in Costa Rica and warned her many times of impending danger, using synthesizers to mask her voice. Whiteman did not know she knew about his daughter; nor did he suspect Sophia had a double life as a CIA special operative.

And now here she sat. The Spanish beauty watched as spectacular green-and-yellow waves of light danced over the heads of a much younger Whiteman and the woman he loved. Tears rolled down Sophia's face, something unusual for a hardcore assassin. She watched, distressed yet mesmerized by the scene unfolding. The captivating lights illuminated the heavens, moving in sync with the symphonic background music and with the heartbeats of the lovers,

hearts forever entwined, beating as one.
Closing her eyes, Sophia dreamed.

About the author…

Dr. Sue Clifton is a retired principal, fly fisher, paranormal investigator, and published author. Dr. Sue, as she is known, can't remember a time when she did not write, beginning with two plays published at sixteen. Her writing career was placed on hold while she traveled the world with her husband, Woody, in his career, as well as with her own career as a teacher and principal in Mississippi, Alaska, New Zealand, and on the Northern Cheyenne Reservation in Montana. The places Dr. Sue has lived provide background and settings for the novels she creates.

Dr. Sue now divides her time among Montana, Mississippi, and Arkansas and enjoys traveling with Woody and the grandchildren as well as with her national fly fishing group Sisters on the Fly. She loves all things vintage, including her 1950 canned-ham camper "Spam I Am" that she takes on Sisters on the Fly events. Dr. Sue supports Casting for Recovery (CFR), a national organization providing fly fishing retreats for women with breast cancer. Ten per cent of the profits from her Daughters of Parrish Oaks Series goes to CFR.

Dr. Sue is the author of ten books: five novels in her series with The Wild Rose Press, Inc.; and one nonfiction book and four paranormal mysteries elsewhere. Dr. Sue appeared in October 2015 in A&E's five-part series for television *Cursed: The Bell Witch*. She was also featured in *USA Today* in articles about her nonfiction book which included the truth about the Bell Witch Legend as told through a young clairvoyant, Angel Leigh, the subject of the nonfiction book and also cast in the A&E series.

Visit Dr. Sue at www.drsueclifton.com and see Novels by Dr. Sue Clifton on Facebook.

~*~

About Kelley Reinemann-Banks:

Kelley is a jack of all trades but master of none. She loves to go shooting, play her trumpet, travel, crochet, paint, write poetry, dabble in photography… the list goes on. Growing up, Kelley envisioned herself blossoming into a productive member of society, but didn't really know what she wanted to do in life. At some point or another, Kelley dreamed of becoming a writer, a meteorologist, an engineer, a forensic scientist, a lawyer, or even an employee of the FBI or the CIA. Fortunately, she was able to pin down an occupation that blended some aspects of each in which she ever had an interest.

Kelley first heard about Dr. Sue through family members who bragged on her writing prowess and vivid descriptions of bygone eras in a place in which they both grew up, the setting in *The Gully Path*, Book 1 in the series. Kelley and Dr. Sue, "long-lost first cousins once removed," began communicating through social media, and established a relationship through their mutual love and respect for the importance of family and the land in which they were nurtured—Mississippi.

Kelley graduated from the University of Mississippi, Ole Miss, with a Bachelor of Science degree in Criminal Justice and a minor in Spanish. Kelley met her husband, a police officer, in their college serial killers class. (Yes, you read that correctly!) They are the parents of three cats, a dog, and a baby girl, who they welcomed into their family in early 2016. Kelley currently is employed with the government and resides in North Mississippi with her family. She lived briefly in Washington, DC, and hopes to never have to pick up roots again.

Thank you for purchasing
this publication of The Wild Rose Press, Inc.

If you enjoyed the story, we would appreciate your
letting others know by leaving a review.

For other wonderful stories,
please visit our on-line bookstore at
www.thewildrosepress.com.

For questions or more information
contact us at
info@thewildrosepress.com.

The Wild Rose Press, Inc.
www.thewildrosepress.com

Stay current with The Wild Rose Press, Inc.

Like us on Facebook

https://www.facebook.com/TheWildRosePress

And Follow us on Twitter
https://twitter.com/WildRosePress

www.ingramcontent.com/pod-product-compliance
Lightning Source LLC
Chambersburg PA
CBHW071520260626
47170CB00002B/447